NICK SILVER
and the
Secret Facility

BY

SEBASTIAN M. PRINCIPATO

Table of Contents

1

Camp Crystalflake

The season of crippling cold was ending as the warm summer approached. A great season for all had arrived on this early June morning. Two tall silhouettes crept along the fields in the shadows, running through a forest not known by many. Hidden by their masks, they conversed. A woman's voice spoke first, nervously, "His appearance won't go unnoticed. You know that, right?"

"Quiet," said a second, rough voice. "Don't worry, the boy will know when he is ready." The two masked figures both stared across the grassy land.

"You don't understand. They know. They've already sent spies," the woman added.

"Mary, don't worry. I've tested the strengths of the boy. For a toddler, he is surprisingly strong. Plus, he knows how to work the You-Know-What."

"Well, I guess that's good, Richard. I hope they finish the construction soon. This relocation of the camp is not the first, nor will it be the last. We should practice dueling next, I think. He will need to know the art of dueling before they find him here." The woman sighed.

"Yes, yes...he should know how to work a sword properly," Richard agreed as he clamped a palm to a scar in his right arm. "And teach him how to talk to –"

"Well, he has been," Mary responded softly.

Richard looked surprised. "He has?"

"Don't you ever listen? I told you yesterday. That boy has been bringing his toys from his bedroom, straight to the dogs. Once, now that I think about it, he held a decently long conversation with Lucy and Lola," Mary laughed.

Richard checked his watch and stated gruffly, "Well, c'mon, Mary. We don't want to be seen here. Reconstruction on the camp starts soon. And it is crucial they finish it before he comes of age."

"You're right, Richard. Let's go," she sighed again. The man walked off, but Mary paused and whispered, "Camp CrystalFlake... take care of my son. Good luck, Nicholas!" Then she caught up to her companion without a word.

Nine years later, in a small town, two kids in the Silver family were getting ready to go to summer camp. Nick Silver was an ordinary eleven-year-old boy, wearing an oversized orange sweatshirt. He had curly brown hair and brown eyes and was decently tall, but not too much. He wore storm-blue sweatpants and his favorite worn-out white sneakers with red on the bottom and the tongue. Although his name was really Nicholas, he preferred to be called Nick.

His sister Madison, thirteen years old, was a little taller, with short wavy brown hair and brown eyes. She usually wore a big sweatshirt, as well, but hers was black and had the name of an art school on it, because she planned to be an artist when she grew up. She wore thick black pants and new shoelace sneakers that were mostly pink with white laces.

On this nice June morning, Nick and Madison were rushing through breakfast so they could head to camp. They had already packed their bags the day before, after they got home from the last day of school. They rushed upstairs to their rooms and simultaneously brushed their teeth, then grabbed their backpacks and raced downstairs.

The kids also bid goodbye to their dad as they stepped out of the house and walked with their mom to the car before piling in. And then they were off toward camp.

The sun shined brightly and filled the speeding car with warmth and light. As they drove, the minutes flew by and Nick imagined what camp would be like. Unlike his sister, he had never been to Camp CrystalFlake before, but it was Madison's third year there. The beginning year is for age eleven and the last year is fifteen. He planned to do all five years at camp and enjoy them to their fullest.

Nick turned towards his sister, who was lost in a whirlpool of thought, and asked her quietly, "Whatcha thinking about?"

Madison took a few seconds to respond. "Nothing. Just about camp."

Nick wondered why her voice was so quiet and unwelcoming. After a minute or so, he forgot all about this and was consumed by happy thoughts of his first year at summer camp. He wanted to do so much when he got there, but most of all, he wanted to make new friends. He wondered what the food was like as he looked out the window. It seemed like they were in a forest-like area, but mainly a park. "Are we there yet, Mom?" he asked impatiently. "Almost, Nick," came the reply.

He was really pumped up, but suddenly getting annoyed with the long wait for summer camp. After months and months of boring fifth grade studying, classwork, homework, projects, and other happiness-destroying work, all he wanted to do was enjoy fun, non-mind-challenging activities with new friends in warm weather. His birthday was on May fourteenth, and on his last birthday, he got a Magic 8-Ball. He pulled it out from his backpack and muttered under his breath, "Will my summer at camp be the most special summer I have ever had so far?" He rattled the ball and read the message on the small triangular screen: "You Can Count on It."

After an hour more of driving, Nick was getting restless. Patience was never really in his nature, especially now. Camp CrystalFlake was all he could think of since early May. And now that the special day had finally arrived, it was taking forever to get to the camp.

They passed a shimmering blue lake in the distance, surrounded by trees. For a split second, as Nick gazed at the view, two glowing red eyes appeared in the lake. For an even shorter moment, two more pairs of eyes glowed on the left and right of the original pair. Amazed, Nick shouted, "Six eyes! In the lake!"

Nick's mom turned briefly and said, "Are you sure? Nick, I think you must be imagining things because you're bored. Nick, Madison – why don't you play a car game to pass the time?"

Madison glanced up from her phone but secretly, neither of them really wanted to. Nick just wanted to get to camp and that was that. He decided to pass the time by going to sleep and eventually, he did. He had a weird dream. At first, he dreamt about the camp he longed for, but then the dreams included things about the camp that he had never seen in the pictures his sister took. Instead, he saw the camp as if he had been there before. He felt like he was flying and he passed the camper cabins, then the small medical cabin, then the big counselor cabin, and a few empty tents. He flew around a grassy hill and dove downward towards a lake. He headed toward it, but there were people coming out of the cafeteria he had never actually seen before and he froze. To prevent them from seeing him, he exploded into a cloud of dark smoke and disappeared on the spot.

"Agh!" Nick gasped as he woke up, feeling numb. "Have a good sleep?" his mom asked. Nick hesitated, then lied, "Yeah. Great." His mother must have noticed he wasn't looking well and said cheerfully, "I have some good news." Nick turned to her and asked doubtfully, "What?" He waited before his mom finally replied quietly, "We're here."

Nick forgot about the dream as thoughts of his arrival at camp took over. The day had come. It was time. Excitedly, Nick yanked his backpack out of the car, crushing Madison as she turned off her phone. Nick waited for his sister as he hoisted his backpack onto his back, then Madison climbed out of the car with her own backpack over her shoulder. They said goodbye to their mom as she wished both of them luck, and they set off to enter Camp CrystalFlake.

As they hurried through the camp gates, they noticed the camp flag wave from a gust of wind. They saw plenty of other kids, too, walking through the camp gates with backpacks and small suitcases. As Nick turned to look at the cabins, a mosquito swooped down and bit him on the arm. He was about to swat it when Madison beat him to it with a triumphant, "Ha!"

Just then, a short kid with messy light brown hair and blue eyes, wearing a gray coat, came over and muttered, "These mosquitoes are so annoying!" He turned toward Nick and added quickly, "I'm Daniel. Nice to meet you. You have problems with the mosquitoes, too?" Nick hesitated and replied, "Yeah. They're annoying." Daniel scratched a mosquito bite on his arm and said, "Lots of them here. Only my first year."

"Yeah, same here," Nick admitted. Madison stepped in and said, "C'mon. Let's go before the mosquitoes come back. At this camp, they bite you just for the heck of it." As the three of them approached the gates, a security guard stopped them and asked sharply, "Names?" Nick didn't expect this, but still answered, "Nicholas Silver." Madison replied quickly, "Year three, Madison Silver. He's in his first year." Daniel blurted out a few seconds later, "Daniel Garring. First year, too, sir." The security guard eyed them and growled, "A lot more of them this year." Then he allowed them to pass and advanced on the next group of kids.

The trio continued along the dirt path, with trees all around, and Nick commented, "Great place here, isn't it?" Madison nodded. "Yeah, it's nice." Daniel agreed, "Beautiful." As they walked on and on, the trees lessened and the camp was in sight off in the distance. Madison cleared her voice and said, "Counselor Philip has been the camp director at this camp for years and is not the type of person to forgive easily. Nick, lay off your sound machines. They have ways of giving detention at camp and Counselor Philip doesn't take kindly to those types of things at all. He decides the detentions and you don't want him deciding yours, trust me." Daniel spluttered, "I've heard the p-punishments from him are really bad." Nick felt kind of let down, but still excited, nonetheless.

They were nearing camp; Nick could feel it. Daniel coughed and accidentally dropped his backpack. He bent down and picked it up as the sound of a megaphone grew loud. Nick was now able to make out the camp easily and the voice of the person talking through the megaphone became clearer. By now, it was a little before noon. They made it to a large gathering where tree stumps on the grass formed a circle. Nick, Madison, and Daniel all sat on three stumps next to each other on the outer rim of the circle. There were loads of other campers on the stumps, too. Through the crowd, Nick saw somebody on a tall, wide, mossy rock, holding a megaphone. He guessed it was the camp director, Counselor Philip. Nick stared intently at him. Counselor Philip was tall, almost skeletal, with long hairy arms and legs. He had short hair, and not much of it, anyway. He had a short mustache that outlined his upper lip perfectly.

Nick looked around as colorful birds pierced the sunlight through the cloudless sky. Counselor Philip coughed away from his megaphone and then started calling out roll call, reading names off a clipboard. "John Jackson. Michael Anthrope. Teal Tinstrip. Are you here?" He coughed again as the kids who he had called out answered him.

He checked his list again, frowned, and spoke into the megaphone, "Tim Ronald. Jack Cullins. Gabriel Golding. Gregory Golding. Dylan Sheimer! Are you all here?" Nick saw a short black-haired, green-eyed kid confirm his name last in a bored voice. As Counselor Philip announced more names into his megaphone, Nick took a quick glance at John Jackson. He looked a little taller than Dylan and had wavy orange hair, brown glasses, and was wearing a yellow t-shirt. Nick started wondering how he wasn't getting hot in his thick sweatshirt when he heard, "David Canscar. Mark Mildred. Daniel Garring. Nicholas Silver! Are you all here?" Nick answered quickly as the others echoed him. His slight uneasiness loosened as the camp director began to read off the paper of names again.

The roll call continued for the next half hour while Nick watched other counselors in the distance preparing lunch outside. When Counselor Philip was done talking about the rules, he led everybody to the lunch table next to the shining lake Nick had dreamt about. The group sat together on the wooden bench, with Nick left of Daniel and right of Madison, who commented, "Lunches here are pretty good." The counselors carelessly tossed menus onto the table as all the campers decided what to order. Nick and Madison settled on chicken fingers, French fries, and chocolate milk while Daniel just got a water bottle and fries.

The other campers seemed to already know each other and all the first years talked to their siblings instead. Gabriel Golding asked, "So, what's this place like?" Nick recognized another first year as Sean Carter, who had swirling brown hair and was tall. "I don't know, but I wonder what activities we'll do," Sean told them. "At my old camp, we had ziplining, canoeing, rock climbing, mini golfing…"

"What about you, Nicholas?" asked Gabriel.

"Hmm, I dunno. I hope we do a lot of fun stuff, though," Nick said, wondering what those things might be.

"You, me, and everyone else, Nick," Dylan Sheimer agreed, grinning.

Fifteen minutes later, drinks and food arrived. Nick and Madison, who were starving, devoured most of their food before realizing they were thirsty and their drinks that were gone in less than a minute. They weren't the first ones done, which didn't surprise either of them. Counselor Philip came back to the lunch table and cleared his throat. "Now," he stated, "we discuss camp rules." There was a short silence while a gust of wind blew.

Rules and Dangers

"It is my duty to hold this camp together while some people will try to 'mess around,'" Counselor Philip announced. "Rules are like money. They are the basis of all human lives and nature. Money supports us and holds us together. Just like rules, which lead us in the right path and direct us from bad." Nick was already getting a bad feeling about this guy. The camp director added in a cold, soft voice, "Rules are more important than humor, which easily distracts from common goals, as enjoyable it is."

Counselor Philip continued his warnings loudly and somberly. "This camp will most certainly not accept campers who have an ego so big that they will go out of their way looking for things that are not meant for them to see." He pointed far back and to the right of the lake, where a line of pine trees stood together. "Such as the area past the trees over there. Meaning, if I catch you in out-of-bounds territory, you will be gone. For your safety, you will have to leave." Counselor Philip left a dead silence behind when he stopped speaking. Nick felt Daniel quiver to his left and couldn't blame him. Nick could only hope that Counselor Philip's attitude would be the only problem at Camp CrystalFlake.

Just when Nick assumed Counselor Philip had finished talking, he began again. "You are not allowed to share beds or be awake past 9:30 pm." The campers all groaned. "You must not share food. You must listen to me and the other counselors. If you have any questions, consult one of the counselors; they are here to help." Nick started wondering if Counselor Philip was the reason Madison wasn't too excited to come back. A bunch of kids started muttering to each other as the camp director was talking to the other counselors

Nick began thinking to himself, "This guy has a punishment for everything, but I'll just have to find my way past..." CRASH! Nick's head spun around and so did every other camper's. The counselors also reacted, but they looked even more scared than the campers did. A skinny, big-eyed man with puffy, dirty hair came running through the pine trees by the lake. He wore brown pants and a ripped shirt with blood splatters on it, and he looked petrified. There was an outburst of talking as the terrified man, who turned out to be a counselor, reached the table and panted heavily, reaching out an arm to help him balance on his wobbly feet. A bead of blood was dripping down his neck as the counselors called the nurse on their walkie-talkies and told her, "Nurse Fletcher, we need you at the outside lunch table. Yeah, next to the lake. Yeah, Robert appears to have been attacked." A full minute passed before anyone saw the nurse rushing out of the medical cabin with a medical kit.

She reached out to the man's face and gently wiped up the blood with a wet rag. She felt his hand next. She moved her hands along his arm, then stopped with a surprised look. "Robert, I'm afraid you have a broken arm. You will have to spend about the next week or so in the medical cabin healing while I examine and tend to the rest of your wounds."

It seemed like none of the other counselors cared about the scared and shocked kids who were still finishing their lunch, with nothing better to do than watch. The nurse quickly ran into one of the tents next to the medical cabin and brought out a wheelchair. She pulled it along the bumpy grass and over to the end of the lunch table, with many kids looking on. Stopping the wheelchair on a flat patch of grass, she gently pushed Robert into it and bent over to examine his legs. She wiped blood off the left one and felt it for any other injuries, then moved on to the right leg and wiped off a streak of dry blood. She felt it a little more and stopped. "Robert, your left leg might be fractured, as well. I'm taking you into the medical cabin for further examination. Do you need anything?" she asked in a worried tone. "No, I'm g-good," moaned Robert. The nurse nodded and pushed Robert's wheelchair into the medical cabin and out of sight.

Counselor Philip led the other worried counselors away from the lunch table toward a sand pit. Nick could see Counselor Philip talking to them but couldn't hear what they were saying. Filled with fear but also with great courage, Nick snuck under the table and crawled out the other side. As the counselors glanced over at the lunch table, Nick hid behind a bush. He could hear other campers whispering for him to get back in his seat, but he didn't want to. He had a feeling the counselors were discussing something important.

He crept into a tent next to the medical cabin as the counselors looked back at the table again. When they turned away, Nick rolled out and twisted around to the other side of the tent. He then sprinted away to the medical cabin as campers gasped and watched with fear. His sister was the most frightened, but she knew he had the courage to make it. He crawled behind the cabin to the other side of the cabin and was now able to hear them.

He put a hand to his ear and heard Counselor Philip say with a quiver of uncertainty, "Listen, whatever attacked Robert shouldn't be much of a threat. Every year before camp starts again, I pay someone to scout around the area looking for dangerous animals that can harm us. If they find something that is a threat, they'll kill it." Nick leaned over a little further and heard somebody ask in a shaky, scared voice, "But what if there are new animals that are living here? And those holes…"

Nick saw Counselor Philip raise a hand in front of the person talking and state firmly, "I said, it shouldn't be much of a threat. Now go file the paperwork. I daresay soon the office will overflow. I have things to discuss with the new campers. Go!" Nick quickly realized what was happening, sprinted around the cabin, ducked under an empty section of the bench, and crawled under the table back to his spot just as Counselor Philip returned and said casually, "Enjoying lunch, kids?" Everybody nodded and Nick, dripping with sweat, nodded nervously, too.

"Good," replied Counselor Philip with forced enthusiasim. "Now, have you all heard about the Zorblin?" he asked ominously.

"Yes," mumbled a large group of campers. Nick just sat there, feeling relieved he didn't get caught spying.

"Well," began Counselor Philip again, "it is thought that the monster lives at this… very… camp. And every year, it looks and waits for a kid to try to sneak into out-of-bounds territory. When he spots one who thinks they can do it punishment-free, its three snakelike necks stretch over each other so that each head is able to eat part of their body. The Zorblin eats kids and you should not be tempted to walk into your own death! The legend is both fact and opinion. You must figure out where the truth lies, as there are some obvious exaggerations to the story. I do not doubt both." When Counselor Philip finished speaking, he stepped away and started doing something on his phone by a tree.

Nick thought the whole story was dumb and made up by the counselors to prevent kids from going outside the boundaries. Nick told his sister this and they started guessing what Counselor Philip could possibly be hiding out there. "Actually, Nick, you're right. There is a good chance he could be hiding something out there and that's why it is out-of-bounds territory!" whispered Madison.

"Exactly. I think he's doing illegal stuff out there – maybe dumping toxic waste into a river or something. I don't know, but the possibilities are endless! Well, probably not actually, but still." Nick whispered back.

As they continued exchanging ideas of what Counselor Philip might be hiding, a kid across the table heard them and whispered back, "You know, the idea of using a fake story to lure kids away from a dark secret actually makes sense!" Nick recognized the orange-haired boy as John Jackson. Then he got an idea. He pulled out his Magic 8-Ball, which he still had with him, and asked it, "Is Counselor Philip hiding anything in the out-of-bounds forest?" He shook the ball wildly and read on the bubbly blue triangular screen in tiny print, "Cannot Foretell Now." Nick had no idea what that meant.

Just then, Counselor Philip let out a low growl and shoved his phone in his pocket as it turned off. He stared right at Nick and opened his mouth. Nick thought it was the end of the road for him and that he would be expelled from camp on the first day. But that's not what happened.

"Mr. Silver," the man said in a low, empty voice, "follow me." Nick got up, every eye of the camp focused on him, and gave his sister a worried look as he walked over to Counselor Philip. When he reached him, he felt the man's grip on his wrist as he was pulled into the woods on the other side of the camp behind the counselor cabins, which weren't anywhere near the very place they departed from. The counselor yanked him around a thorn bush and by the time they reached the other side, Nick still had no idea what was going on.

Counselor Philip finally let go of Nick, who stumbled slightly, and before he could ask anything, the counselor announced calmly, "We're going to play a game. Can you guess what game that will be, Mr. Silver?" Nick weakly raised his scraped head and groaned, "No."

"Well, then. Let me explain. But let me ask something first. Why did you think you could listen in to our counselors' conversation? Did you think you would hear anything about the legend being fake? Because it's real. And I hope you don't go down that path of thinking you can waltz into the forbidden forest. Because too many deaths have been caused by kids thinking the legend isn't real." He paused, shaking his head sadly, and pointed into the vast area. "Now, we will have a scavenger hunt. I'll forgive you for your transgression – if you find my silver watch si…."

Nick looked around and interrupted. "But this forest is huge! How am I supposed to find it?" The counselor handed him something and told him, "Here is a stopwatch. You will have all the time you need. No crossing into the out-of-bounds forest. Do you hear me?"

Nick stared at the stopwatch and muttered, "Yeah," before the camp director turned and left the forest, saying, "Good luck, then," and abandoning him to find a silver watch lost in a forest that could take weeks to search completely. Nick wondered what everybody was doing right now and then winced with pain. He was starting to wish he never came to camp. It seemed as though he would not be able to control the camp situation himself. At the very least, maybe he could get rid of Counselor Philip somehow, but he had to admit it was sort of his own fault this was happening, Nick thought guiltily.

He began walking as he set the stopwatch to two hours. Although it was really a natural setting, it seemed like the entire forest was just a set-up built by Counselor Philip to make him suffer because of how many dangerous obstacles were in it. He walked around a thorn bush as a gust of wind blew a heavy branch right smack into Nick's face, launching him backwards into a pile of poison ivy. As soon as he landed on it, though, there was a flash of fiery orange light from beneath him and when he looked at the poison ivy, it had been completely burned to ashes.

Ten minutes later, he had to cross a lake to get to near something silver that he saw shining. As he crossed, a twig under the dirty water grabbed hold of the bottom of his sweatshirt, pulling him so his foot slipped on an underwater rock and he fell backwards into the water.

When he got out of the lake and reached the silver object, he discovered that it was nothing more than a tin can.

Nick was getting exhausted. More than an hour later, he could see the sun's light fading as he went deeper into the forest. It had been a long time since he was dropped off at the camp by his mother and he now thought that this wasn't camp, but more of a prison. All Nick had wanted to do at camp was enjoy himself, relax, have a good time, and make new friends.

While looking for the watch, Nick started questioning why he had decided to listen in on a private conversation anyway. It wasn't open to him, so obviously, Philip had a point. Nick was already mad enough with himself when a flash of yellow light covered the forest and the loud, crackling sound of lightning crashed in his eardrums. Heavy rain drenched him as it poured down. CRASH! BOOM! He sprinted back toward the beginning of the forest, with no care anymore for Counselor Philip's punishment, as this was already punishment enough.

Nick stopped for a second to breathe next to a heavy fallen tree being held up diagonally by another older tree. Suddenly, lightning struck, and for some reason it was so loud and intense, the flash of light seemed stronger and brighter than any other lightning strike. As he heard the sound of a tree snapping, he realized exactly what and where the lightning had struck. The old tree lay dead and destroyed on the muddy ground and the big heavy tree crashed into the pile of leaves where Nick had been standing just before he jumped out of the way. BANG! CRACKLE! He was sprinting again as the rain hit him hard and fast. He reminded himself that he should have seen this coming, since he had watched the weather report for the whole week on the news yesterday.

Camp was rapidly turning from good to bad to worse. Nothing was going right at all. For all Nick knew, he was out of the state by now. He was lost, with no idea where he was, where to go, or what to do. He was already getting hungry again, just because of how much work he had to do to try to find a stupid silver watch. He had been traveling along the same path for around five minutes when he came upon a golden-colored metal poster on the ground. He picked it up and read the silver lettering aloud: THE SILVER WATCH CLUB. WATCH OUT FOR SILVER BEARS. HUNT SILVER BEARS THIS TUESDAY AND WEDNESDAY.

Nick was outraged. He wasn't even looking for the right kind of silver watch all this time. But the real reason he was angry was because he'd seen the back of the poster a few times already and the gust of wind must have flipped it over. The stupidity of the entire situation was equally annoying. He dragged the cardboard poster along the muddy ground, with only one goal repeating in his head: to find the edge of the forest.

CRACK! Nick raised the poster over his head. BOOM! "No!" bellowed Nick as a lightning bolt crashed somewhere nearby. "I won't die. No!" He breathed heavily and then a bolt of lightning flashed right in front of his very eyes with another loud crack. He was flung into the dirt and the metal sign slipped from his hand. As smoke surrounded the area, a cold, toneless voice whispered, "Not now but soon, my child. Soon." Before he got the chance to yell out loud, another bolt of lightning crashed down on his right side and in a cloud of smoke, a tall figure appeared, but then was gone. Nick rolled over onto his right side. His poster was on the ground, half of it vaporized by the mini-explosion and the other half steaming with hot smoke.

"What the...?" croaked Nick. He seized the remaining half of the poster and set off again, walking toward a light he saw ahead of him. He heard a loud boom coming from far behind and twisted his body around immediately. With a gasp of fear and curiosity, he looked into the darkness, where six glowing red eyes flashed brightly and then vanished as quickly as they appeared, beside the location where a tree had crashed down mere seconds before.

Nick reached the edge of the forest and found Counselor Philip there. He dragged the poster off the ground and showed it to him. The director stood there for a moment, his expression blank, then his mouth curled into a smile. "Good job. You have done well." Nick threw the sign onto the mud and said, "Alright, good. Grand. Can I go back now?"

Counselor Philip chortled, "Of course you can. I know you think that punishment may have been a wee harsh, but you must understand that some things are necessary. The legend of the Zorblin..." Philip shivered. "Too dangerous. And thank you for retrieving the sign for me. I needed to promote the Silver Watch Group because recently, a lot of bears populated this area. Now be good, Silver." He then pulled a silver watch from his pocket, checked the time, and said, "Dinner should be starting soon. I think they had to do dinner early. So much paperwork. Now get back to camp, Silver. I'd be sorry to have to give you two punishments in one day...and I'll have to make an announcement soon. I have a couple of new rules." For a second, Nick considered telling the camp director about the figure he had seen, but he didn't want to push his luck any further.

Nick followed him out of the forest, through the sand dunes, past the counselor cabins, and then to a big, grimy, rusty, old shack. When they entered, Nick realized right away that this was a cafeteria. Counselor Philip brought him to a dirty bench next to Madison, who sat to the right of Daniel, and warned, "Now, don't try to sneak off again to hear things you shouldn't." With a sinking feeling, Nick remembered seeing the man's eyes stare at his hiding spot, although he hadn't thought then that he had been discovered.

Madison sighed and demanded to know, "What punishment did he give you?" Nick groaned and told her, "I had to find a silver watch sign in the forest." He was surprised to see his sister perk up. "What?" he asked. Madison faced him with excitement. "The out-of-bounds forest?" Nick frowned and said, "No, the other forest. I saw the red eyes again, though – the same ones I saw in the lake on the way here in the car." Madison's eyes widened. Daniel realized what they were talking about and said with a shudder, "I don't ever want to go in those forests. And I think you went into the Forest of Tappers."

Nick only heard some of this because he was remembering something else. "Hey, why are we having dinner less than three hours after lunch?" he asked. His sister and Daniel gave him a stony stare. "Oh, right. I forgot to tell you," said Madison. "Counselors had to have dinner early." Daniel added, "Yeah, because of a delivery problem, I think. And the whole thing with Counselor Robert." Nick glanced at the stopwatch he still had as the counselors set the menus, which were only crumpled papers with food items scribbled on them with pen, on the table. Nick sniffed the cafeteria air and although it didn't smell as bad as the forest, the smell was still awful.

Counselor Philip entered the cafeteria, sighing, and Nick scowled at him. The counselor brought out his megaphone and stepped up on a grimy wooden stool. His low voice came out sounding loud. "Due to certain circumstances, we will be making a few necessary changes at Camp CrystalFlake!" Nick got worried. Who knew what Counselor Philip could be referring to now? After Nick's punishment in the Forest of Tappers, the man was probably planning something horrible.

"This camp makes enough money to supply food, games, etcetera – yet in order to do more and raise enough money, we have planned an idea," he continued. "I don't really enjoy the idea much, but it's the best thing we have been offered." During Counselor Philip's speech, Nick saw him glare at some of the older kids. "Now, we are going to. . ." He paused, and every kid crossed their fingers and put their hands together as if to pray. Finally, he announced, ". . . have fundraisers that include campers sending votes to Town Hall." There was a loud burst of outrage that sounded like an explosion, forcing Nick to clap his hands over his ears while trying to hold back on joining the angry protests because he was already on the counselor's bad side. Counselor Philip boomed into the megaphone, "SILENCE! Settle down. There is still more. To help with our new fundraisers, we will be giving you all… a camp dog!" The counselors cheered and some of the kids got excited, while others looked worried. Nick didn't know what to think. Coming from Counselor Philip, it would be some aggressive dog that'll bite everyone, he thought. But on the other hand, Nick had always been an expert with dogs and enjoyed them. "Now, the rest of the new rules will be posted on the camp bulletin board tomorrow morning," the announcements concluded. "That is all."

When dinner came, everybody else ate like pigs but Nick ate slowly, thinking. He wondered what Counselor Philip was hiding in the forest. And it seemed that he was also trying to hide it from the other counselors, who seemed as if they already knew what it was, anyway. Nick told this to everyone at the table, trying to speak over the noise from the other two tables near them but not loud enough for the counselors to hear. Sean Carter said, "The thing is, even Philip seems worried about it." Jacob Hayonds, a second-year who was said to have explored every little crevice of the camp, commented, "The whole situation is crazy, if you ask me. It can't be real. Nothing's in the forest. Believe me, one time I snuck in and I quickly left before old Philip found out. I found nothing." Naturally, Nick remained stubborn. A few people seemed to agree with him but some people didn't and had different views, but not much to offer. Nick looked at his dinner and felt hungrier than he ever had in his entire life, but something inside him told him not to eat it. And so, he didn't.

The Legend

———

Pit! Pit! Pit! Pit! As everyone remained gathered in the cafeteria, the rain outside rushed down from the dark, dismal clouds and whoever stepped outside would be pelted with sharp blades of raindrops. Not only was there teeming rain, but there were powerful bolts of lightning shooting out of the clouds like the tentacles of an octopus. Nick stared at his food as he began trying to guess what a Zorblin might be and why it was dangerous. Whatever it was, though, seemed to really shake up some of the campers. He had already asked his sister twice during dinner if she knew, hoping for a proper answer, but always getting the same, "No, I have no idea. And besides, didn't you say you think it's fake?" He was getting tired of not knowing things but was looking forward to finally getting some sleep later.

Although he was still hungry, a small and vague voice inside his head kept telling him, "Don't eat the food. You will regret it. You wait and see. Don't eat the food." He wondered why his mind kept telling him this, but after a while, it felt like the voice wasn't even a part of his own mind. He was getting restless thinking about the Zorblin and the no-food thing, so he finally mustered up the courage to ask Daniel. But he didn't have the answer Nick expected. "The Zorblin? That creature – no, that's bad. If it is real, that would be bad. Not sure if it's real or not, though. But you shouldn't try to look for it like everybody says that they're going to do. That would be…well, pretty high up on the no-no list." Nick wondered

what Daniel meant when he said some campers said they would go looking for the Zorblin. He started to imagine what the Zorblin would look
like, since Daniel made him even more curious. He noticed, however,
that Counselor Philip looked like he was in a bad mood. Nick tried to
stop thinking about the Zorblin because he was still scared what the
counselor would do to him if he kept asking about it.

After a few minutes of talking with the others at his table, the light
hanging above his head flickered and turned off, then back on. At the
exact same time, a mental lightbulb flickered on and shone brightly inside
his head. He had asked a few kids about the Zorblin and they suggested
that he look in the camp library. A high schooler told him that the camp
had a person who made custom magazines of the goings-on at camp,
which were in the library along with other books. Nick didn't even know
they had a library, but the campers told him the small shack between the
cafeteria and the counselor's cabin was the old library that some kids still
used.

This was definitely a game-changer for Nick and he wanted to know
more. He asked the other kids if there were any rules for the library, still
worried about slipping up in front of any counselor with a connection
to He-Must-Not-Be-Named, as he had come to refer to Counselor Philip.
They told him the library only opened on Mondays and Wednesdays,
and the counselors wouldn't work in it any other day. But a third-year
camper from Cabin A, who was a friend of Madison's, gave Nick hope.
She told him, "I remember going into the library once and I'm positive
I saw, like, half a shelf full of Zorblin books and folklore about them."
He grinned and thanked her.

Nick continued picking at his food, still determined not to eat but
tempted by his hunger. He sat watching his sister conversing with some
campers at the other table and he tried to theorize answers in his head to
all of the questions he had. He felt he was beginning to get obsessed with

this Zorblin thing. Soon, the counselors escorted all the campers to three cabins. Nick would be sharing a cabin with a large group that included his sister, John Jackson, Daniel Garring, Dylan Sheimer, Gregory Golding, Shea Arte, David Canscar, Gabriel Golding, Allissa Helga, Tony Trustfinler, Jackie Gordon, Jack Karoff, Isabella Laney, Stewart Bones, and many others.

Counselor Chris led them into Cabin B and told them they could pick whatever bed they wanted. Nick counted how many bunkbeds there were as the counselor explained the rules. The counselor grimly explained that they were one bunkbed short, and until the order for another bunkbed came in, one person would have to sleep on the floor.

Everybody just stared at each other, as if waiting for someone to step up and make the sacrifice. But that moment never came. A full minute had passed before David Canscar spoke up and stated, "I have an idea. What if we alternate who sleeps on the floor each night?" Everybody agreed with this and they decided to vote on who would go first, so David ripped a piece of paper from a notebook sticking out of his backpack, grabbed a pen, and wrote Floor-sleeper Chart. He then wrote down every cabinmate's name on a list to indicate who would sleep on the floor when. David put Shea at the beginning of the list, meaning she would sleep on the floor that night, and put his own name at the bottom of the list — obviously so he wouldn't have to sleep on the floor for a while.

Everybody looked over and approved the list (except Shea, who groaned) and heaved their backpacks onto their beds. Nick gave Madison the top bunk of their bed, which was up against the wall with one side against a window, and he took the bottom bunk. He looked at the stiff sheets on his bed, but he and his sister had come prepared. They both ripped off the sheets and piled them into a corner, allowing Shea to use them, then pulled clean sheets from their backpacks and placed them onto their beds. Nick put a thick, heavy white blanket over his sheets and spread out a smaller red blanket, decently comfortable, onto the side of his bed. He and his sister looked at each other's beds and grinned.

By around nine o' clock, most of the younger kids had already fallen asleep. Madison told Nick about the variety of camp exercises they had done that day while he was in the forest and he was at least happy he missed those, as he found his adventure in the forest kind of fun. As he half-listened to his sister drone on about camp, Nick started to think about the secret forest and how his first camp day had gone. When he turned over to get more comfortable, he spotted something that wiped his thoughts from his mind. John Jackson, on the opposite side of the room from him, was reading a book called Zorblin: Facts, Life, and Origins. Nick could barely resist. He leaned over and whispered, "Hey, whatcha reading?" John turned toward him and whispered back with a grin, "Book about Zorblins." Nick, ready to take risks, asked, "Can you tell me about some?" Instead of putting him off, John brightened up and replied, "Sure," which surprised Nick.

John almost immediately began to explain, "A Zorblin is a creature created from magma in the deep underworlds from a planet known as Mezort." This immediately fired red flags for Nick, as none of this made sense. "They have three long, tentacle-like, scaly, hairless necks and three heads with two beady red eyes each, that are roughly the shape of a tri-angle. They have long, skeletal torsos that lack arms but end in a stubby, sharp tail. If you get stung by it, you'll be injected with deadly poison. Right before the torso meets the tail, there are two stubby but strong veined legs with sharp claws that can sink into almost anything." He paused to take a breath, then grinned and said, "So now you know." And he turned back to his book.

Nick, satisfied but craving more, paused a second and dared to ask quickly, "Can you tell me their origins?" He hoped John wouldn't turn him down, but was positive he would, and was surprised to hear him say,

"Yeah, okay. Sure. I was thinking about reading about that soon anyway." Nick leaned against the backboard of the lower bunk, his pillow propped up against it, and listened as John began, talking aloud as if he were reading the words directly from the closed book at his side. "People can only guess how the Zorblin was made. But hundreds of years ago, an anonymous source from Planet Mezort stated something that might be the truth. The source claimed to be a victim of a dark villain who practically ruled the planet and forced to help in his schemes." He took another breath. "From what the source said, we can assume that the dark ruler of Planet Mezort, who had overthrown the original king years before, had been starting to face problems. As he constantly dealt with relatives trying to stop him, he also had to stop the attacks of countless soldiers who had worked for the king.

"The Dark Ruler, that's what they called him, would conquer new planets and then mold each planet into his own. A citizen of one of the victimized planets claimed he knew someone who created an object that was able to prophesy that one of the Dark Ruler's future conquests held the type of power and control he sought. Ever since the ruler heard that, he had been attacking other planets, trying to find the one the device prophesied. But while he was gone, the few people who hated him and weren't forced under his control would attempt to raid his base. One day, when the Dark Ruler was working on special plans for Planet Mezort, one of his greatest servants called him down behind his base. There was a large canyon in the ground, full of fiery magma, which had recently cracked open. A large, burning red fragment of the Great Star of Power floated above the canyon." John paused and took a breath.

"The Dark Ruler reached out his hand and grabbed the fragment. Its powers were transferred into him. He used the powers of the Lava Fragment of the Great Star of Power to morph the magma into monsters. His personal favorites, the Zorblins, were the strongest. He killed off the other monsters and kept producing new Zorblins to do his bidding. After years of searching, he thought he had found the planet he was seeking. Earth. Our planet, the one prophesied to hold the power he was seeking. He traveled to Earth with the Zorblins and made new ones to guard his base." John took another big breath and added, "Oh yeah. Did I mention the middle head of the Zorblins can spew lava and the left and right heads spew acid?" Nick murmured, "Typical. Typical."

John continued, looking upward, trying to keep the story straight. "Anyway, he and his Zorblins killed lots of humans. But someone, possibly one of his relatives, overpowered him and sent him back to his planet. The mysterious relative thought he killed every Zorblin that was sent to Earth. It is rumored that the relative forgot one, however, and it escaped and hid within this very camp. When the Dark Ruler returned to his base, he noticed another family member running away from it and realized that another relative had somehow killed the rest of the Zorblins and sealed the crack in the ground. Later that day, all the Dark Ruler's relatives captured him and threw him into the prison he created. He had put every bit of his power into building the Mezoar Prison, which is what he named it. And since that time, the Dark Ruler has been patiently waiting for his faithful servants to return and release him." John paused again before adding, "But that's just a legend."

Nick thought over what he had just heard. "Thanks," he said, and wished John a good night. Nick lay back down in his bed, imagining what the Zorblin would look like. Although he was extremely tired, he didn't feel like sleeping. He had so much on his mind, but one of his questions was now answered. Zorblins were – well, very likely real. And one of them could be lurking at Camp CrystalFlake. But what did the prophecy mean about one of the planets the Dark Ruler would try to conquer holding the type of power and control he sought? What was the prophecy referring to there? The last Zorblin? "No, it can't be," thought

Nick, remembering that the prophecy was made before the Zorblins. But that meant nothing. What if the prophecy was talking about another fragment from the Great Star of Power? He felt excitement running through his body. He believed his theory was right and couldn't wait for Monday to arrive so he could go to the library and research this further.

But for now, he just had to keep guessing. It was about 9:30 and Nick saw Counselor Chris coming towards their cabin. He strode towards the door and opened it reluctantly, then walked in and turned his head twice, making sure every camper was asleep. Nick simply rolled over and shut his eyes. When Counselor Chris left, Nick remembered what was said about that 9:30 sleep thing. "This camp is insane," he thought, "but it does offer more than it was supposed to."

The Lake Trip

"Yawwwwn!" Nick raised his head off his cold pillow and noticed it felt heavy. He looked around. Some of the other kids were awake already. The rest were sleeping. Nick looked over at the clock on the wall. It was seven in the morning. He yawned again and leaned his back against the backboard of his lower bunk, flattening his pillow.

He wanted to enjoy the quiet time while he could before Counselor Philip would wake them all up or whatever the next encounter with him would be. He looked outside, wondering if it was still storming. The storm had gone, the sky was almost cloudless, and the hot sun was blazing through the camp. The ground was still damp from the rain, but the sun shined so brightly, it looked as though it had never rained.

It was Sunday, one day before the library opened. Plus, it was day two of camp. It took him a few seconds to remember the story from the night before, about the Dark Ruler of Planet Mezort and how he had created the Zorblins. He got up from bed and sat on its edge. That's when Counselor Chris entered the cabin and attached a few sticky notes to the clipboard. When he finished, he said gruffly, "Everybody needs to get dressed and ready. We're going on a special trip today."

Surprised, Nick asked, "On the second day of camp?" He expected a trip to be planned in the middle or end of camp, but not on the second day. "Yes," Counselor Chris responded briskly. "Counselor Philip is too busy today to do the activity he planned, so he assigned us to bring you without him." Nick took in all of this happily, though slightly disappointed as he had wanted to make it up to Philip. Everyone who was still asleep was told to wake up and get ready.

Once the counselor left the cabin, everybody rushed into the bathroom. Nick approached the clipboard and read the first sticky note: "Lake Trip on Sunday. Special Activities." He read the second: "Eat delicious food on the water. Enjoy the lake breeze." Then he read the last: "Prizes and games for campers who win the challenges." He lit up with excitement. Even though Philip had planned it, it sounded like the trip would be fun. Nick got dressed, brushed his teeth after waiting forever in line, and glanced again at the clipboard. He noticed a fourth sticky note hanging off the edge that he must have missed. This one was the best one yet: "Campers are permitted to bring one of your own personal items from your backpacks." About a half hour later, Counselor Chris returned to Cabin B and filed them outside in a line, with everybody talking excitedly and showing one another what they were bringing, besides bags with their bathing suits in them. Madison brought her phone, but Nick had decided to take his Magic 8-Ball. It had never, ever failed him and he felt it could help answer a few new questions he might have from the trip to the lake.

Counselor Chris led them all onto a yellow bus. Two other counselors were leading the other campers onto two more buses. Nick got crammed into the window seat, with Madison in the middle and the kid Nick recognized as Dylan Sheimer in the aisle seat. It was highly uncomfortable, but Nick decided to make the best of it by chatting with Dylan.

"What do you think the activities will be for the lake trip?" Dylan asked.

"I dunno," Nick shrugged.

"Hmm. Maybe a swimming contest because…where are we visiting again? Oh, right! The lake – the place where people go to swim!" Madison interrupted sarcastically. Nick and Dylan laughed as the bus drove along a bridge above a stream. They passed a line of trees on their right and on their left was a patch of sandy land. Beyond that was the large lake. Even farther in the distance was a tall, rocky, mountain.

It was only a few minutes before they reached a dirt field. The bus stopped and the counselor driving told everyone to get out. They stepped onto the sand and saw a wooden deck raised about nine feet off the ground that they reached by climbing a small wooden staircase with thin, sappy railings on both sides. Glancing behind him out of the corner of his eye, Nick saw two counselors carrying a few heavy-looking boxes, filled with games. They all sat down at the long wooden bench, at a long oak table. The two counselors hauled the boxes up onto the deck. One of the counselors came to the middle of the patio and said aloud, "My name is Counselor Jacob." The breeze from the lake blew as he continued. "First, we will be having lunch supplied by the local pizza restaurant a few miles down the road." A few kids cheered. "Then, we will set up a few of the games and activities, and one final competition with a big prize…" This got everyone excited, but he doubted nobody was as ecstatic as Nick. He was happy to finally have a day full of fun activities after a long year of school. And after yesterday, he wanted to have as much fun as physically possible.

After a few minutes of chatter among the campers, the food finally arrived. By now, it was around 10:30, so it was really more of a brunch than lunch. Counselor Jacob chimed in and told them, "We were planning on having this as breakfast, but the breakfast place we tried ordering from was closed." They all ate the food immediately, except Nick, who hesitated until he heard that same, weird voice in his head saying, "Eat it. It is not the same." And so, Nick ate, wondering if the voice was even real. He was starving and had four big slices before he finally felt full. When everyone had finished eating, the pizza boxes were empty. Pigeons must have smelled the pizza, though, because a second later six of them swooped down and attacked the crumpled boxes, grasping at the remnants inside.

The campers sat at the oak table like ticking timebombs, waiting as the counselors set up activities and games on the sand right next to the deck. They were barely able to restrain themselves from running down the deck and playing every game at the same time. Finally, after about ten minutes, which seemed like an eternity to the campers, the counselors climbed back up to the patio and announced, "The games are ready!" There was an outburst of excited screams and commotion as the campers rushed toward the staircase and onto the sand. Nick pushed his way through the crowd and jumped down the entire staircase, then sprinted around and faced what the counselors had planned for them.

There were three long tables, filled with games, piled with boardgames, and surrounded by many other enjoyable things. There were two full rows of arcade games and in the middle and off to the side closer to the water, there were activities like horseshoes, pin the tail on the donkey, trust fall, and even a map for a scavenger hunt. The counselors had set up so many things, it was hard for Nick to try them all, which was never really a problem he faced. He realized that all it would take to have a good time at camp was for the owner of the camp itself to not be running it at all.

After about an hour and a half of scavenger hunts, cotton candy machines, and other things, every kid lost track of the time. It was the middle of the day, and the sun was burning up the breezy beach. Nick was so positive that this was going to be the best day of camp, he asked the trusty Magic 8-Ball, "Can anything possibly go wrong today that makes it bad?" He shook the ball powerfully and read the words on the screen. "You Can Count on It." He looked confused. For the first time ever, he questioned the Magic 8-Ball. The sun was blazing through the cloudless sky, as the lake shimmered a bluish green.

"Is everybody ready for the big reveal?" Counselor Lily called out. Nick spun around, as did every other camper. "Here's the reveal of our grand competition!" chimed in Counselor Jacob. Everybody forgot about what they were doing and grew silent while expectedly staring at the counselors, waiting for them to announce the news. "It's a . . ." chorused Counselor Gabe. "Swimming competition!" bellowed Counselor Lily. Over the uproar of excitement, Nick heard his sister's voice adding cynically, "Because nobody here figured that out sooner, what with being told to bring our bathing suits?"

"Yeah, maybe that should've been obvious," Nick admitted to himself. The counselors gave everybody a choice: either participate in the competition for a prize or, while everyone else does that, you could swim in the lake freely. A lot more people than Nick expected decided to swim on their own. That meant there were only nine kids competing with him: his sister, Dylan Sheimer, Ronald McKenzie, Kenzie Berto, David Canscar, Stewart Bones, Justin Swabble, Sean Carter, and Leah Dortle. Counselor Chris stood outside the locker room building, waiting for anyone who wanted to race. All the people not racing were already in Counselor Lily's long line. The minutes crept by, feeling so much longer than it actually was, but when the last of the ten competitors had run out of the locker room, it was finally time. As Counselor Chris led them towards the lake, some kids started making bets with each other about who they thought would win. Of course, they usually they bet that they themselves would win.

Counselor Chris showed them their section of the lake, which was about fifty feet long, with those little swim rope barricades that are usually used to keep people in their own lane. There were no ropes separating the competitors, though. There were only ropes to prevent the competitors from going too far out in the lake. Everybody lined up next to each other and eyed the finish line. Counselor Chris announced lazily, "So, the rules are: no pushing, no shoving, no going out-of-bounds, and no pulling back or grabbing onto the other competitors. Am I clear?"

"Yes," replied all ten voices stiffly.

"Then on my mark . . ." began Counselor Chris. The pressure grew tense. "Get set . . ." The campers held their breath, waiting to dive underwater but still waiting for the counselor's command. "GO!" And then they were off. They dove underwater and when they resurfaced, they didn't stop. "OW!" shouted someone near Nick as another voice gasped, "Sorry!" Nick swung his arms through the heavy water, penetrating it and swimming through the crowd. He had to stop for occasional breaths and to rest his arms and legs, but he didn't have much time because every second mattered.

He took in some air quickly and raised an arm to wipe the water out of his eyes as the blurred image of the finish line became clearer. Counselor Chris bellowed, "First, second, and third place winners will all get a prize!" That put Nick into pure competition mode. There were still about thirty yards more to go and he noticed he was in sixth place. Determined to win, he pushed himself as much as he could. Gasping for air, he quickly moved into fifth place, then took a wild breath and dove underwater, swimming right underneath the person in fourth place who had been blocking him. When he resurfaced, he had made it to fourth place, but he was running out of energy quickly. His sister was, no doubt, in first place, Dylan Sheimer was in second, and Sean Carter swam just behind him. Nick strained more than any other time in his whole life, making speed a priority to get into third place. He was gasping for air at this point, trying to pass Sean Carter, who was now neck-and-neck with him.

He pushed himself past his own endurance level and just barely made it in front of Sean.

Through the lake water, Nick screamed at himself, "Come on!" He wheezed and gasped for air and painfully swung his arms harder, thrashing at the water. But as he passed Sean Carter, he had to slow down and rest, and by the time he was swimming fast again, they were neck-and-neck once more. As Nick moved forward, an image in his mind stirred. He couldn't make it out very well because it was too blurry. As he swam, he tried focusing on the image he saw in his mind. For a split second, he saw the blurry motion of a lake, then six red eyes glaring down at him, and then... "Aggggggggggggggghhhhhhhhhhh!" The entire picture in his mind shattered completely as he focused his eyes onto Dylan Sheimer.

Dylan yelled as he was being mysteriously pulled downward underwater and then outside the ropes. Nick and Sean were the first to notice. Dylan gasped and gurgled underwater. Nick stared at Sean, and Sean nodded back. They swam out beyond the ropes towards Dylan, who was being dragged underwater and further away from the race. They swam as fast as they could, but Nick was so weakened from the race, he couldn't push any faster or further. He had to stop and rest. As he did, he felt something hard, squirmy, and slimy wrap around his left leg, pulling him underwater, too. He felt Dylan and Sean pulling on his bathing suit shirt, trying to bring him to the surface. Nick realized he was drowning. The beast, or whatever it was, was surely about to rip his leg off. Dylan and Sean pulled on his shirt with all their might, but Dylan was too weakened from the attack on him and Sean was tired from the race. Nick yanked his leg up, but the beast just would not let go. He was running out of air fast. He felt the terrible agony of his leg being pulled from his socket. Spitting out bubbles, Nick was pulled farther away from Dylan and Sean. His head ached and he saw a blurry image of a transparent-looking person, male or female. He wasn't sure, looking worried, and fast. And the screaming of desperation, as if something bad had happened. Or was happening. Nick's headache subsided as the image was wiped from his mind. He was still drowning...deeper...and deeper...and... splash! He suddenly felt two arms under his arms, holding him up. His sister had finally noticed what was happening.

"Yes! Air!" Nick gasped as he was lifted, waist deep in the water, far from the ropes. And every camper was watching. Dylan and Sean were still swimming, but suddenly the beast struck again. Dylan cried out as he was pulled from Sean, who grabbed onto his hands as Dylan's legs were being pulled the other way. Dylan screamed in pain as Nick and Madison swam over to him.

"Help! Heeelp! Arrghhh!" Dylan splashed around, waving his arms as he tried to resist the beast forcing him downward. "Noooo!" He spit out water as he resurfaced again after resisting the beast that had just pulled him back under. Nick tried to reach Dylan, but he didn't have the energy. Neither did his sister, who had also just stopped to rest. Nick looked hopefully at the counselors, who were too far away to see. Nick shouted, "Help! Dylan is being pulled underwater by something! He's drowning! Help! Help!" From far away, he saw the dots that were the counselors coming nearer. They had gotten onto a raft lying on the ground under the deck and quickly paddled towards Dylan. When they reached him, one of the counselors grabbed the oar and shoved it at the beast. Dylan was finally freed and the counselors lifted him onto the raft to safety.

As the counselors paddled back, Sean, Nick, and Madison wearily swam back to shore, with every camper's eyes on them and Dylan. Nick had just noticed that Dylan's left leg was bleeding. There was a huge mark on it, while on the other side was a gaping gash, with blood dripping down. The counselors on the raft made it to shore and carefully placed Dylan on the sand as he began to fall unconscious. One of the counselors spoke on a walkie-talkie as another counselor paddled on the raft again towards the three kids who were still making their way back. Nick listened carefully and heard the counselor say into the walkie-talkie, "Nurse? Nurse Fletcher. Dylan…what did you say your name is, kid?" Dylan's eyes fluttered slightly as he groaned weakly, "Dylan S-sheimer."

"Uh, Dylan Sheimer, injured his leg. It's bad…pulled into the ocean… loads of blood… come now!"

"Hey, kid!" Nick swung his head around and saw Counselor Jacob on the raft, with Sean and Madison already next to him. Nick climbed onto the raft. His bones felt like rubber and he was happy to rest his legs and clear his mind. But after what had happened, he was worried. Every time he tried to clear his mind of all thoughts, a cold feeling would slip through his bones and blurry images would pop into his head, unconnected to his own thoughts. He ended up lying down on the raft, thinking about all that occurred.

The counselors decided to end the trip early, announcing it right after the last three soaking wet campers headed towards the bathroom to change. Nick peeled off his drenched bathing suit and squished it into the bag as he pulled out his wrinkled clothes. He got dressed as fast as he could, sighed to himself, and then left the stall, where he ran right smack into Daniel. There was a second when both looked at each other without saying a word before Daniel asked in a confused voice, "What happened? And how did you fight back?" There was an even longer silence then, since Nick had no idea how to respond at first. "Fight what back?" he finally asked.

Daniel's face turned completely pale in a split second. "The monster!"

Nick found his words. "Well, I had to get it off of me, and Dylan… wait, what do you mean, 'fight back'?"

Daniel looked as though he had completely lost all patience. Exasperated, he said, "Not that! When it was drowning you! You did something to it…there was a flash of light…and then it backed off and went for Dylan again." He left a blank pause.

But a question nagged at the back of Nick's head. "What do you mean, I 'did something to it and it backed off?' I was drowning! I assumed it thought I was dead or something and then went for Dylan!" The color in Daniel's pale face reappeared as he pointed and blurted, "No, it didn't! I saw a light over where you were from that dock and heard a loud thud and then a screeching noise. Then you floated upward and just b-barely resurfaced, and your sister got hold of you! B-because of that, that monster nearly killed you!" Nick stared at Daniel's face, which had gone completely pale again, and heard him answer the question bubbling in his head.

Nick took in everything Daniel had just said. He felt more campers' eyes staring at both of them and knew they were trying to listen to their conversation. Finally, Daniel opened his mouth again and said, "Well, I'm glad you're alive. I just hope Dylan . . ." He broke off, but Nick got the point.

Soon after, the smell of the lake breeze left everybody's nostrils as they piled into the buses and left the shore, ending their disastrous trip.

5

The Holes

———

I t started to storm again. Brilliant yellow lightning bolts struck the
seaside and the rain beat down hard as the three buses drove along the
bumpy road. It was only when Nick, sitting between John and Madison,
felt his Magic 8-Ball inside his pocket did he remember what it had told
him hours before. He had doubted it when the ball told him disaster
would strike…but it did. He wanted to talk to John or his sister, but the
truth was nobody really wanted to talk after what had just happened.
The nurse had taken Dylan into her truck and drove him back to camp,
letting him sleep on a stretcher.

Things at camp were truly going from bad to worse. The excitement
had died, the fun had ceased, the trip had ended early, the counselors
were a wreck, and Dylan had been attacked. Nick had suffered injuries,
too, but he figured they must not have been that bad, because by the
time they were on the bus, the gash and blood had both faded and
washed away.

"Why did this bad stuff have to start on my first year of what was
supposed to be a good camp?" he wondered. Why had disaster struck
them? What had pulled him and Dylan down to the lake bottom? Could
it have been the infamous Zorblin? And what had Nick's visions meant?
Things were getting weird quickly and the summer had just begun. The
day's summer light subtly faded as the drenched bus continued driving

/as about two o'clock when they reached the camp.
rs from Cabin A was already there and the Cabin C
later. It was still decently warm out by the time every-
. had been an excruciatingly long day and they were all
ha... .k.

When Counselor Philip saw the campers retreating to their cabins, he stared at every single one of them, a confused look in his eyes. As Nick reached his own cabin, Jack Karoff blurted out grimly, "He knows. Counselor Philip. He knows what happened." Everybody agreed. Nick gave a vigorous nod and slumped down onto his bed, feeling the Magic 8-Ball against his leg. He stretched out and immediately caught sight of a trickle of blood running down his left arm, then he wiped it off with his sleeve.

The campers all rested for a few minutes, but soon started getting bored. Multiple buzzing voices soon broke the silence. Nick was bored, too, but didn't feel like talking. He searched vigorously through his stuffed backpack and pulled out a notebook, then dug even further. From a clear, long container, he removed a pencil with a large eraser and a small, red sharpener. After twisting the pencil into a fine point, he pulled the notebook closer, opened it to a clean page, and thought about what to draw. He hesitated for a second, wondering if he should do what he wanted before deciding he should. "Hey John?" he asked quietly.

"Yeah?" responded John after a moment or two.

"What should…what do you think I should draw?"

John took a bit longer to respond. "Maybe a… yeah! Try drawing a Zorblin!"

"Alright," Nick said brightly. "Let's do this." And so, he started drawing. He tried to use John's details of the Zorblin from the night before, but he couldn't remember exactly what he had said. Still, Nick was pretty happy with the way the drawing was coming out. He drew a long, slimy, bony, snake-like body with a long tail and two stubby-clawed legs. The snake's body twisted into three skinnier versions that extended into three, oval-shaped heads, with long serpent tongues sticking out. There were four large fangs in each ugly head. After about ten minutes, Nick was done and told John triumphantly, "Finished!" He held up his picture and bent the other side of the notebook where John couldn't see.

John grinned widely but observed, "No. Not really!" Nick frowned. "Okay, then what does it look like?" John bent over his own bed and pulled a book from under his mattress. He held it in his arms, flipping through the pages. "It looks like..." He found the page and held up the book. "This!" Nick gawked at the picture. The Zorblin had a skeletal back, not anywhere close to a snake's outer structure. The body extended to a scaly tale that looked like the one from his own drawing, but it got even worse. Extended from the neck, three scaly, raw, cold, blood smeared, but bloodless boneless necks writhed and extended into faces in a shape between diamonds and ovals. They had countless sharp teeth on the side of each long, vertical, outstretched mouth with a dry scrunched-up interior, full of blood. They had tiny slitted nostrils that leaked with thin streams of blood, topped off with two beady eyes on each head, each eye small and beady and full of a dark scarlet gleam. They were hairless and hideous . . . and a creature Nick had seen before.

"John!" Nick shouted, shocked and happy. "The Zorblin! The legend says it's fake, but it's not! I've seen those six beady red eyes before!" He was excited to have learned another part of the truth. So excited, in fact, that he immediately devised a theory. "You know what? What if…" Nick stopped abruptly, as if someone had just told him to go and live in the Forest of Tappers. "I bet the Zorblin was what pulled me and Dylan under the lake!"

John stared at him in confusion. "Well…" he began, but Nick stopped him. "No, no! It makes sense! Hold on. Check your book! Check your book to see if they can swim!" John silently looked again at the book. He read for a few seconds, then replied, "Well, I guess they can swim, but…" Nick stopped him again. "See? Exactly! The Zorblin pulled us into the lake! But why?"

"Nick, wait," John interrupted as Nick went silent. "Let me finish. Like I said, they can swim but when they do, it evaporates some of their skin. A Zorblin definitely wouldn't go swimming and evaporate their skin, in a public place, just for a quick lunch." Nick understood what John meant. But then a new idea came to him. "But what if it was a different monster? No, no…like, what if the Dark Ruler accidentally forgot to kill one or it escaped to a different planet?"

With a curious look, John replied blankly, "Nick, if there is anything this book is sure of, it's the fact that the Dark Ruler killed every monster he didn't care about, which was every type of monster except for the Zorblins." Defeated, Nick simply muttered, "Oh." John shrugged. "Good theory, though." Nick put an elbow in his lap and his head on his hand. An icy feeling swept over him as he sat on his bed, facing the window. He realized his mind was completely blank before a blurry image swirled to life in his head. He forced himself to think of other things as the blurry picture dissolved from his memory and the cold feeling subsided.

He was bored with himself. Resisting an urge to go out and about and just explore, he remained seated on his bed and caught a glimpse of Daniel eyeing the other campers. As Nick watched, Daniel stealthily jumped off his bed and slowly crept over to the door, opened it slowly, and sprinted out. As he did, a small piece of paper dropped from his pocket onto his bed. At first, Nick didn't care. He assumed Daniel got a letter from home, saying something about an allergy he had, and that he forgot to tell the counselors about. It was a stupid guess, but it was all

Nick could think of. But after almost a minute of guessing why Daniel might have snuck off, Nick got suspicious and was dying to know more. And when Nick got that curious, he would not shrug it off. He glanced at his sister, who shared his talent for art and was distracted with her marker set and sketchbook, and then crept around slowly, walking towards the bathroom that was next to the slightly open door, making it look like he had to use it. The other campers were distracted and Nick bolted to his right. He squeezed through the slightly opened door, trying very hard not to force it open any further, and rushed out into the grass fields at last.

"Yes!" he muttered under his breath. He saw no one in his path as he quickly snuck away from his cabin. He scanned the whole camp, looking for Daniel, and found him half-hidden by the grassy hill, staring at the out-of-bounds forest with a look of terror on his face. Next to Daniel, on his right, were holes in the ground. Nick looked to his own right and stared at the counselor cabin. Nobody there. He held his breath and ran over to Daniel, stopping as the other boy turned to him with a look of horror on his chalk-white face. "Hi, Daniel," Nick greeted him quietly. "What are you, er, doing here?" Daniel took a while to respond as he tried to look anywhere but at Nick's face. "Nothing."

"Are you sure?"

"Yes."

"Then why aren't you in your cabin?"

"Well, why aren't you in your cabin?"

"To see what you're doing."

"Just looking," Daniel shrugged.

"So, you're just looking around?"

"Mm hmm."

"Didn't you say you never wanted to get on Counselor Philip's bad side?" Nick questioned him.

"Yeah…"

"Well, you're not really supposed to be here. Right?"

Daniel didn't respond, but instead glanced at the forest and then at the holes. Nick followed his eyes and looked at the holes, too. There were a lot of them. Nick wondered aloud, "Where do all of these holes keep coming from?" Daniel turned to him and replied, "That's the thing. I don't know. I first noticed them this morning. At first, I thought they were just normal holes. Then I noticed that they looked . . . well . . .." Nick looked at the holes. There was no way normal animals could dig these. They were too wide and just big in general, and way too deep. Daniel must have figured what Nick was thinking because he immediately replied, "Well, probably a bear, actually. I really don't know."

Nick looked at Daniel, then back at the holes. "I guess that could make sense. Yeah," he agreed blankly. Daniel sighed and told him, "They've been getting worse. Bigger, more of them. This morning, I wrote a quick letter to my dad, asking about the holes. On my way back to Cabin B after the trip, I picked up my letter from the mail bin at the fireplace. He said not to worry about them, but . . ." Nick examined the holes more closely. They were leaking with a greenish-light blue mixture. Without thinking, he bent over and touched the mixture. He scooped some up, then straightened back up again, watching the mixture oozing in his hand. It was slimy, soft, and cold. Nick looked around. There were similar holes from this area all the way over to the entrance of the Forest of Tappers, behind the sand dunes, and in front of the counselor cabins. He had remembered seeing them before, but never this many. With a sigh, he looked up to the sky and wondered when Dylan was coming back. "Hey, Daniel?"

"Yeah?"

"When do you think Dylan will be back from the medical cabin?"

"I'm going to guess . . . about a day or two."

"Okay," Nick nodded disappointedly. The truth was, it had been a grueling day for him and right after they had started bonding, Dylan nearly got his leg torn off and was rushed to whatever medical facility Nurse Fletcher used. Nick surveyed the variety of holes again, noticing more of the odd ooze in every hole...but what could that mean? There were already enough questions in his head. "It's been almost two days," Nick said grimly, "and I've already been nearly killed. This camp isn't for me. I usually like solving puzzles. But this? This is too much." He turned to Daniel hopefully, searching for advice. Finally, Daniel stopped looking so worried. A tinge of color returned to his face as he looked Nick in the eye.

"Things can get bad, Nick," He glanced at the out-of-bounds forest and the counselor cabins and added, "but there's always going to be a way to flip a situation around. It's the only way you'll figure this out." Nick stared at him, dumbstruck at first, and then smiled. Daniel's chalk-white pallor was gone as he smiled back. "See, I'm good at motivational speeches!"

"Campers! Attention, all three cabins! Meeting outside!" Nick and Daniel spun around immediately to see a distressed Counselor Philip marching towards the cabins, yelling into his megaphone. Nick felt relieved he stood where he was with Daniel, because they were far away enough from the megaphone to avoid having their ears shattered. Not like it really would shatter anyone's ears, he thought, but you never know. They watched as every camper from every cabin slowly spilled out, looking tired. They stared at the crowd for a second before running over to join them. As Counselor Philip closed his eyes and bellowed into the megaphone again, Daniel and Nick raced as fast as they could. Nick almost fell into a hole but didn't. However, when he turned to see what he had tripped on, he accidentally ran straight toward another deep hole and fell into it with a long "Aaaggghhh!" He hit the bottom with a loud squish and looked down. Although it was dark in the hole, he could still see the shining ooze up to his ankles. Luckily, Daniel heard him as he yelled and came over to help him climb out.

Finally, they trudged into line, with Nick covered in slimy, dripping ooze from the ankles down. Counselor Philip stared at him and sighed, "Why do you have slime on your feet, Mr. Silver?" Nick didn't know how to answer. He simply shrugged and stayed silent as Counselor Philip announced in a tired, grim voice, "Like I said yesterday, we have to institute some changes. This will include writing letters to the Town Hall, so that is what we all will be doing tonight." Nick's stomach contracted and there were cries of protest, but Counselor Philip merely frowned and continued, "Silence! We will be writing to vote about what we think about a new town museum." Some of the campers looked curious, while others looked bored. "A museum about ships." Nobody had any verbal reaction to this. "I want your essays about your thoughts on a museum about ships to be on my desk tonight by six-thirty. That is all."

Nick, unable to resist the urge and remembering one of the camp director's previous announcements, raised his hand and asked out loud, "When is the stress dog coming?" Counselor Philip scowled and replied in an exhausted voice, "Soon. Any more questions?"

"Um...counselor?" A girl with a tiny voice raised her hand. "How – how long does the essay have to be?" Counselor Philip screwed up his face and pondered before telling the crowd, "Hmm...let's see. How about...five pages, then." This time, nobody argued. They knew it was pointless. "And, answering Mr. Silver's question, the stress dog is coming on Tuesday."

"WHAT?" Nick yelled to himself inside his head. He had been excited for the stress dog to come ever since he heard about it, and the thought that he had to wait even longer for something he really wanted stung him.

"Now follow me," Counselor Philip commanded, leading everyone into the cafeteria. "This will be a working dinner. You can start your essays as you eat." The campers scowled. "I'm sorry, but just this time. Oh, and I almost forgot," he said calmly. "Since our cafeteria ladies here didn't have enough time to prepare dinner, we had to order from the restaurant down the road, but luckily, they did have enough time to make . . . special vegetables!" Yay, Nick thought glumly as the cafeteria ladies handed out plates of vegetables, plus plastic trays with chicken wings and fries and bottles of water. Once the food was sitting in front of Nick, he stared at it hungrily, but first…

"Also, there have been some complaints from parents, so you have to eat the vegetables," Counselor Philip announced sharply. The lunch ladies nodded as the other counselors stood against the far wall, staring aimlessly. Counselor Philip muttered something to the counselors and they hurried outside. A minute later, they returned with piles of paper and a box of pens. They gave everybody six pages – one describing the museum, the other five for the essay – and told the campers, "You may eat now." Nick was devastatingly hungry. He wanted to eat the chicken fingers first, but Counselor Philip was staring in his vicinity. Nick guiltily jabbed his Brussels sprouts with a plastic fork just as the same nagging voice in the back of his head muttered, "Don't eat it. It is dangerous." Feeling a prickle of annoyance, Nick looked up and noticed the counselor had looked away, so he pierced the chicken finger with his fork and strained to listen for the voice. This time, it told him, "Eat it. It is not like the others. It is different. You can eat it." He grinned and dipped the chicken finger in ketchup before shoving it into his mouth in one large bite.

Remembering the essay, he seized the paper and read: *Brand new Ship Museum is the newest idea from Town Hall. It will be a three-story building entirely made out of marble, dedicated to ships of the past. It will be a place where you can study ships, their past, present, and future, and learn more about their origins. It will replace the old town theme park. Town officials say the Ship Museum will benefit the city and create revenue, unlike the theme park, which did not. Additionally, with the funds made from the museum, Town Hall will be able to bring more amazing changes to the town. Although town officials say it will benefit the community, some people disagree with that opinion. There will be a vote on the eighteenth of June (Monday) to decide whether or not the park is demolished for the museum. As of right now, there appears to be nearly an equal vote between the museum and park, although the park is slightly behind the museum. Now, the campers of Camp CrystalFlake will help decide the final verdict.*

When Nick finished reading, he was annoyed. That theme park was a place he planned to visit during the summer and on weekends to have fun. All he really cared about, though, was that Town Hall should not tear it down. He could see that other kids had the same hopes as he did. Turning his attention back to his food, he picked up a chicken finger, dipped it in more ketchup, and took a couple more bites, washing them down with a drink of water. He stared at his Brussels sprouts and spinach, then at Counselor Philip, who had been watching over each table for five minutes. Nick had a strange feeling something bad would happen if he ate the vegetables, but at the same time, he would probably be punished if he didn't. After the hunt in the Forest of Tappers the day before, Nick was completely done with punishments. He stared hopefully at his sister to his left, but she was completely focusing on writing her essay, although it looked as if she hadn't even touched it. He looked wistfully to John on his left, who was already on his second page and taking a break to eat some of his fries.

Of course, Nick couldn't just tell them, "Okay, guys, I need help. This voice in my head tells me I can't eat the vegetables, but I have to. What do I do?" Bothering anyone about it was hopeless, so when nobody was looking, he grabbed a handful of the vegetables and threw them under the table while faking a confused look at his five blank papers. He did this two more times until his plate was empty. He ate more fries and drank some more water, and then focused on his papers. He read the first paper again and began writing, "I don't think they should demolish the theme park because…" and immediately hit a roadblock. He didn't know what to write. Finally, he continued something adults would probably like, "…this is a place where families can connect. A place where families can join together and have fun. By replacing it with a museum…" He considered what he should write next, staring at his mostly blank paper and thought deeper…deeper… An icy feeling showered over him, like a tornado of cold winds while being drenched in heavy rain. In his mind, a picture started to form of a ghostly man, screaming in rage. Another figure, someone, was comforting him, telling him they were going to fix the problem. The screaming man continued to rant as the second person, male or female, pleaded with him, assuring him their next plan would work, unless…

But was the first figure really a man? Nick swung his head upward, straightening his back, and forced his mind on the essay as the picture in his mind dissolved. He wrote, "…you remove the fun, happy times families gain with each other. Sure, they can recreate new ones at the museum, but it wouldn't be the same. Kids will be unhappy when they see their favorite theme park destroyed and replaced with a museum they didn't want." And so it went on like this for an hour, as he switched between the essay and his meal. Nick thought that he was the farthest behind on completing the essay, but soon realized that wasn't true after stealing glances at other campers' pages for ideas.

The clock said six o'clock, half an hour before the essay was due. Nick was nearly done, but completely worn out in the process. After all, Dylan wasn't the only person to be pulled to the bottom of the lake. Nick finished his fourth page and started the fifth and final sheet. Meanwhile, John had already finished and was helping other people finish theirs. Nick was waiting for inspiration to pop into his head. The only problem was that that wasn't working at all. He remembered that the library would open the next day and he forced himself to get his assignment completed. But of course, he was fresh out of ideas. Finally, with ten minutes remaining, he decided to ask his sister for help. She had just finished and told Nick, "Write about . . .that. Yeah…no. Don't bother with that. Let me do it. Yeah, that's good, one more . . ." After about five minutes, he was done. After thanking his sister, he relaxed and finished his dinner – still aware of the vegetables on the floor – and talked to her about his visions and the holes in the ground outside.

"Hmmmm. I wonder what those holes are all about. And what did you say was in them again?" she asked curiously.

"Some weird, slimy oozy stuff."

"Weird, isn't it? You don't think…the Zorblin?"

"I dunno. All I know is that the Zorblin wasn't the one that pulled me and Dylan into the lake."

"You sure John's right, though?"

As Nick thought, he looked at John. "Positive. I trust him. I just wish Dylan would heal already. I want to talk to him and ask him stuff," Nick sighed.

"Like what?" Madison asked.

"Well," Nick began, "first, what happened when he reached the lake floor? And did he see it? And I also kind of miss him. You know, when we talked on the bus this morning."

"Yeah," Madison nodded. "That was pretty fun."

It was a real bore fest once everyone had eaten their dinner as they waited for Counselor Philip to come back in. And when he did, people regretted wishing that he would. He looked pale-faced with shock as he entered and asked, "What happened at the lake with Dylan Sheimer?" Nick had a bad feeling about what was coming next. The counselor looked around the room, glaring at everyone. He asked loudly, "Why did a camper get sent to the Medical Cabin?" Nobody answered since only a few campers knew, and none of them even understood it. "Alright, then. Now, I will come around and collect your work. And please, campers, be more careful from now on. We really do not need a repeat of today's distressing events." Counselor Philip muttered something to the counselors and then he strode over to each lunch table, collecting the essays one by one. When he finished, he gave them a quick look and then announced, sounding exhausted, "Counselors Chris, Lily, and Jacob will lead each camper to their cabin. The library will be open tomorrow." Nick cheered inside his head. "Also, Counselors Chris, Lily, and Jacob will inform you all about tomorrow's activities. That is all. Goodnight."

Camp Activities

"C'mon campers."

"Okay."

"Alright."

"Mmhmm."

As the sun sank, red and bright orange skies colored the landscape. Stars appeared every here and there. The clouds that still remained were a bright pink as the warmth of the summer day slowly subsided. Counselor Chris led his line of campers to Cabin B and said dully, "Now go inside, and I'll explain tomorrow's events." Every camper tiredly trampled into the cabin, falling onto their beds. "Okay, tomorrow will be the day that this camp hosts a variety of activities, each harder and more challenging as you progress. If you are one of the five that do the worst, you will be eliminated."

There were lots of tired, "Ooohs!" and "Aaaahs!"

"Now get some sleep. You'll need it for tomorrow."

Each of the campers peeled off their clothes in the bathroom one at a time and put on their pajamas. Counselor Chris was long gone by the time everybody was changed. The brilliant red sky darkened in the night as the sounds of hooting owls disrupted the campers' peace and quiet. Nick, however, didn't even notice the hooting and was tirelessly looking forward to the next day, when the library would open and the camp would be hosting a contest. He dreamed on about this as he heard everybody murmuring about the contest. They kept saying how it would be an upgrade from the swimming challenge and they named it "The Big Thing." As the others all around him began to relax and sleep, Nick wanted to do a few things. But first came the bed list. "Okay, guys. On my list, it says the next person to sleep on the floor is... Stewart Bones!" yelled David from across the room in a fake excited voice. "Congratulations, Stewart! You have now entered the Floor Sleepers Club!" Stewart frowned as he hauled his stuff to what they'd dubbed the Corner of Shame. Shea happily brought her things to Stewart's old bed. After some of the campers gave him extra sheets and blankets, Stewart began accepting his fate a little more.

Outside, the sky turned to purple, then faded to a dark night. Nick sat in bed, silently thinking. All was calm. He looked around the cabin at the kids sleeping, talking, and laughing and then he saw John, who was looking down at a book. He moved his head even further to the right and saw Daniel was lying in bed, under the covers, with a tired look on his face. He leaned over out of bed and looked upward above his bunk, to see his sister asleep. He thought about camp, the library, the counselors and holes, the lake trip and Zorblins, the new friends he'd make and had already made. Before he dozed, he felt one last feeling of warm happiness running along the sweatshirt that was too comfortable to take off and finally fell asleep, drifting into a world where all was possible.

"Chirp! Chirp! Chirp!" A cold breeze blew through the silent cabin. As this happened, Nick was in a dream that he was thoroughly enjoying, where he battled, struck, and dodged. The asleep part of him was immersed fully in the dream. In one corner of his brain, however, was a part of him that was aware he was sleeping and didn't want to wake. In his dream, he was fighting off a towering icy slug with a death ray. He strained as he used his ability to gain fire power. He flew towards the slug that had just shot off a wave of ice as snow fell to the ground and breathed fire when the two collided. The ice was beating down the fire…Nick was panicking…he shot out beads of fire from his palm, which the slug easily avoided as his ice ray overpowered the fire and…

"Too cold. Stop. Warmer. Make it warmer…" he muttered. Nick snapped his eyes open as another cold breeze flew past him. His head was up, neck turned, while the rest of his body remained motionless as he stayed flat on his back against the frigid sheets. He dropped his head onto the pillow carelessly.

"Can't, Nick." Nick rose his head again, feeling heavy and cold, as he heard his sister repeat from above him, "I told you last year, when somebody tried to touch the thermostat, it required some code." Nick, realizing what must have happened, let his head fall onto his fluffy, cold pillow for a second time while trying to remember his dream. Irritated, he got out of bed slowly and saw the problem: the door was ajar. He trudged over to it and closed it with a loud slam. A few kids woke up from the sound but dropped back to sleep. Now that he was already up, Nick decided to quickly go to the bathroom. Afterward, he covered himself with his blankets and enjoyed the new warmth. But it was hard to fall back to sleep now that he was awake. He decided to check the time, pulling himself further out of his covers to read the clock. It was only 7:12 in the morning. He let out a heavy yawn and rested his head on his pillow. He remembered everything the second his head touched the pillow. The competition…the library…Dylan…

Nick heard grunts and shuffling all around him and realized everyone else was waking up. Rays of sunlight shone through the windows of the cabin as the flag outside whipped in the wind, the sun slowly rose, and the moon disappeared. When a good portion of the campers in Cabin B had woken up, Counselor Chris burst through the door, giving everybody a grin. "Ha! I got to wake you all up early. So," he began curtly. "I think you all know why today is special, don't you?" Everyone nodded as a chorus of "Yes" was heard around the cabin. "Spot on, campers. Now follow me. It's breakfast time. Oh, and one of our campers will be joining us again."

"I guess we'll have to after breakfast."

"If we even have time to, John."

"Well, if you were paying attention, we will be going to the fields at noon to begin the tournament."

"Well, good for you, John."

"C'mon, we're lagging behind. Do you think they'll have the books we need, though, Nick?"

"I hope."

Creaking sounds filled the warm air as campers dropped onto the wooden bench at the outside table, engaged in conversation. Nick and John plopped down next to each other, with Nick to John's left and Madison's right. Daniel came and sat down to the other side of John. "Hey, guys."

"Hey, Daniel," the three chorused. As they talked, the counselors walked around handing out menus. Nick stopped and looked around, watching birds fly around the camp as flowers blossomed by the lake. Finally, just as he had been anticipating, Nurse Fletcher walked toward the table, passing the camp flag on the edge of the sand dunes, joined by a short, jet black-haired kid with green eyes. Before the two reached the table, just out of earshot, Nurse Fletcher whispered things that Nick assumed were safety warnings and then let Dylan take a seat. Nick caught his eye and waved. Dylan took a seat next to Madison and grinned. The first thing he said to Nick was, "Medical Cabin: boring. Horrible tentacle thing that grabbed us, you know?"

"Yeah, that was – er – painful. And, well, slimy."

Dylan laughed as the birds chirped a high-pitched tune. "Yeah, it was pretty slimy. And for a monster that was trying to drown us, I personally don't think it did a good job." The boys laughed together this time. "So, um, guys – what did I miss while I was in that boring medical cabin?"

"Well, the counselors announced a tournament for campers with a series of challenges where you have to be the last person to get eliminated." Madison stated.

"Cool. Anything else interesting going on?" Dylan asked eagerly.

"Well, Madison, John, Daniel, and I are trying to figure out the mystery of the final Zorblin."

"Oh, you mean the legend about that what's-its-name creature made by some Dark Ruler?" Dylan remembered.

"Yeah, how'd you know?" Nick asked curiously.

"Who doesn't know about it?" Dylan said and pointed at one of the lunch ladies nearing their side of the table. "Alright guys, let's just order our breakfast before we run out of time!" After scanning the menu, Nick, Dylan, and Madison decided on chocolate chip pancakes and John and Daniel wanted scrambled eggs. When the lunch lady came, she said hoarsely, "What will you be eating?" They placed their orders and the lunch lady marched off. Then Nick remembered. "Guys…"

"Yeah?" chorused the other four. Nick attempted to explain the voice the best he could. Even though it was a serious question, it sounded stupid saying it out loud and he knew it. Their responses were just what he had predicted: "Hmm. Maybe you should just ignore it." and "I don't know. Maybe you only think it's a voice? It might not be real." Nick found none of these explanations helpful. As the food arrived, he stole a quick glance at the holes. There was only one new hole. The biggest yet.

They all ate like royalty that morning. Even Nick. For some reason, the voice in his head decided, "You can eat this. It isn't like the other food." When everyone was full, they relaxed in the sunlight daze. When Nick started wondering about the library again, John voiced his thoughts by saying quietly, "So, are we going to the library after this or what?" Everybody agreed and they waited for the counselors to lead them back to their cabins. Nick filled Dylan in about why they were going to the library. That's when Counselor Philip showed up and asked enthusiastically, "Nice breakfasts, campers?" Everybody nodded as the lunch ladies nodded curtly, smiling.

"Okay, everyone!" The sound of every camper's least favorite megaphone echoed through the grounds. "Before the tournament begins, we will allow you campers to explore the campground and get familiar with it. No going out-of-bounds or you're out!" added the counselor fiercely. As soon as they were allowed to go, the five kids sprinted off. But as they were running, Daniel stopped them and said grimly, "Sorry, guys, but I can't join you at the library. I have to do some extra work that, you could say, my father asked of me." Everybody said their goodbyes and hurried towards the library. It was an old, musty shack, with almost-clear windows all around. It was painted white, with some spots of mud on it, but otherwise not too bad. On the front white door, a sign hung from a little stump that stretched an inch out that read, OPEN. They walked closer as Madison reached for the golden, smudged doorknob and pulled. It didn't open. "Should've known," she groaned as Nick gave her a confused look. "The librarian always shows up late... and that door is always broken." They tried opening it a few more times; everyone taking a turn and all failing. Unfortunately, they wasted their time because just as Madison expected, the librarian showed up late and unlocked the door. She asked nicely, "Did you all want a book that badly?" Nobody answered but instead nodded impatiently. As the librarian walked across the cold, stony floor toward a wooden desk, the rest of them briskly stepped over the threshold.

There were four shelves, filled with books, which went from one side of the room to the front of the desk. "Alright!" said the librarian cheerfully. "Go find your books!" Each of them took a shelf. Madison took the first, Dylan the second, John the third, and Nick the fourth, all the way at the back of the room. Nick searched through different books, sliding them away with a finger every time he saw a book unrelated to Zorblins. He was shifting aside a book about presidents when he saw a title on the back of another one: The Legend of Zorblins and the Rise and Fall of the Dark Ruler. He grabbed the dusty book and blew on it, watching the thick sheets of dust take flight. He examined the leathery, hard cover. There was a thin slice right down the side, with a yellow strip extended from the back of the book. Nick identified it as a bookmark at once. He swung his head around to see a small chair. He dropped onto it and turned the book over, revealing a text that read:

The legend of the Dark Ruler remains in pieces, as some people try to glue them together. This book can help identify the Dark Ruler's past, present, and future, while also bringing the knowledge of his favorite inventions: the Zorblins. Unlike every other, this book will use pure fact and truth to help the reader identify the life of the Dark Ruler, who once lived a life of woe. This book tells how the Dark Ruler came to be, why he began his life to rule his home planet, and why he began the quest of hunting down the Fragments of the Great Star of Power. Warning: Do not let this book fall into the wrong hands. The author of this book died by unknown forces shortly after finishing writing it. He claims to have made this book for a special purpose. This book still remains under the title of the true author. Do not let this book fall into the hands of anyone with Mestephan-like features.

Nick finished reading the back of the book with a look of utter confusion. He had barely understood some of what he had just read and had an urgent feeling not to show anyone what he had found. Just by reading it, he knew if anybody at all found his book . . .but how would he get it out of the library without the librarian noticing? "No," he thought. "If it is in the library, then it will be safe to check out." He clutched the book right to his side, shielding it from gaze, even though he was going to have to show everybody anyway.

"Yes!"

"What?"

"A book on legends! That has to include Zorblins, right?" John figured as he saw the book Madison was holding.

"Yeah! This is it!" Madison cried. The librarian flinched but didn't look up from the book she was reading.

"Anyone else find one?" asked Dylan.

"Well . . ." Everybody stared at Nick as he slowly lifted his book from his side.

"Nick, what is that?"

"Well, it's a book on the history of the Dark Ruler," he said simply. They all looked at it for a few seconds and that's when Dylan said, "Oh, shoot! Look at the time! Counselor Idiot…er…Philip, should be calling us down soon!"

Right on cue, the voice came. "Every camper please get in lines in front of your cabin in five minutes' time!" exploded Counselor Philip, no doubt through his megaphone.

"Come on, hurry! Let's check these two out!" said Nick as he flew across the room in a hurry. Madison went first. She dropped the book, Legends and Tales of Dangerous Creatures, onto the librarian's desk and said loudly, "I'd like to check out this book."

"I'm sorry, miss, but I'm afraid that book is written mostly in another language," said the librarian sadly as she held up the book and handed it back to Madison, who looked disappointed and went to put the book back. Next came Nick. Reluctantly, he handed his book over to the librarian, whose face twitched as her features grew dark with fear. "Where did you find this?" she hissed in a harsh, venomous voice.

"In…it was on the back shelf!" Nick told her.

"Put that book back where you found it!" she shrieked, her voice sounding slightly different.

"But I found it and I want to check it out!" Nick interrupted before she could continue. She had abandoned her happy tone completely now. Her face was demented and screwed up with anger and horror, looking strangely like a whirlpool of darkness as she screamed, "You can't read that book!" Nick stared at everybody hopelessly. That's when Dylan retorted, "He found the book. This is a library. He wants it, so he should keep it!"

"That book is off-limits and will be thrown out! Now please, leave both your books, put them back, and go!"

Shocked, Nick slowly spun around and slumped towards the back of the room, book clutched tightly in his right hand. He had an idea. When he was at the back of the room, he saw a vent that led outside. He slowly took the cover off the vent, which creaked quietly, and carefully placed the vent cover on the floor. He saw a two-foot gap between where he had removed it and the cover on the other side of the vent, outside the building. He placed the book in the middle of the vent, made a mental note of where the vent would be when looking from outside, then gently picked up the cover and snapped it back in place. The book was hidden inside the vent for him to secretly take later. "Perfect," he thought as he rushed back over to the front of the library, forcing a sad expression. "Goodbye," said the librarian, looking confused as the campers exited.

They jogged over to the cabins as Nick briskly told them what he had done and why, and they seemed pretty impressed. Once they reached the front of the cabin, they all stopped talking and got in a horizontal line in front of Counselor Chris, who was saying, ". . .should be here any second now, and when he is, he will explain the rules and lead you to your first challenge." Counselor Philip walked over to the crowd of campers a few minutes later. "Alright, campers! Are you ready to begin the tournament?" There were loud cheers as he boomed, "Then follow me to the first challenge!" They walked over to the sand dunes, where Counselor Philip stared at the sand and said loudly, "Alright! Your first challenge is to find the hidden treasures buried in the sand. You will all be given plastic shovels. You will have to dig to find pennies. If you find a penny, you're safe. There are about forty of you left here, as of yesterday. Some parents decided to take their kids home after the lake issue…" He paused. "So anyway, there are forty of you looking for pennies. There are thirty-five pennies in total. The five campers who don't get a penny will be eliminated." Lots of campers were pumped up, prepared to beat the challenge. Nick was ready, determined to win. Counselor Philip went around the line of campers and gave them one plastic shovel each. "Is everybody ready?" he bellowed.

"YES!" cried the campers.

"GO!"

Nick could barely make out what happened next. All he saw was the blur of thirty-nine kids rushing past him, sand flying anywhere, even in one of his eyes, and getting elbowed and then shoved into the sand with his thigh two inches deep in sand. He winced and noticed his hands were empty. He reached around and seized his shovel, pulled himself onto his feet, and dove toward the mound of sand. He swung his weak right arm that held the shovel straight into the sand and withdrew it as somebody's foot propelled into his wrist. He stumbled for a second, got to his knees, then began digging rapidly. Sand shot around everywhere as voices yelled. Nick wasn't sure if he could do it; there were kids already jumping around showing off their pennies. He crawled over to a less crowded spot and began flinging sand out of the way. After a few minutes, he had devised a plan: he would try his hardest to fling sand into other kids' holes and crawl out of the way once they turned to see who had done it.

Time was running out and Nick still didn't have a penny. He looked around and saw Dylan holding a penny, next to John. He turned to Madison, who had been looking restless, and now changed expressions as she held out a penny, too. Nick dug furiously as the sun beat painfully onto his neck. He anxiously grazed the top of the sand with his shovel and stopped still when he felt a bump vibrate through the tool. He knew what it was. Throwing the shovel aside, he reached into the sand and pulled out a small, shimmering, and sandy penny.

As Nick ran into the line of campers with pennies, he saw another camper joyfully carrying a penny, as well. As soon as they stepped in line, Counselor Philip yelled into the sunny breeze, "One more penny remains!" Looking back at the sand dunes, Nick noticed that none of the kids still there were anyone he knew, and lost interest. The six kids still searching for pennies broke out into small scuffles, elbowing each other aside and kicking to knock each other over despite the counselors' shouts. Finally, one kid leapt into the air with joy, holding out a shiny new penny and leaving the other five kids looking disappointed and angry.

"Now, campers!" Counselor Philip announced, gesturing to the line of winners. "Thirty-five remain, and five sadly lost! And now we continue the tournament! Follow me! Yes, the ones who didn't win, also." They all followed the counselor to a big tree behind the counselor cabin. There were ropes hanging from the top of the tree and the campers' breathing intensified. "Our next brilliant challenge...is a tree climbing race! The first thirty to the top of this big camp tree progresses! The ten who don't are out!" Quiet muttering broke out. "And yes, I did decide that some rounds eliminate more than five people." The counselors positioned everybody all around the tree and called out, "The Great Camp Tree! Race to the top going live in three…two…one!" Everyone rushed toward the Great Tree all at once and Nick noticed they actually were going live. Somebody was recording them with a big camera a few feet away.

He circled around the bottom of the tree, looking for the best place to start climbing. He lifted his right foot onto a stump that stuck out, reached a left hand out, grabbed a branch with it, and hoisted himself up while setting down his left foot on the curved bark. He climbed up into a tangle of heavy branches, he forced his way around them, and leaned his back against a heavy one while lifting his feet up onto a smaller branch. Campers climbed right over him, leaving him immobilized. Nick pushed his back slowly up the big branch as his feet walked up the skinnier one, which two other campers were climbing over. He made it to the top of the tangle of branches and bent low while grabbing onto the huge trunk of the tree. He focused on sliding his feet into the grooves of the trunk and balanced himself as he clung straight to the side of the Great Tree. He lifted a hand up higher to another branch, but a foot squished his hand and he retracted it painfully. The camper above him slipped and fell, hanging over one of the bigger branches above Nick. He reached his arms up onto a huge branch next to the one the other camper was stuck on. Nick pulled his legs onto the branch and nearly fell off when he shot his hands out to wrap them around a small branch. He pulled himself back towards the heart of the tree while balancing his knees on a steady branch.

The fragile branch in his hands gave a short crack and fell as he released it, dropping between all of the branches and onto the ground, right out of the way of the counselors. Nick advanced on the heavy branch and climbed up the thick bark of the tree, arms wrapped tightly around the trunk, ascending out of sight behind the colorful leaves and small branches. As he stuck a foot into one of the tree's holes, another camper climbed along on a branch next to him and shoved him sideways. Nick yelled out as he swung around the tree, the side of his sweatshirt tied up on a small branch. Another camper came up behind him as two more passed him on the other side while he struggled on the side of the tree, swinging back and forth, foot and sweatshirt stuck. He grabbed his sweatshirt firmly and pulled hard. He grunted as it dislodged suddenly, then removed his foot from the hole and stepped onto a small stump to grab a better branch than the others.

Campers powerfully climbed up the tree all around him. Some were forced to let go and fall back. Nick was sweating as he painfully lifted his feet onto one of the highest branches in sight. He gripped one of the holes above his head tightly with both hands and used it to lift him-self up onto a curved, thick, heavy branch directly above him. A few more campers reached the area above him, spit down at the ground and other campers that were lagging behind, and continued up the final, curving branches.

Nick pushed with all of his might up the final levels of the tree, latch-ing his feet onto any rough surface, and finally brought himself to the top. It was a small sunken area, surrounded by thick branches that extended into thin ones on all sides, with yellow flags on each branch. He pushed aside one of the campers that had tried to shove him just as the head of another camper appeared between two of the curved branches. Nick leaned on his stomach, reaching out his right hand with all of his might at the top of the branch, charged at one of the flags, and missed.

He slashed his dirty hand again and missed again, then strained one more time . . .and grabbed hold of it.

Nick released all his nerves and unclenched his muscles as he leaned back and admired the small yellow flag in his right hand. Suddenly, he got shoved aside and twisted on the spot, tripped over a rough twig, and grappled onto one of the branches. Without much strength left, his hands slipped and he fell. He dropped a few feet down and latched onto a rope, all air in his lungs emptied on impact. Crumpled, he slowly lowered himself down, hands throbbing. Between his bended arms lay the small yellow flag, the wood splintered in two pieces. When Nick landed on his knees on the ground, he stared at the part that held the flag, and the longer portion that now was just a long stick. He heard the counselors muttering behind him as he got onto his feet and picked up the broken flag. Counselor Jacob walked over to him, put a hand on his shoulder, and said softly, "I'm sorry, but since your flag broke . . ."

Another voice interrupted, "You're still in the game." Nick and the counselors spun around to see who had said that. They stared back at an impatient looking Counselor Philip. "It's fine," he grunted, "Remember the rules? I don't care if it breaks, as long as they bring back the flag." The counselors had no choice but to leave Nick in the game and he walked triumphantly towards the line of kids who finished. Nick felt a rush of gratitude towards the camp director suddenly. When everybody had made it safely back to the bottom of the Great Tree, the man who had been recording stopped and said, "Pretty good. That got a lot of views." He and Counselor Philip started murmuring to each other and when they were done, Counselor Philip took a wad of cash from the man, who smiled and left.

Counselor Philip looked back at the campers. He pointed at ten campers who walked grimly to the side with the others who had been disqualified earlier. "Well, ten of us are gone and thirty of us remain! Now follow me to your next challenge!" They ran behind him and stopped in front of an open field. "Get ready..." he began dramatically, "for the . . . obstacle course!"

"I knew it," thought Nick, who had been guessing ever since he had finished the second challenge what the next one would be. "Your third challenge will be quite different. Two of you will race each other at the same time. One will fail, one will succeed. In the end, half of you will progress and the other fifteen will not." Nick stared up at the obstacle course. He wanted to at least know what he had to do before doing it. First, they had to run up the stone stairs and jump onto the stone pillar, jump again onto a raised stone horizontal ledge that would connect the two racers' platforms, then jump again onto a wide ladder, cling onto it, and climb to its top. Next, they would have to crawl across the top of the ladder as it curved upward into an arch. Once they made it across the ladder, they would have to jump again onto one giant trampoline. Third, they would have to jump from the trampoline to a small platform in front of a balance beam and, once past that, had to jump one more time onto another staircase that the racers would have to share, this one wider than the first, and race to the top. First one to reach the top, wins.

The counselors paired up everyone with a partner and then the first two racers were off. Nick was with someone his age named Gabriel, who was tall, wore glasses, and looked like he could run a mile within five minutes. They were waiting next to each other on the line as other campers ahead either raced or cursed under their breath at their opponent. And when every spectator watched Dean slip and fall onto the grass, Counselor Philip called out, "And did I mention that if you fall onto the ground, you have to restart the whole course?" Dean swore so loudly, Counselor Philip had to yell at him, but in the end, Dean ended up winning because his opponent faked trying to win and slowed down instead, because he didn't want to continue in the competition.

There was race after race after race, when finally, the pair that was in front of Nick and Gabriel began theirs. They finished after a few minutes. Harry narrowly beat Joseph, who was too exhausted to move as fast during the final run. Nick looked up at Gabriel, since he was taller than him, and Gabriel said, "Fair game?"

"Fair game."

They were off as soon as the whistle blew. Nick ran up the steps and heard Gabriel rushing right next to him. Nick took a large breath and jumped onto the first pillar, then took off flying onto the ledge in front. Now came the hard part. He bolted off the ledge and latched onto the ladder as he became completely unaware of where Gabriel was. Everything around him dissolved into a blur except for the curved ladder, which he climbed with great difficulty. He slammed his finger into the ladder and fell over backwards as something caught hold of his sweatshirt hoodie. "Fair game," repeated Gabriel. "Thanks," Nick choked as he straightened himself against the ladder. They both sped upward rapidly and Nick lost track of Gabriel again. He slowly started to crawl as he reached the top of the arch, then more quickly as his knees protested in pain. CRACK! "No!" The ladder swayed violently as he felt Gabriel twist behind him. They both yelled out as the ladder shifted again, nearly knocking them both off.

"Wait!" boomed the voice of Counselor Philip as he worked hard to connect the broken beam of the ladder that continued to shake. Nick rocked back and forth as the ladder vibrated against his ribs. He didn't even notice Gabriel, who tried to crawl to the other side of the arch despite its powerful swaying. "Stop! Stop!" yelled Counselor Philip. Nick and Gabriel abruptly stopped moving as the arch rattled dangerously. When the counselor finally got a firm grip on the beam and was able to hold it together, he hissed through gritted teeth, "I fixed it. Go!" The two boys began racing towards the other side of the ladder when it gave one last, slight shake. Sweating, they reached the end of the arch and leapt onto the trampoline. Gabriel jumped a second after Nick, who lost his balance and toppled over as Gabriel hit it, sending a ripple across the trampoline and nearly knocking Nick over again. After perfecting his jump onto the balance beam, Gabriel hesitated for a moment, then began walking slowly across it.

Meanwhile, Nick had slowly raised himself off the trampoline and jumped onto the balance beam. He slowly edged along the beam sideways with Gabriel still out in front. As the audience gasped, Gabriel jumped onto the staircase merrily, winked at Nick, and began racing up the stairs. Nick paced to the other side, feeling balanced as he tried to even his arms, then jumped onto the staircase and hurried up to Gabriel, thinking, "Yes, I can still do this. I just have to get around Gabriel."

Gabriel was almost at the top of the staircase by then, panting heavily, every bone in his body on fire, when Nick croaked, "No!" He stretched out a hand in front of Gabriel, pushing him behind as he wheezed and sprinted higher. Gabriel chased him and Nick watched him surge in front. Desperate, he ducked and weaved under Gabriel's outstretched arm and passed him once again as the audience gasped and some even clapped. Neck and neck, the two, without realizing it, extended their legs slightly and ended up tripping over each other at the same time and landing onto the top of the stairs. Nick groaned as Gabriel mumbled, "What…? Did we both…?" The crowd murmured as the two untangled themselves and muttered, "Sorry," remembering their agreement to play fair.

"They both tied. Surely, we'll need to have a do-over?" someone asked. "No," said Counselor Philip firmly, "We need the time. We'll just have to leave them both in." Nick joined his friends as Daniel said brightly, "Still in!" John and Dylan mumbled things that sounded like, "I'm out." "Not fair." "Cheaters."

Madison recounted how she narrowly beat Anne, who tried to push her onto the grass but missed. Daniel spluttered out excitedly how he swerved around some older kid who tried to knee him and won. And Nick explained how the beam of the ladder cracked so that he and Gabriel had to stay put, and how they ended up tying for first. And so, the day went on. Nick, Madison, and Daniel, who was a pro at mazes, worked their way to the end of a maze together, after the kids who lost had slumped out of the maze looking weak and tired. Later, they had a race around the camp, which Nick triumphed in, getting last place and Madison just barely lost. After that, they had a contest to create the best replication of a picture. Nick won that easily and Daniel was runner-up. Finally, when it was the second-to-last challenge, they had an eating competition that Nick won by eating four slices of pizza ordered from a local restaurant. "This thing about not eating some food has made me hungry," he decided. Daniel managed to choke down three and a half slices, and Gabriel had to give up after trying to begin a fourth.

Nick and Daniel were competing in the final challenge of the tournament. "Congratulations to both of you! You made it to the grand finale! Now, watch as these two battle it out in . . .an advertisement!" The words entered Nick's mind, but he didn't think he understood them correctly, although he was sure he had heard Philip perfectly. "Yes, that is right! The camper who creates the best advertisement for the new CrystalFlake Apple Juice wins!" Nick expected to look at Daniel and see an expression to match his own, but instead Daniel showed comprehension and determination. He sat down at one side of the bench in the middle of the cafeteria, with a glass of CrystalFlake Apple Juice in front of him. Counselor Philip watched while Counselor Lily started recording Daniel. "Okay!" began Daniel in an enthusiastic voice, "Have you seen the brand new CrystalFlake Apple Juice? What? You haven't? Well, come on down to your local grocery store today, and buy some! It's good for parties, families, schools, anything!" He took a big gulp out of the juice and grinned even wider. "Come and buy some today! It's delicious!"

When Counselor Lily pulled her phone away, everybody knew the recording for Daniel was over and clapped. When the applause stopped, Counselor Philip spoke in a loud, clear voice, "Next up is Nicholas Silver!" Madison, Dylan, and John moved to the front of the crowd. "You got this, Nick!" whispered Madison.

"Yeah, don't let that dope get to you!" responded Dylan.

"Just focus and you'll come out on top!" finished John. Nick sat down on the bench nervously as Counselor Philip placed another glass of CrystalFlake Apple Juice in front of him and pushed the old one out of the way. Though he wished they had given Daniel support as well, he was still thankful they were trying to help encourage him. When Nick was ready, Counselor Lily said, "Get ready..." and started recording. Nick looked into the camera and began, "So, er, CrystalFlake Apple Juice has reached your stores today! It's very good. Mmmm. I've had about fifty so far." He flinched nervously as the crowd of campers stared. "And you should definitely have some yourself!" He picked up the glass, felt a lump of cold and pain slide down his throat, and drank it down as a voice in his head burst hoarsely, "No! You shouldn't have!" Nick was too nervous to care about the voice as he groaned and set down the glass. He looked weakly at Counselor Philip, who appeared impatient and tense. He felt sick. An empty, bubbling pain gripped him as even his sweatshirt started feeling uncomfortable around his contracting stomach. His skin hardened and his color turned pale as his vision of the room slowly dissolved with it.

Nick's eyes bulged as brown liquid poured from his mouth. He coughed multiple times as he felt his throat seizing up. He saw the blur of Counselor Lily moving back and stopping the recording nervously, Counselor Philip looking concerned, his friends watching, and the room around him. A searing pain stretched over his lungs as bubbles erupted from his mouth and he fell over. The room grew dark…he felt pain all over . . .still falling . . .

The Glowing of the Eyes

"Lucky it didn't reach his brain."

"Don't say that!"

"I know, but still..."

"But who would've poisoned him?"

"Don't ask me just because I'm his sister! I don't know!"

"I don't see why you would."

"Look! He's waking up!"

"What are you three doing here?"

"Sorry, Nurse Fletcher, but..."

"Oh, forget it now, he's waking up."

Hearing voices around him, Nick raised his head as the morning light stroked his face. "Wha-what happened?"

"You were poisoned, bud," replied Dylan grimly. "Poisoned?" asked Nick confusedly as he struggled to lift his head. "Keep your head down, Silver. You need rest," interrupted Nurse Fletcher. "Has the tournament ended?" Nick demanded weakly.

"The tournament? Nick, that was yesterday. It's Tuesday, ten o'clock right now," John answered nervously.

"What...?"

"Yeah, you've been…well, unconscious for a while. Are you okay?" his sister replied.

"And since you've been poisoned, or whatever your body's reaction was, and probably both confused and weak," Nurse Fletcher interrupted again, "we brought in the camp dog to help with your recovery here in the medical cabin."

"Really?" asked Nick brightly, although his voice cracked and his throat stung.

"Yes. Also, your friends here," she gestured towards the other three, "convinced me that maybe you should name him." A small brown puppy with white spots and big floppy ears jumped on Nick's bed and sat down next to him. "I'll name him…" Nick thought for a second. The dog had a sort of golden coat of fur that stuck up like fire, as if the dog was a small flame. "Flame." He scratched Flame on his head affectionately as the dog moved closer and sniffed him.

"Flame. What a marvelous name for a dog," Dylan snickered.

"Now, here is your breakfast." Nurse Fletcher laid a tray of pancakes and sausages down on the table next to Nick, along with a glass of milk. "And your friends here suggested that perhaps it's best that you don't eat the food served here." Nick nodded, not wanting to explain the voices. He ate a bit and curled up next to Flame as Nurse Fletcher led everyone else out, telling them that he needed to rest. Nick remained still on his bed. "The Zorblin can't be real," he thought, not for the first time. "That's absurd, impossible…" And how could Planet Mezort exist – a planet that nobody's ever found? Surely, they would have to notice it. He had believed so much in the Zorblins' existence after what John told him, he had barely thought about whether it could be a lie. "If only I had that book, I could sort through the facts and see if it's true. But how can I, when I'm stuck in here and that book is in a vent within the walls of the library?"

Nurse Fletcher returned. "How are you, Silver?"

"Good."

"I'll be back soon with some things to entertain you." She left as Flame woke up from his nap and looked straight into Nick's eyes. A warm, calm feeling swept over him. "Do you like this place better than your old home?" The words came out of Nick's mouth before he could stop them. The air around them glowed as his covers lit up with a bright light and Flame softly whimpered, "Noohh." Normally, Nick would have backed away, but for some reason he felt that this was normal.

"But I didn't like my old home much."

"Why not?" whispered Nick.

"Old owners didn't feed me much. Bored, constantly . . ." If a dog could shrug, Flame managed it.

"Well, at least you might have fun here," Nick commented faintly.

"That is true, Nicholas Silver."

"How do you know my name?" whispered Nick again.

"I heard it a few times."

Nick straightened up and leaned his back against the wall. When he looked at Flame again, he noticed his vision seemed to make colors more vibrant, as he glanced down at his sweatshirt. The light around them bounced off the bed onto Flame, who seemed to be enjoying himself. But Nick yawned and tried going back to sleep. He emptied his mind and got comfortable, a cold wave of air passing through him as he fell asleep, Flame at his side. He dreamed about a small child, lonely and terrified, walking in the middle of an unknown forest where he knew no one would find him. He couldn't handle his mission and broke down, coughing. Then a ghostly figure screeched at him, "You wouldn't fail me now, would you, dear boy?"

"N-no," the boy stammered quickly, looking anywhere but at the ghost. "Good. I will be back soon and when I am, I am hoping it will be ready. Will it?" Terrified, the boy stammered again, "Y-yes. It will be ready."

"Good," hissed the sharp, clear voice of the tall ghost. "But I need help from you." The terrified boy winced and whispered, "How so?" The ghost sneered. "Keep an eye on our little friend, would you? I've been fearing something that I think may be caused by the two things we share." For the first time, the small boy looked up at the ghost and murmured quietly, "Alright, I will."

"You take after your father. You would make a good soldier for my army." And as the ghost cackled madly and faded away, the boy ran out of the forest as fast as he could.

Nick's brown eyes shot open as cold sweat trickled down his neck and he reflected on his dream. He had just watched a boy and a ghost have a conversation. The ghost had asked the boy to keep an eye on somebody that shared a connection with them. The ghost had found the boy in an empty place and asked him if something was ready. What could this mean? As Nick scratched Flame, he felt the painful, cold stabs in his stomach and forehead fade.

"Ah, good. You are awake." Nick looked up to see Nurse Fletcher standing next to him. "Here is your backpack and a remote so you can watch television. And here's your lunch." She set down a tray of fries and a cheeseburger on the table next to him. "I will be back at dinnertime to deliver your food." The rest of the day was boring as he listened to the laughter of kids outside, watched TV, did some drawing, and ate his dinner. As night fell, he put away his things and resumed questioning the Zorblins' existence until he fell asleep.

Wednesday morning delivered dreary skies and clouds. Although it was not raining, it was still dark and windy. When Madison, John, and Dylan came to visit him, he recounted what had happened after they left and his sister explained, "We wanted to get your book back, but the counselors didn't let us go anywhere near the library since it wasn't open. They kept us as busy as possible, making us do an hour-long exercise video to make money for this cheapskate camp. And for the rest of the day, we all did a Camp Trivia challenge made up by the counselors. It was awful. Even worse, Nurse Fletcher kept saying that you needed rest and we would disturb you by asking you questions about the apple juice."

"But we were able to do something good this morning . . ." John began.

"We raided the library for your book!" interrupted Dylan, who couldn't look or sound happier with himself. John pulled out The Legend of Zorblins and the Rise and Fall of the Dark Ruler and tossed it to Nick, who eagerly caught it and flipped it open. Dust flew out of the old book. Squinting at the faded words, he read aloud, "Chapter One: The Childhood of the Dark Ruler. The Dark Ruler, lonely and friendless, had a difficult life growing up on Planet Mezort, unable to be seen by those who weren't Mestephans. He never liked his relatives, who would always get in the way of his ideas of fun." Nick took a breath and commented, "Classic villain story. Had a bad childhood, blah, blah, blah." He continued to read, "He was an independent worker who was never able to pull off something big on his own. He hated getting help, even if he wasn't able to do one of his projects on his own. However, he had Mestephan powers, while others did not. He was born with a rare mutation that gave him an unstable source of powers. He discovered this one day when he was working on a project and one of his relatives in their second life tried to head them off.'"

"Second life?" repeated Madison. "What does that mean?" Nick stared at John, who shrugged, "I don't know. Maybe it means when you... maybe on that planet you die, then your life restarts from the beginning?"

"Anyway," Nick went on, "The Dark Ruler remained just a young boy, with powers like no other. He hid in the shadows when his relatives looked for him; he lurked in the darkness when no one else was stirring. His secretive attitude was misjudged by others as hatred and greed, although the real meaning behind it was bitter doubt that anybody could help him." Nick stopped reading for a moment and studied the width of the book. "Man," he said, "this is a long book." Everybody looked at him expectantly, as if to urge him to read more, but he hesitated. "I...er...I think I'm just going to sleep a while. Just a quick, nice refresh," Nick sighed. And his plan worked. As soon as he said this, Nurse Fletcher hurried over and said, "Okay, everybody out. We need to give Silver some rest." And within half a minute, they were gone and Nick was alone. He wanted them to leave because he still felt like this book was his and he should be keeping it a secret. It was a strange feeling, sure. But after what happened with the tournament and the voice urging him then, he didn't want to repeat his mistakes. After everyone left, he was about to start reading again when he asked Flame, "Should I have done that?"

"Whatever you think tends to work in your favor. I found that out at my old home," Flame barked softly. Nick nodded and smiled, then continued to read, "The Dark Ruler always hated school. On Planet Mezort, school was nothing more than Mestephans learning to control their powers, about other planets, and to build extraordinary things that only Mestephans could build."

"What is a Mestephan?" Nick whispered under his breath, too quietly for Flame to hear. "Of course, the Dark Ruler never shared his name at school willfully. He always wanted to operate alone and keep his identity concealed from the unworthy. Only a few kids at his school ever learned his name and the Dark Ruler would always deny it. At his school, The School of First Life Mestephans, they would make him play to his skills. He embraced his condition, the Quarelenza Disease, because it was what made him so smart and powerful." Nick stopped reading when the page ended, slightly annoyed by how much the book talked about Mestephans but didn't say anything about what they were. He breathed deeply in and out. "The Dark Ruler, as his life carried onward, started being an arrogant, talkative, gloating, mischievous boy. In his later days of school in his first life, he began carelessly abusing his powers and made the other kids fear him. The ones that sought guidance and friendship were tricked into following his path without knowing their wrong. He would attack kids with his powers, which grew stronger each day. On his planet, the powers he used were considered illegal to use on people, but the boy who would become the Dark Ruler didn't fear the law as others did.'"

"Are you doing well, Silver?"

Nick snapped the book shut on his thumb. "Mhm," he assured the nurse.

"Well, that's good. I've run some tests on your blood while you were asleep."

"Wait…what?"

"And I daresay you will be ready to return to the camp's activities and your cabin tomorrow, Thursday afternoon. Your blood has been badly contaminated, but over the course of these few days at rest, the poison has dissipated."

"Well, that's good," said Nick.

"Indeed, it is," Nurse Fletcher agreed as she turned to step out. "I will be bringing your lunch up soon."

Nick sped back to his book and whispered as he read, "Growing up, the pathway of the Dark Ruler's life began to twist. Only scrambled information about his life in his teens was ever found. When school ended for him, he ditched his gang and ran away from his family. What exactly he was doing, only some can explain. The few who met him during his time of exploration, after his school years ended, were able to inform the authors of the Dark Ruler's goals. The Dark Ruler had been searching for the complete collection of Fragments of the Great Star of Power." This was just what Nick had feared. He had hoped, really hoped, that the Dark Ruler had not known too much about the Great Star of Power. If, by some slim chance, the Dark Ruler was real, then maybe Nick could get others to help stop him from gaining power. But the boy who had tricked and deceived so many had discovered such plans all along. Nick's thoughts deepened. "What if…what if the Dark Ruler didn't manage to get all of them before he was thrown in prison…?"

A few minutes later, his lunch arrived and he wolfed down an entire pizza pie. The rest of the day passed the same way as the other days in the medical cabin, but as night descended over the fields and Wednesday was ending, Nick thought about the vote to demolish his childhood park… then the possibility of Zorblins being real. . . then the book . . .and the poison . . . As he slipped into sleep, whispering voices from counselors broke the silence and he was hurtling down a lake. . . down . . . down . . . red eyes. . .

Warmth surrounded him, but it was not enough to wake Nick on the hot, humid, wet Thursday morning. Butterflies fluttered in and out of the Medical Cabin through the window that was open slightly and allowing the warm outside air into the cold cabin. Suddenly, soft, furry paws were on Nick's face, tickling his skin, and he woke up gradually, his dreams dissolving in his mind, as Flame sniffed him. "Morning, Flame," yawned Nick. "Hello, Nick!" the pup yapped back. Nick raised himself up as Flame slowly edged backward off his chest. He looked forward to returning to his cabin and being with his friends and sister again. He got out of bed, packed his things, got dressed, and seized the Magic 8-Ball as it rolled out of his backpack. He reached over and the second his fingers touched the ball, it spoke. "The X-Ball Zero will guide you through your path of life. The creator of the X-Ball Zero requested that at this age the owner, Nicholas Silver, must know about me."

Nick yelled and stumbled backward, throwing the ball into the air. Flame immediately leapt off the bed and caught the X-Ball Zero tightly in his mouth right before it hit the ground. "Why did you throw it?" the dog asked irritably. Nick gently took the ball from Flame's mouth and felt the saliva drip onto his hand, but he didn't care at the moment. "Because…oh, I don't know…why do you think I chucked away the talking sci-fi ball, Flame?"

"Nick, it's your special X-Ball. They are made for important people."

Nick looked at the ball skeptically. Maybe this was why it would never fail him. It was special. He asked it quietly, "Are you special, then?" He shook it and read words he had never seen on any kind of Magic 8-Ball before. "Well, duh, Nicholas Silver. Or would you like me to call you Nick? Indeed, I am special." He pondered the words multiple times before accepting that the message was real. Nick sighed and stuffed the X-Ball in his backpack, hoping to study it more later, and sat on his bed next to Flame. Then he remembered: Flame wasn't his dog and did not belong to him, even if they had made such a strong bond. Flame was a camp dog for every other camper. They smiled at one another as Nurse Fletcher came into the room and told him, "Good news, Silver. You have healed overnight quicker than I imagined. Usually, it would take a few more hours, but for some reason . . ." she stared at Nick, then Flame. "Anyway, you have healed enough to return to the other campers just in time for breakfa-"

"Hooray!" cried Nick happily, cutting her off.

"As I was saying," she responded warningly, "you and Flame will walk over to the breakfast table and then you will introduce him to the other campers, since you have grown such a bond with him."

"But why haven't they met Flame yet? There was plenty of time to do a meet and greet while I slept or rested, or. . ."

"He didn't want to," Nurse Fletcher interjected sharply. "He wouldn't leave your side. Now c'mon, Silver. Let's go." She led him out into the long, open fields where birds flew back and forth, towards the wooden table where the other campers ate their breakfast. Nick cheerfully joined his friends as Madison said sarcastically, "Great going. You've already become famous by the third day of camp! That's a record!" They laughed as Nick enthused, "Awesome! I'm doing great, then!" and continued to joke together through breakfast. He didn't bother telling them about talking to Flame or the X-Ball but did tell them how he started to question the obvious: whether Zorblins or the Dark Ruler were real.

Dylan commented, "Yeah, I actually doubt they're real. Like, it was probably a squid or something in the lake. I dunno, but the idea of a three-headed worm thingy...now that's just insane."

Madison chimed in, "Well, I don't know. As stupidly crazy it seems, there is actually lots of proof pointing towards it, but still...I don't know. John?"

John shrugged. "I think it just might be true. I mean, I didn't believe it at first, but when I read more about them...and there were a lot of weird things going on in the world."

Nick nodded silently. His friends and sister around him talked, but their voices faded from his mind. He was deep in thought, wondering about the world and what other weird things it had produced. "Nick?

Hello? Can't pay attention for one minute, huh?" laughed Dylan. Nick focused again. "Um, yeah. Whatever you said."

Breakfast passed quickly until they had to return to their cabins. Cabin B was quiet. Nick replied to campers that asked him about the poison, although he didn't like talking about it, while he unpacked his things. Sean Carter questioned if there was something wrong with the juice or whether Nick had just gotten sick, when somebody else asked, "Did it hurt?" Nick spun around, trying to find the person who spoke. "Did it hurt?" Daniel repeated nervously. Nick answered bitterly, "Well, yeah. It felt like somebody was trying to squeeze a plastic tube down my throat as it shrank and completely dried up. It was something like that." He hoped to close the subject.

Thursday turned out to be a boring day. The kids waited in their cabins until it was time for lunch, then were allowed to roam the camp. While waiting for dinner, Nick revisited the holes and saw there were even more. But it wasn't just that. Some of the older holes had more slime in them and they were wider. He stared until he felt a familiar sense of coldness and became numb, then looked away. Sean Carter, a second year, and a first year from Cabin A were with him, discussing whether they could swim in the lake or not. Meanwhile, Counselor Philip was patrolling the camp until he gave orders to the other counselors and hurried off into the counselor cabin. Nick never got a chance to continue reading The Legend of Zorblins and the Rise and Fall of the Dark Ruler, mainly because he never had time alone. At dinner, Nick noticed he had stopped hearing the voice, but the food he received was the normal camp-made food. He assumed his poisoner must have taken a break, but he found it hard to relax when it was obvious to him that there was an impostor at Camp CrystalFlake.

By Friday morning, Counselor Philip seemed as if he couldn't care less about him anymore, but Nick was almost positive he still hated him because of something Nick had found out that day before breakfast: during Madison's first year, she told the counselor about Nick and how he did basically everything the man despised. Cabin B was empty after breakfast except for Nick, Madison, John, and Dylan. Everyone else was outside playing tag and hide-and-seek with the other campers or laughing as they flew kites. Nick looked happily out the window, then found a piece of paper and a sharpened pencil, wrote the word SUSPECTS on the top of the paper, and asked his friends, "Okay, who do you think, if we're talking about anybody at this camp, poisoned me? I want each of you to say who you think is behind all this."

Dylan said, "Librarian."

John said, "Lunch people."

Madison echoed Dylan, "Librarian."

The others were surprised by John's answer. "Well," he began, "it makes sense. Wouldn't the CrystalFlake Apple Juice be made by the people that make the food? I think they might have something to do with this. Plus, at their age, nobody – I repeat, nobody – would ordinarily even be working. And why do you think it's that old librarian, anyway?"

"Well, brainiac, that's obvious," Dylan answered sarcastically. "When Nick tried to check out a book on Zorblins and that Ruler guy, she went berserk!"

"Yeah! Because if Nick were going to find out about some murdering monster thingy, they'd do all they could to stop it!" Madison added.

Nick stopped paying attention to their conversation and then wrote on the paper:

SUSPECT ONE: LIBRARIAN, MOST LIKELY.

SUSPECT TWO: LUNCH STAFF, LESS LIKELY.

"What do you mean, less likely?" asked John. "I put enough evidence for you all to understand! You need new batteries for your brains."

"You know what?" Nick said, laughing. "C'mon. Let's stop worrying and go outside. We never even stopped to think if that 'poison' was just an accident with the ingredients."

"Yeah," Dylan said shakily.

"That's way more likely," Madison agreed. "Alright, come on!"

Together, they all walked outside. Within minutes, the four were sweating as the summer heat beat down on them. They watched campers running up and down the camp fields, around the lake, through the sand dunes, and around the hideous holes in the back of the camp, between the two forests. Then Madison noticed a basket of kites and they each grabbed one, racing each other and laughing hysterically as the temperatures rose rapidly and the kites swirled. They couldn't find anyone who looked grim, not even Daniel, who was staring at the holes with a kite in his hand. There was a kid talking to him and Daniel smiled on and off.

Nick and Madison swung their kites like swords at Dylan and John's, knocking them out of the sky. They raced each other behind the counselors' cabin as Nick's colorful kite flew high in the sky behind him while he ran. Daniel joined in and easily outran them. Nick passed the Great Tree, ran up to the tree stumps and empty campfire ring, and then into the sand dunes before he tripped and fell. His kite was flung from his grip and twisted and writhed as it landed in the sand beside Nick. He burst out laughing as Daniel ran toward him and tripped himself, launching forward headfirst onto the other side of the dunes.

Nick was having so much fun as he and Daniel got up and smoothed out the kites that he didn't even notice the flash of bright, neon orange when he laughed again. The two of them ran to the edge of the lake and saw John and Madison on the other side, pulling something out of a hole.

Daniel and Nick's kites become airborne again as they ran towards them. "What's up?" Nick asked quickly, breathing heavily in the heat.

"Kite got stuck, in this hole. . ."

Nick looked. The hole was wide, rough around the edges, steep, and oozing all over with the same mysterious, sticky slime as the others. Madison's dark kite was ripped and covered in ooze, half of it completely submerged at the bottom of the hole. As Nick pulled on the kite string handle with the others, he relived a happy memory from the day before, when he had introduced Flame to all of the campers. He decided not to tell anyone about his bond with Flame or the X-Ball Zero, but when he told everybody about Flame and all the tricks he could do, they clapped.

SQUIRCH! "What the…? Okay, that wasn't necessary. "

"Sorry Nick, but next time you should pay attention."

"Yeah, not my fault even though I was the one who, well. . ." Dylan butted in.

"Dylan, I think we all know you purposely yanked the kite that way to send some slime flying," said John blandly.

"Whoops, my bad."

Nick's eyes focused back on them briefly as he blurted, "What?" A moment later, he lost interest and stopped paying attention again.

"Come on, the kite is almost out," John said. They all pulled on the kite and finally, with a snap, they felt it release. Unfortunately, it was the string connecting the kite to the handle that had snapped. With disappointment, they watched as the kite in the hole became fully submerged in the ooze and disappeared from sight. Everyone sighed, realizing their hard work only made things worse. They walked away, with Nick, Daniel, Dylan, and John tugging their kites behind them while Madison dragged her useless handle. After lunch, Nick finally had the chance to get back to the book. While every other camper continued playing outside or

relaxing by the brilliant blue lake, Nick lay on his bunk and began reading aloud to himself, returning to the page about the Dark Ruler's search
for the Fragments of the Great Star of Power.

"Chapter Two: Adulthood. He spent years of searching for the fragments, but without success. No matter how hard he tried, he never knew
why he couldn't obtain the secrets. But one day in his later life, he knew
he had to face the facts and to stop being completely independent. So,
he gathered some of his circle from school and evaluated their strengths
and smarts. He kept the ones who would be useful to him and abandoned
the ones who would not. The young boy who had now entered adulthood
took his gang and set off on months of journeying through Planet Mezort,
the planet impossible for all non-Mestephans to find, in search of a home.
Eventually, they found themselves a tower and the young leader commanded his followers to take over the tower. They obeyed, killing everyone who stepped foot in the tower the days that followed until nobody
else returned."

Nick stopped reading and took a long breath. He tried to take in all
of this, but it sounded so unbelievable. "Once they had conquered the
tower, the fierce young leader named himself the Ruler of the Querzelan.
The details of that are not too well known, but it is fact that it has a special meaning behind it. Over time, the Ruler of Querzelan raised an army
and gathered new soldiers. One day, however, his relatives found him at
his tower and he was furious. He ordered his soldiers to kill them because
he was so filled with hatred at the sight of his relatives – all but one: his
younger brother, who he had been close to in a secret sort of way.
However, he controlled his emotions and ordered the Querzelan to kill
them and leave none behind. His soldiers and his relatives fought and
ultimately, neither side won. The Ruler's relatives escaped with enough
information to have him arrested.

"'The Ruler knew however, that it was time to flee. He took a map of the dark universe around him, his notes of where fragments of the Great Star could be hidden and commanded his soldiers to defend his base while he continued his quest independently, since he always believed working in a group was the source of failure. He searched far and wide for the fragments and found none. On a certain unknown date, one of his enslaved servants came to him on a distant land and held out an invention in the shape of a round toy. The servant gave it to the Ruler, who asked the object a question and turned it thrice in his hand. The result was immediate, and the orb told him where he could find the fragment he craved the most: on a planet called Earth. The Ruler took the orb and traveled to Earth.'" Nick readjusted himself, his neck growing stiff against the backboard.

Determined to proceed, he returned to his book and read some more.

"The Ruler reached Earth with a variety of his favorite weapons and started to plan his raid. When he asked the toy again where the fragment he sought would be, it revealed that one day in the future, it would show up at what would eventually be a small summer camp in the woods of upstate New York. He immediately traveled to that place and found just open land surrounded by trees. But he trusted the invention and built an underground facility of secrets. He made it out of iron, a metal he associated with himself. He supplied the facility with an armory, a healing room for Mestephans, labs, and other areas. The rooms of the Secret Facility were built around four long hallways that connected into the shape of a square and it was finished after months of work. The Ruler made sure no humans would find the Secret Facility by placing the entrance where only Mestephans with brains and brawn that matched his own would be cunning enough to enter. He constructed the underground facility for months while the mortals began work on the camp he would someday destroy. He built mechanical suits, armor, weaponry, labs, medical bays, and a room where only the best-kept secrets were held…and that are still unknown to this day."

Nick closed the book carefully, still thinking over what he had read. "An underground facility?" he thought. "But. . . how?" He concentrated until his head started to hurt, then decided to take a break from reading and go outside to meet his friends. He found them relieving their boredom by climbing up the hill and rolling back down. When Nick rolled down, he suddenly shot forward, glanced off a rock, narrowly rolled around a tree, and spiraled across the field into a soccer net, ruining some fourth-year campers' soccer game. Daniel, laughing, plowed straight into the goalie's legs, knocking him over as the ball soared into the net. "Nice shot," John told him on their way to the dinner table. "Perfect ten pointer."

At dinner, Nick decided to be honest with his friends and catch them up on the story of the Dark Ruler and the Secret Facility. They all seemed to be interested and their reactions were similar to his, more or less. Later that evening, Cabin B had fallen quiet. It was past ten and everybody was asleep – counselors and campers alike – except for Nick Silver, who lay in his bed, thoughts swirling in his mind. He loved trying to solve mysteries, but at the same time, was annoyed by the lack of answers. Then it hit him. What if he had been poisoned because he was the one to get the fragment? "Yeah, right," he laughed to himself. "I have never even seen a fragment like that in my whole life. It must be someone else. Maybe the enemy thought it was me and they made the poison in the facility! Or maybe they realized I might learn about them and try to hunt down the fragment before they get to it!"

He sat up straight, eyes bloodshot. Not because of what he had just considered, but because of a loud shuffling noise outside. The ground shook beneath him as he remained silent. He was alone in the dark as everyone else slept. He heard a heavy breathing, as his heart beat against his ribs. There was a high-pitched groan from outside and Nick froze completely, holding his breath, petrified with fear. The ground rumbled as what little light there was in the cabin diminished and with a crunch, the window next to him folded inward. His sweatshirt felt weird. Unnatural. Earlier, it had been bright and comfortable, but now he was scared and it felt extremely uncomfortable and the color turned a pale gray. What was going on here? Nick stared outside the window as his body grew frigid with fear. His heart pounded against his ribs as the ear-shattering sound of loud breathing filled the air. He peered out through the window frame, feeling small, and looked straight into a face, lit up by the moonlight, which had haunted his thoughts for days.

The beady red eyes were soaking into his brown eyes as they met. The Zorblin's eyes turned darker and darker, finally transforming into the very color of his own. Sweating all over, Nick noticed he couldn't move. The eyes of the Zorblin's middle head were giving off a special radiation that prevented him from moving a muscle. His sweatshirt looked pitch-black by now and felt like a leathery metal against his pajama shirt that was under it.

The moon illuminated the scene perfectly a second later. Nick, still rooted to the spot, stared into all three waving heads of the final Zorblin. The four-remaining red, beady eyes found his and darkened in color as the first pair had. The grip that kept him from moving grew stronger. With its skeletal tail swaying to the side, the Zorblin headed closer toward the cabin. It opened its middle mouth, the other two still closed even as a light green liquid steadily poured from them. With the window still open, only half of a wall separated it from him. Nick knew that the Zorblin was going to kill him right then and there, with nobody else able to help him as they slept without a clue. Nick's throat seized up and he was unable to use his voice anymore. . .

Suddenly, with a burst of fiery light, Flame appeared on his bed and stared into the six glowing brown eyes of the Zorblin. Its eyes drifted over to Flame hungrily, and Nick was released from his pain. He could move again. As Flame's eyes glowed a bright golden hue, the Zorblin's six eyes turned that same color. But Flame wasn't affected by the Zorblin like Nick had been. The dog began to bark ferociously at the Zorblin, who stepped back. Feeling the courage he had needed earlier, Nick felt a calming warmth and he glared with rage and pride at the Zorblin, whose eyes bore into his own. But it wasn't affecting him anymore. Nick and Flame exchanged grins and Nick raised his arms, elbows bent as if he were flexing his muscles. He felt his sweatshirt swell with a great, amazing, uplifting warmth as it glowed, expelling a bright gold and orange light. Then, out of nowhere, an aura of fire appeared around the sweatshirt that didn't hurt Nick but felt slightly like he was being poked with half-sharp knives of heat. The flames also enveloped him with a warmth that kept him safe from the deadly stare of the Zorblin just outside.

Instinctively, Nick turned to Flame and hugged him around his neck. His hunch worked and he felt all of Flame's power leap into his sweatshirt. It soon glowed and erupted with fire so strong, it lit up the whole cabin with a blinding light. The Zorblin backed away and disappeared from sight as all of Nick's energy died out. His sweatshirt returned to its regular orange, the fire was gone, and he collapsed sideways on his bed, Flame falling at his side.

The Sweatshirt

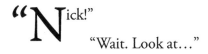 ick!"

"Wait. Look at…"

"OUCH!"

Nick woke up, dried blood covering his weary face. "What…what happened?"

"How would we know?" said Dylan. Nick sat up straight in his bed. He looked at Flame next to him. Then he remembered everything from the moment he first heard the Zorblin he had believed was fake, just outside his window. "Zorblin!" he blurted out breathlessly. "They're real. I saw one last night and…and…the Great Star of Power that you told me about? John, that must be real, too. That Zorblin couldn't have been created by anything else. You should've seen it. . ." He felt pain all over as he noticed his sweatshirt flicker with light and then dim in color. A realization came to him. "Wait a minute. AHA!" he cried triumphantly, surprising the other three so much that they stumbled backwards. "My sweatshirt! It glows when I'm happy and feel comfortable, but when I'm in mortal danger or angry or something, it's uncomfortable and loses color!"

Nick didn't stop there. "Last night! Flame and I, we…well, he protected me from the Zorblin's stare, and my sweatshirt glowed and lit on fire. Friendly fire, I guess you could call it, and he scared off the Zorblin!" He noticed now how shaky he was and how dry his throat felt.

"Nick, that's…that's…" stuttered John. "Awesome!" Dylan interrupted.

"Don't you understand what this means?" John asked. "The Secret Facility has to be real, then! And that would be…well…labs! Bioweapons! The Zorblin's hideout! This is not a good thing!" As the truth sank in, Nick's heart also sank like a stone. "He's right, that's bad," he agreed. Nick had just realized that every camper in the cabin was watching him and that outside, Philip and some other counselors were trying to fix the bent window above him.

"How are you, Mr. Silver?" Counselor Philip asked, peering in. "Fine," he lied. If Nick were to tell anyone about the legend of Zorblins somehow being true, it wouldn't be him.

"I see. Getting yourself injured multiple times on your first week here. . ."

Nick pulled himself up as the heat of the sun through the window prickled his cuts painfully. "Well, Silver, do you think you need to go to the Medical Cabin?" asked Counselor Philip.

"No, really. I'm…I'm fine. I can stay here. Just have to wipe off this blood. . ."

"I'll of course be informing your parents again, Silver," continued Philip. "Now good day to you and do try not to get yourself in any more predicaments like this, please."

At lunch, later that day, mail came. Nick was elated and other kids were so homesick that they instantly tore open their letters from home and read them before even sitting down. He and Madison opened identical envelopes and Nick began to read his.

Hello, Nicholas!

I hope you're doing well at camp. I am still shaken up from my call with Counselor Philip about you getting sick from some "sour" apple juice. I hope you're feeling better.

I've also heard about all of the new friends you made. I'm so proud of you. As for this recent sickness, I have asked Counselor Philip to keep you away from apple juice until we can figure out what actually happened. The day you and your sister come home, I'll be ready with a plate of fresh cookies. I've also asked Counselor Philip nicely to take care of you and treat you well.

Mom

He quickly scanned the page over again. "Nick, there's more," Madison said as she flipped Nick's letter over. He became disappointed as he read:

P.S. Nick, good news: the theme park isn't getting destroyed. The Ship Museum will be in a different location. Bad news: some strange new factory is being built all across the area and people seem to really be supporting it. See you soon!

Nick finished reading while his sister started talking to some girls in her year, then yawned quietly and finished his lunch. Afterward, he decided to take a walk around the camp, eventually finding Daniel at the holes. He pointed out, "They're getting worse, Nicholas." And sure enough, they were. Now there were thick beads of slime leaking from the holes, connecting into the beads from other ones. Plus, the holes had grown wider.

"Forget it," Nick said suddenly, a smile spreading across his face, "It's a nice day. Let's try to enjoy it." And he walked off, leaving Daniel slightly stunned. A nice breeze had penetrated the heat. It was the perfect mix of hot and cold to put Nick in a good mood. He joined his friends, who were still looking slightly shaken from the truth of the Secret Facility. Trying to hide his own underlying panic, he straightened his expression and said calmly, "C'mon. Things may be tough, but we should enjoy the good stuff while we can." At that moment, he felt a sense of happiness grow inside of him. With all worries forcefully pushed to the side, his sweatshirt flashed with a blazing fire for a few seconds, but the instant Nick noticed, it flickered and died. "I don't understand this. Why?" he wondered aloud. He had finally cracked. "How? Why me? Why is my sweatshirt glowing and how? What does this mean?"

"I wouldn't be able to tell you that if I tried," whispered John.

Nick began shouting, wanting to break the whispering hum of the other campers around him as they stared curiously at his sweatshirt. "This has something to do with that facility, I'm positive!" he bellowed. And at that moment, without any control whatsoever, his sweatshirt froze around his body as an image burst into his mind. He saw a long gray hallway, the air filled with voices... "Aha!" he cried triumphantly. All he knew was that the sweatshirt he had worn for years must…"have something to do with the secret facility!" The surrounding campers were casting odd looks in their direction, so Dylan and John felt like it was a good idea to keep their group moving along. Daniel caught up with them and asked, "Whatcha yelling about…?"

"Nick," John implored once they were out of earshot from the other campers, "you can't just go around saying that!"

"Saying what?" Nick responded.

"You can't just say you have something to do with the Secret Facility! Haven't you heard the rumors that have been spreading for the past few years?" Nick had no idea what John was talking about, but he didn't care. Before he could respond any further, Madison asked the obvious question. "Why is the world going so weird all of a sudden? How are these things real?"

"Doesn't matter," Nick said shakily. There was a horrible flash of an image in his mind of the night he had faced the Zorblin and eluded a probable death.

"Nick, please, be reasonable here!" John cautioned again.

"Yeah, Nick. C'mon, who knows? It might just be a glow-in-the-dark sweatshirt or something. Oh, never mind. But still, don't try looking for that underground death trap," Dylan warned. Nick looked at all of them hopelessly and finally spoke his mind. "I don't care! I have voices in my head, I keep seeing weird flashes of stuff, and I can talk to Flame!" The three others became quiet all of a sudden. They obviously didn't know anything about the last two things he had just revealed.

"You...you can talk to Flame?" wheezed Madison breathlessly.

"Yeah, so?"

"That...that isn't a good thing, Nick," John said.

"What do you mean?" Nick asked, deflated.

"The rumors . . . well, for the last few years, there have been weird, um...afflictions happening to people. Stuff like, er, this," Dylan murmured.

"And?" added Nick, trying to escape this conversation. Madison was unable to talk and Dylan was panicking. "And?" John said. "And all of those people, all of them..." He drew a breath. "Vanished – without a trace." Nick took this all in, breathing heavily as his mind saw more unpleasant flashes of the Zorblin.

"And what about the poison? What if it really was poison?" Madison asked.

"Yeah! The poison! Try saying how that was a misunderstanding! You really can't!" Nick reminded them. There was an impenetrable silence where they all considered this, then Daniel frowned. "Well, maybe you have a point, Nick . . ." he broke off. They could not think of anything more to be said. Numbly, they all headed back to the cabin without a word. As Friday came to an end, the temperature dropped overnight. Saturday morning brought a breezy wind and slightly warmer weather conditions. The campers sat around in their cabin for most of the day, talking, and when Sunday came, they played soccer and basketball or made things with items in the Arts and Crafts Tent. On Monday afternoon, Nick finally pulled out the old leathery book from under his mattress. He hadn't read it since he had seen the Zorblin, and he suddenly decided he wouldn't read it at the moment either. Instead, he stuffed the book away again.

However, although he didn't want to read the book much anymore, he had no intention of returning it to the library. That's why, on Monday morning, he made sure it was hidden carefully where he could still find it and he had marked his page. It was drizzling that day and foggy the next, so Nick and Madison made up their own game that they called Blinded Tag-and-Run, where the tagger had to run through the fog with their eyes closed, trying to tag the other players who could barely see with their eyes open through the thick fog all around. The game ended with a few small injuries, but nothing serious. John and Dylan devised a game of races, where one pair would race while the other two decided what type of race it would be: jogging, skipping, crawling, or hopping. It was fun to race crazily through the fog, still half blinded, to the entrance of the Forest of Tappers.

By the time the fog cleared up, the campers were finishing their lunch. Feeling overheated, Nick ran back into his cabin and threw his sweatshirt onto his bed to be more refreshed. At his feet was Flame and Nick greeted him happily. The dog stared for a second, licked the air wildly, then let out a soft, excited yap that Nick could not understand. For the next few minutes, he debated with himself before deciding to open up the old leather book and review it again. Returning to the book-marked page, he continued where he had left off.

"Chapter Three: The Revolution of the Dark Ruler. The young Ruler wandered the planet far and wide. Every so often, he would return back to his home planet and meet his army. Then he would return to planet Earth and continue his research down in the Secret Facility. On one of these occasions when he returned to Planet Mezort, the Ruler of the Querzelan was surrounded by King Cracious and his own army. The Dark Ruler did not give up, though; at once, he called in the Querzelan. They came to his aid at once and a battle broke out, which was known as the Battle of the Lords.

"The Battle of the Lords lasted for days as the Querzelan fought valiantly against King Cracious' army. This battle brought the destruction of many lands. In the end, the Querzelan conquered the soldiers, and, with intense strength and immense power, the Ruler overthrew King Cracious. Within days of the king's defeat, he died while held captive by the Querzelan. The Dark Ruler immediately became the leader of all and started off his new role by destroying the castle of King Cracious, a good man who had been broken by a terrible, power-hungry one.

"The citizens of Planet Mezort began to fear their new leader, the Dark Ruler, who fashioned himself a new name: Ruler Quarzolon. He was rising in power steadily, slowly taking over and gradually manipulating the lives of many with his powers."

Nick went no farther and slipped the book away again, taking more time to digest all that he had read. Tuesday and Wednesday swept by and Thursday brought with it a horrible storm. Everyone was forced to stay inside their cabins all day, and when they had to eat, they'd sprint through the pouring rain to the cafeteria. The storm continued to rage on through the night, finally passing by the time they woke on Friday morning. But there was one problem: there was too much water everywhere, as the grounds were damp and flooded, so there could be no outside activities. However, none of that could overshadow the shocking news that arrived Friday morning after a long breakfast in the cafeteria.

Counselor Chris trudged through the wet and muddy grass into Cabin B. He pulled a few pins out of his pocket, then three crumpled notes, and pinned the three notes to the board. Then he dropped the rest of the pins in his pocket and walked off, grumbling. Everybody hurried over to the board as soon as the door slammed behind him. Nick expected to hear bad things coming from the campers who read the news first, but they got really excited instead. He jumped off his bed and looked at the notes. His jaw dropped. He was in total shock as he read:

BRAND NEW CAMP, BRAND NEW FUN! Camp CrystalFlake is now getting a brand-new design. A whole new expansion plan is in the works. Get ready for a new building, courtyard, towers, and more!

Towers? A building? A courtyard and a whole expansion? Amazing, Nick thought as he reread the note. Then he read the second one.

ENTIRELY NEW CAMP AND BETTER SECURITY! A wall will be constructed around the new camp's boundaries. This will

help security and also prevent access to the Forest of
Tappers and the Quarren Forest.

"Woah…wait a second!" Nick got an idea after rereading the words
he had missed the first time. He staggered across the room through the
crowds of celebrating campers, dodging paper airplanes, where he finally
bumped into Dylan.

"Dylan…" he panted.

"What?"

"Didn't you see that note? The Quarren Forest!"

"Oh. Oh yeah, the out-of-bounds forest. What about it?"

"Dylan, the Quarren Forest. The forest where we guessed Ruler
Quarzolon made the Secret Facility. The forest was named after him."

Sports and a Forcefield

Nick was lost in thought. If the secret forest was really named after the Mestephan from years ago. . .

He looked at Dylan, who still hadn't moved from the spot where he was when Nick ran into him. Nick decided to speed off through the crowd of celebrating campers to find anybody he could ask. "John," he thought. "I need John." But John was nowhere to be found.

"John? C'mon John. Where are you?" Nick murmured silently. He never noticed how big Cabin B was until he was running back and forth, passing other campers, and finally calling out, "John!" At that second, as he uttered that single word, his sweatshirt flashed with painless, bright light. Everyone gasped and backed up. Nick walked through the crowd calmly, his sweatshirt's fire already receding. He felt exhausted, but he found John. The flames died out because Nick had done what he needed to do. The sweatshirt had merely helped him do it by parting the shocked cluster of people.

Seconds later, the campers had started talking again, but this time their voices were more subdued and much quieter than before. Nick whispered to John, "Come with me. I've got some stuff to tell you."

"What do you mean?" John questioned as Nick directed him to an empty corner of the cabin.

"I mean, this camp...c'mon, you should be able to see the resemblance, even if Dylan couldn't."

"Nick, just tell me."

"Okay, fine. Didn't you see that note? The *Quar*-ren Forest? And Ruler *Quar*-zolon? Don't you also think something is wrong here?"

John pondered that. "I guess, yeah, but we still don't really know much about that Quarzolon guy."

"Yeah, well, I don't care about knowing him. I just want to understand that confusing mess, Quarzolon...OUCH!" It was as if Nick's bones from his skull down through his spinal cord had just been sliced with a sharpened knife. "Owww. . ." The pain ended as fast as it started.

"What is it?" John said, concerned.

"My back – it hurt when I said, 'that confusing mess, Quarzolon.' OW, again!" Once more, Nick had a split-second pain that ran from his skull downward.

"Stop saying it!" John warned. "Obviously, it's going to hurt."

"Funny enough, I think I found that out for myself," Nick contorted, wincing from the pain that had already subsided.

"Probably a curse or something. I don't know," said a familiar voice. Nick spun around and John looked up.

"Madison, were you spying on us the whole time?"

"That doesn't matter," she said. "I'm just guessing here. All this weird stuff going on about that Ruler guy? I think the name is cursed. You can't say it in a bad way without getting pain thrown at you."

"Yeah. Probably," nodded Dylan, who had just made his way over.

"Geez, is everyone spying today?" said Nick, his head spinning.

"Guys, did you hear about Swaying Swords starting tomorrow?" Dylan asked.

"Swaying what?" asked Nick. Then it hit him. "YES! Swaying Swords! I forgot about that!"

"Yeah, Nick, remember? That awesome sport? You asked me about it constantly," Madison reminded him. "You know, the game where you're tied to a rope by a harness and use swords."

"That's a weird way to put it, but yeah," said John. "The tryouts are tomorrow. That should be fun to watch."

"I think I'm joining the team," Nick stated suddenly. "I feel like I'll be able to make great swords . . . and use them well."

"Well, that's not a bad idea," Madison told him. "You'd probably be good at it. And besides, for the entire time I've been coming to this camp. . . yeesh, Cabin B always lost."

"What do you mean?" asked Dylan.

"Well, Cabin B was always the first team to get eliminated. Usually, two random teams get selected to fight first."

"And?" Nick pressed on.

"And Cabin C or A always beats Cabin B, and when the two other cabins fight each other first, the winner between those teams will always beat our team into the dirt."

"Well, that stinks for our team!" John summarized pretty well, in Nick's opinion.

"Well, I'm joining Swaying Swords. It seems like an incredibly fun sport, and I want to try boosting our cabin to success!" Nick declared triumphantly.

On Saturday morning, Nick's excitement had not diminished. The camp sport, Swaying Swords, was all he could think about. He raced through his breakfast – ever since getting poisoned, he had not heard the voice in his head at mealtimes – and jumped up as Counselor Philip called loudly through his megaphone: "ALL CAMPERS TRYING OUT FOR SWAYING SWORDS, PLEASE JOIN US AT THE LAKE." Nick got up and a few campers at the table clapped, bidding him good luck while his friends and sister gave him words of encouragement. He traipsed outside with the rest of the campers.

"Now, kids," said Counselor Philip as he walked them over to a short, balding, smiling man. "This is Coach Razan. He is going to train you, select a captain, and teach you how to play the sport of Camp CrystalFlake: Swaying Swords."

"WHOOOOOHOOOO!!" the campers cheered.

"Alright, quiet down!" Counselor Philip admonished them.

"Oh no, Philip. It's fine. I'm glad that these kids are excited!"

The counselor groaned. "Alright. You kids be good to Coach Razan, you hear? Now, sort yourself by stepping on your team names."

Nick was about to ask questions when he looked down and saw three mats on the ground. One said AIRFORCE RANGERS. "That must be Cabin A's name," he thought.

BIO BOTS. "That must be our team's name. Pretty lame, to be honest."

CRUMBLING CURSERS. "Must be Cabin C's team," Nick thought again. He walked forward and stepped on his team's mat. When everyone had found their team's place, Coach Razan told them, "Now, this." He pointed at four beams coming out of the lake. They were rising high, shaping a square, and bending sharply horizontal, as if to form the exterior of a box without any faces. One metal beam ran horizontally between the two beams at its side, with platforms on top, next to the other two beams in the opposite direction. Two ropes hung from the middle beam, with harnesses attached. Two huge metal pillars rose up and had what looked like a metal plank attached to them, one plank facing the other right across from it.

Then there were two more pillars, one on the side of one pillar, sticking out of the beams resembling an incomplete box, closer to it than the other, and another pillar on the opposite side, closer to the other beam with a plank, platforms on the two beams, connecting to each other. The jet-black harnesses, dangling above the planks, looked like high-tech gear. Finally, there was a ladder leading up to one beam with a plank, and another ladder on the other.

When all of the campers were done observing the arena, Coach Razan cleared his throat and started explaining. "There are seven players on each team. The Captain, the five Fighters, and the single Defender. The Defender wears armor and bears a shield and stands on one of the platforms next to their teammates' beam, and closer to it, as well. When a Fighter is up, they get tied to the harness attached to a rope. When the round starts, they jump off the plank, swing in the air above the platform, and use their swords. They make their swords – not real, of course – and armor in the Arts and Crafts Tent. The main goal of a single round is to get one hundred points. Once you get one hundred points or more, you climb back down as the Fighter you beat gets down. A new Fighter from that team is up and faces another one of you for another round."

Coach Razan paused as everyone listened closely. "The round only ends when a rope is cut by the opposing side and one of the two Fighters drops into the lake after their opponent slashes it with their sword. But you must have one hundred points or more to win. If you and your opponent both have less than one hundred points, then the one who slices the rope loses the round. If someone with less than one hundred points cuts the rope of someone with one hundred points or more, then the one with more points will win anyway.

"Now, matches are the number of rounds it takes for one team to get five hundred points or more. Now, you might be wondering: how do you get points? Well, if a Defender blocks the blade of an opponent, they earn their team fifteen points. When a Captain spots an opponent cheating, the team the cheater is on will lose twenty points.

"Most importantly, though, when a Fighter stabs their opponent in the shoulder, stomach, or lower area, their team is granted ten points. When a Fighter stabs an opponent in the chest, they earn their team twenty points. That is how you gain points and lose some, too. Matches will happen every so often during the summer until the final match happens, when the winning team gets the trophy: the Sword of Gold award."

Many kids were intrigued by this, but few of the older ones seemed to care.

"Now, of course, I will be picking the Captains. Three Captains, three teams. Ah, yes. Cabin A… Avery, fifth year, if I'm not mistaken? Come over here." The coach indicated a spot to the left of him as Avery walked over, grinning. "Now, Cabin B. . .always most difficult. Gabriel, you have an older brother, yes? Oh yes. Gregory, come on up. Fifth year, too? Oh, yes, fourth year. You'll do good all the same."

Gregory, tall like his brother, with untidy light hair and looking nervous, walked through the crowd and stood next to Avery, who clapped him on the back. Gabriel was standing next to Nick. "Didn't know you had a brother," Nick whispered to him.

"Yep. He's been playing Swaying Swords since his second year and he almost carried the team last year, from what he told me," Gabriel whispered back.

"Hmm. Nice," Nick commented.

Coach Razan cleared his throat and said, "Hmmm, I wonder, Cabin C . . . why, of course! Where…? There! You, Ronald Hills. I heard you were good." Ronald Hills, a fifth-year camper who was almost as tall as Coach Razan himself, strutted over to the other two Captains, looking like someone had just offered him a mansion for free.

"Now, for the Fighters. There was someone I definitely wanted to meet. Yes! There you are, Nicholas!" Nick felt his stomach leap. Coach Razan might have meant him. Maybe not, but how many campers here with his name did he know?

"Yes, you, Silver. I recall your sister telling me about you once. Yes, you have the proper body of a sword fighter. You seem to be a good Fighter. Now, come over here." He pointed to a spot to his left. As he walked over to Coach Razan, Nick realized he was the first Fighter to be picked. This was great and he imagined bringing the Bio Bots success at last. Suddenly, he was filled with determination to do the best he could to raise his cabin's team position in the Game of Swords, more commonly known as Swaying Swords. The other four Fighters for Cabin B turned out to be Gabriel Golding, Alissia Helga, Jack Karoff, and David Canscar.

After the Fighter selections for the Airforce Rangers and the Crumbling Cursers, the Defenders were picked. The Defender for the Bio Bots was Isabella Laney. When the three teams were all sorted, Coach Razan called out to the crowd, "Our first match will be tomorrow! It's a shame some of our old players left, but our new ones will do well, too!" He beamed and continued, "I will give you from now until tomorrow at noon to create your own sword out of any bronze or scrap metal or anything you find useful in the Arts and Crafts Tent. Now, I wish you good luck!"

The three teams marched back to their cabins, which were already filled by the other campers. "So?" Dylan asked eagerly when Nick walked through the door. "Yeah, how'd it go?" asked John, springing from his bed. "Did you make it in?" Madison wanted to know.

"Well, yeah! I was the first Fighter chosen!" Nick explained to the three of them what happened at the lake.

"That's great!" said Madison, as she jumped off of the top bunk.

"I know. And, oh. . . I have to make my own sword by tomorrow!"

"Well, better get working, then!"

Nick headed into the Arts and Crafts Tent. It was bigger than he thought; a long table with two benches on each side and loads of supplies on the table, stuffed into buckets, jars, containers, and other things. "How am I supposed to make a sword? Who puts ingredients for a sword in an arts and crafts place?" he wondered. But his question was soon answered when he saw scraps of metal and hot glue being pulled out of two different buckets by three campers of the Crumbling Cursers. Nick thought, "Well, then. This camp does. I don't even..." And then he walked smack into Daniel Garring.

"Ouch! Nick?"

"Huh...Daniel? What are you doing here?" Nick asked.

"Eh, nothing really. I'm bored, so Sean and I decided to make a clay statue." Nick squinted and saw Sean Carter working on a two-foot-tall clay statue of a building.

"Nice statue," he commented quickly. "Anyhow, I'm here because I need to make a sword for that sport that's starting up, Swaying Swords."

"Oh, yeah. I wish I could play it, but I can't," Daniel added grimly.

"Why not? You should've gone with us to the..."

"Doesn't matter. I wasn't, er, allowed."

"Why not?"

"Well . . . you know, my dad. Anyway, you should probably start working on your things. I'd work on the armor, especially, if I were you.

The kids that got picked for the other teams . . . yeesh!" Daniel rolled his eyes.

"Oh. Yeah. Thanks for the tip, Daniel."

"No problem. See you around," Daniel grinned as he walked back to the table with Sean. Nick thought about what he had said about the armor, although a sword seemed easier to make, so he decided to do that first. He headed over to an empty space at the table and thought about what kind of sword he wanted. "A not-too-long, straight, light, sharp sword," he thought. "Maybe I can make it shoot out fire, too." He raised his arm above the leftover scrap metal on his tray, pointed his finger at the pieces, and whispered with a jerk of his finger, "Turn to fire!" Nothing happened. Nick honestly expected nothing more.

He spent the next several minutes trying to make a sword, resulting in several painful cuts on his fingers, hot glue-covered hands, and a fresh batch of impatience. He took a break and focused on making armor instead, starting with the legs. He found four straps, which turned out to be a perfect size on his legs and found four identical long shards of red bronze. He spent even more time learning how to properly work a hot glue gun, then when he figured it out, he used it to glue one large shard of bronze on one strap, and one on the another, and so on. He waited for the glue to dry and then put on the straps. The bronze hung perfectly in place on the straps that locked around his upper and lower legs.

"There," he thought. "Armor for my legs. . ."

Just then, the voice of Counselor Philip came through his favorite ear-splitting megaphone, echoing loudly, "ALL CAMPERS, COME TO THE OUTDOOR TABLE FOR LUNCH! ANNOUNCEMENT!"

Nick found an empty bucket, took a marker to print his full name on it, and then dumped in the scraps he would use for his sword and chest plate armor, followed by his finished leg armor. Then he put the bucket in a corner of the tent, next to some of the other campers' buckets. He quickly crawled through the opening of the tent and found his way to the table next to the lake, where the large architecture for what would be a giant closed metal box stood in place: the arena for the sport he wanted to win.

Nick swallowed his lunch while talking to John, Dylan, and Madison about his progress with the armor. Everything seemed peaceful until Counselor Philip made another announcement, disturbing the calmness. "Hello, campers! As we all know, tomorrow begins a new year of the Camp CrystalFlake sport, Swaying Swords! This year, after the payments were made for getting it set up here," he gestured at the lake, "it cost more money than expected. Now, this means that to continue feeding you kids, we will have to do a few more activities!"

"No," Nick moaned. "No way, you won't..."

"So, to start, I will be giving everyone a two-paper essay on how to survive a night in the forest. Just a nice camp-related paper that I thought appropriate! The paper is to be turned in by seven o'clock tonight." There were groans that echoed through the fields.

"Wait – but how does that help get money?" asked a third-year girl.

"It doesn't," stated Counselor Philip. "But I thought you all should still have something to do anyway. Another announcement...construction on the renovated Camp CrystalFlake starts tonight and continues after the first match of Swaying Swords. So, I arranged a little mining fieldtrip in the Klark Cave, down by the rocky hills. The challenge will be to collect as much materials as we can and then donate them to factories for money, to help pay for the camp's renovation and other things. The top three campers to get the most minerals for the factory will win a prize!" He passed out the papers and put three cups of pencils and erasers on each table, then marched away toward the Counselor Cabin.

Nick stared at Flame, who was prowling the grass, waiting hopefully for food to fall off the table. "That's not fair," he thought. "Doing that now, of all times, with campers having to get ready for Swaying Swords tomorrow. You guys agree with me, right?" Flame nodded and Nick recognized a grim look in his eyes, but Madison asked, "What?"

Nick was confused; it didn't seem like they understood him . . .all but Flame. Wait. . . but Flame hadn't understood him once, which happened to be the only time he had tried talking to Flame without his sweatshirt on and then he finally understood. The sweatshirt, the magical sweatshirt: it allowed Nick to speak to animals – or at least dogs – while he was wearing it.

How had he never noticed it before? He flashed back to his seven-year-old self, when he was in a store with his family. There was a lady with her dog there and Nick was wearing his sweatshirt – but how did it still fit him? He had talked to the dog. He heard his own words come out of his mouth and the dog seemed to understand him . . . but he also heard a strange growling coming from his own mouth. He remembered how confused he was then, looking around for a second dog, and none of his family seemed to understand what he said. And at that moment, they also looked around, expecting to see another dog.

Could it be that the sweatshirt was growing with him, which was why it always fit perfectly? It seemed like he had to look at a dog and concentrate just a bit in order to speak with it. He wondered whether this was a good thing or a bad thing, but decided to keep it a secret for now.

"C'mon, Nick." His thoughts were obliterated as he came back to reality. "Yeah, I'm coming, guys. . ."

Nick spent an hour trying to add more to his Swaying Swords equipment, but he had no luck at all. He ended up crawling out of the Arts and Crafts Tent, having completely wasted his time. Exhausted and hot, he dragged an oak log to the edge of the lake and began his essay. It was getting later and later into the evening and distractions kept popping up. Finally, he gave up and took a break. Placing the half-finished essay on his bed, he took a stroll around the camp. But unluckily, a familiar voice soon boomed out with another announcement.

"CAMPERS! RECONSTRUCTION WILL BEGIN NOW! ALL CAMPERS, RETURN TO YOUR CABINS AT ONCE!" Reluctantly, Nick tramped back to Cabin B as Derek, another first-year camper, exclaimed happily, "Hooray!" Nick rolled his eyes.

Gabriel walked up next to him and asked, "Hey, Nick, did you get anything done?" Nick sighed and admitted, "No. Not much. Only the armor for my legs, but that's all, and I'm half-done with my essay." Gabriel nodded. "Yeah, same. I finished my legs and started my sword, but didn't find anything for a chest plate, and I'm only half-done with the essay, too."

When they pushed the cabin door open, voices greeted them.

"Hey, Gabe! Hey, Nick!"

"Did you make a sword yet, Gabriel? Nicholas?"

"Can I try out your swords, please?"

"You're so lucky. I wanted to be on the team so much!"

"I'm surprised you two are on the team, Nick and Gabriel. First-years aren't often chosen."

It went on as campers bombarded them with questions and exclamations. Nick thought his head was going to split open from all of the noise. Suddenly, the construction workers decided to begin their work with a loud bang that shook everyone up, because it rocked the whole cabin. A fifth year poked his head out of the window and hollered out, "What happened?"

In a slightly worried voice, a balding construction worker yelled back, "It's all fine...all fine! Go back to what you were doing!"

After that, it was peacefully silent for a while. Some campers decided to draw on the floor, some worked on the essay, others talked on their beds, while others played board games at the table in the back. Nick laid on his bottom bunk, Madison above him, and imagined himself fighting in Swaying Swords. . . charging another. . . the opponent trying to hit but missing. . .

Nick knew he had to finish his essay, but then he thought, "Well, I do have a lot of time. I'll relax for now." And he joined his friends at the back of the cabin. By dinnertime, he still hadn't touched his essay. It was a quarter to six, but he decided he didn't need to bring his essay with him to finish. He still had time. The campers scampered off to the cafeteria while the construction workers remained outside.

Nick, Madison, John, and Dylan joked and laughed while they ate.

"Did you finish your essay yet?" John asked him.

Nick hesitated and murmured, "Um. No."

Madison was exasperated. "How? You had half a day to finish it, so you decide to wait until after dinner?"

Flame whimpered at Nick's feet. "True, true..." murmured Nick, distracted as he watched the pup sit down next to him on the floor. "Oh, fine," said Nick, aware that his friends thought the low growl Nick made actually came from Flame. "Here's a piece for you." And he dropped a bit of his chicken at Flame's feet.

After dinner, Nick realized it was already half past six. Half an hour to finish his essay. He immediately asked his friends for help, since they had already finished their essays hours before, and was grateful as they helped him through the entire essay. Thanks to them, he finished with ten minutes to go. He rushed outside, bursting through the door triumphantly, and went to the large patch of dirt by the entrance, sur-rounding the empty fireplace. Nick dropped his paper on top of the stack of others sitting on the tallest log in the patch. Then he ran back across the field. He stopped suddenly, still breathing heavily, and stared at the holes. He thought he caught a glimpse of movement. The holes, slimier than ever, now had wood planks built between them, with a pile of bricks stacked behind them in an area where more trees used to stand.

The construction workers had left for the night already, and the coun-selors were in their huge cabin. All was well. He stared at the platforms towering above the lake, where he would soon be competing. He returned to Cabin B, deciding he was too tired to work on his sword and armor.

At ten o'clock, Nick was still wide awake, anxious. He was worrying about the next day and couldn't sleep. When he finally dozed off, he had a weird dream about a figure was lying on the ground. Suddenly, fire exploded from the figure's chest. He saw a dark brown handle with a sil-ver-colored metal diamond-shaped pendant around it. There was a sym-bol on it, with red jewels on either side of the leather handle, which erupted from the figure's chest. The figure remained limp and still. Then more fire erupted as a burning, shiny white or silver-colored iron sword emerged as if it were being pulled from a rock. With one last burst of fire, the flaming iron sword rose so high, it fell away from the figure, landing flat on the floor next to it.

And in the morning, when Nick awoke, that same iron sword was lying at his side.

While the campers ate breakfast in the louder-than-ever cafeteria, Nick wasted no time in telling his friends about the night before. They were all shocked, confused, and bewildered and started offering various possibilities at once.

"Maybe your parents ordered it and had it delivered to you last night?" suggested Dylan.

"Maybe someone, a counselor maybe, left you that sword?" suggested John.

"Maybe the dream might actually be real? Well, I doubt it…but maybe someone in the cabin accidentally left it on your bed somehow?" suggested Madison, who was the most confused.

There was a real sense of anxiety for the Swaying Swords players, and more excitement than ever before throughout the rest of Camp CrystalFlake, as everyone impatiently waited for the competition to begin. After breakfast, Nick and the others stood in the sand dunes by the lake as John gave him suggestions for swordplay, Madison helped him learn the best way to hold it, and Dylan showed him really useful sword movements to help attack and block the opponents.

Finally, in the middle of lunch, Coach Razan walked in and asked loudly, "Who's ready for the first match of Camp CrystalFlake's Swaying Swords?" The campers cheered, their echoes bouncing off the walls. "The first match: the Airforce Rangers versus the Bio Bots!" The campers cheered louder. "Everybody come outside!" Coach Razan and Counselor Philip led them out to the Swaying Swords arena, where blankets were strewn about for the campers to watch the competition. Coach Razan beckoned the Bio Bots and Airforce Rangers over to him as everybody else sat down on the blankets. "Okay, Captains, go with your teams to your side of the arena. Line up the Fighters at the bridge and bring your Defender up to the platform. Go!"

Avery Lukan of the Airforce Rangers and Gregory Golding of the Bio Bolters separated. The five Bio Bolters Fighters – Nick , Gabriel Golding, Alissia Helga, Jack Karoff, and David Canscar – and the Defender, Isabella Laney, ran over to Gregory and headed to their side of the arena. The bridge had a blue team flag across it, which bore the image of two swords crossed, a lightning bolt in between, and the letters B.B. in the middle. The Airforce Rangers went to their bridge, with their symbol of a fighter jet between two swords on a red flag, with the letters A.R. at the bottom. Coach Razan yelled, "Get your Fighters and Defenders into their stations! Swaying Swords begins…now!"

Everything was a rush. Gregory, Gabriel, and Isabella climbed up the ladder connected to the bridge above the lake. Gregory tied Gabriel to the rope as the opposite team did the same with their players and Isabella stationed herself on the large platform, ready to defend. The whistle blew and Gabriel jumped as the A.R.'s Fighter jumped, also. They both swung in midair, a few feet above the Defenders' platform, which was a few feet above the water. Clutching their shields, the Defenders readied themselves. Gabriel swung forward, his outstretched arm holding his long, sharp blue sword. He lunged as Gregory, behind him on the platform, carefully watched his brother. The Airforce Ranger's Defender quickly raised a shield in front of their Fighter and, unfortunately, Gabriel didn't have time to raise his sword. The sword and shield collided, rewarding the Airforce Rangers with fifteen points.

"AIRFORCE RANGERS TAKE THE LEAD, FIFTEEN-ZERO!" bellowed Coach Razan below as the crowd cheered and booed.

Gabriel swung forward, looking determined, and the Airforce Ranger's Fighter yelled, "Ha! You think you'll win, don't you? But I'm Luke, the best player…" But Luke wasn't focused. Gabriel curved his sword around the Defender's shield and hit his chest plate squarely.

"BIO BOTS ARE NOW IN THE LEAD, TWENTY-FIFTEEN!"

This turn of events made Luke more aggressive. Fortunately, after Gabriel caused the Bio Bots to have a score of forty-fifteen, Gregory spotted Luke attempting to kick Isabella off her platform. This put the

Airforce Rangers at negative five. Down below the brawl, half the crowd cheered loudly as the other half yelled, booed, and screamed.

Luke swung forward, brandishing his sword madly as Gabriel swung to the side. Luke lunged forward, his sword about to collide with Gabriel's chest plate when Gabriel swung to the left and Luke's sword slammed into Isabella's shield.

"BIO BOTS IN THE LEAD BY FIFTY-FIVE TO NEGATIVE FIVE! AT LAST, THE BIO BOTS MIGHT WIN..."

Luke's anger was preventing him from getting a hit on Gabriel until finally, SWOOSH! His sword feigned Gabriel into lunging towards the Airforce Ranger's Defender's shield's direction, causing Gabriel to hesitate as Luke struck his chest firmly.

"AIRFORCE RANGERS NOW RETURN WITH FIFTEEN TO FIFTY-FIVE, BIO BOTS STILL IN THE LEAD!"

It went on for a few minutes, until finally the score announcement loudly changed from "THIRTY TO FIFTY-FIVE, BIO BOTS!" to "THIRTY TO SEVENTY-FIVE, BIO BOTS!" Soon it became "SIXTY TO EIGHTY-FIVE, BIO BOTS!" and later turned to "NINETY TO ONE HUNDRED-FIVE! BIO-BOTS CAN WIN! C'MON, GABRIEL GOLDING!" After five more minutes, Gabriel cut Luke's harness with a clean slice and Luke tumbled onto the previously flat terrain of water that was the lake. The Bio Bots won with one hundred twenty-five points, and the crowd roared with happiness and fury.

The next Fighters to face each other were Jack Karoff and Joseph Herrals. They each swung out of the other's path, the Defenders blocked blades, and Nick noticed Jack's move where he spun really fast in a circle, making it so Joseph couldn't hit him properly.

With Jack's amazing moves and sword slashes, the Bio Bots beat the Airforce Rangers narrowly by one hundred-ten to one hundred-five.

The Bio Bots had two hundred thirty-five points in the match so far. And then... "Next, Nicholas Silver versus Evan Mester!" Nick hardly noticed how loud the applause was the second his name was announced because of how nervous he was. He climbed up the ladder after putting on his bronze leg straps – overhearing some kids whisper about his lack of armor – and walked to the platform where Gregory was. As Gregory tied his harness, he whispered, "Don't worry, Nick, you'll do great." And on that thought, the whistle blew and Nick and Evan both jumped at the same time.

The feeling was marvelous. Nick felt like he was floating on air in the midst of action. He swung around, bounced off the Defenders' platform from the momentum, and swung back up into the open air freely as Evan raised his wide, green sword. Evan swooping towards him brought Nick back to reality. He raised his right arm and lunged his iron sword. The blade began to burn. Its iron was glowing, and it was coated with a thin layer of energy that looked vaguely like faded . . .fire?

Nick barely paid attention. Remembering the moves Dylan taught him, he pushed his body weight backward and Evan's blade just barely reached the place where his chest had been a second before. He lunged forward with great speed, and with a loud swoosh, Nick's iron sword pierced Evan's leather chest plate, which was singed by Nick's sword.

"TWENTY TO ZERO, BIO BOLTERS! GOOD JOB, NICHOLAS!"

Evan slashed his sword at Nick's knees, but Isabella came just in time. She reached up on her platform and lowered her shield. With a bang, the green sword met the shield.

"WOOHOO! THIRTY-FIVE TO ZERO, BIO BOTS IN THE LEAD!"

Nick concentrated. He could see where Evan was tensing, where he didn't expect Nick to attack, and where he did. Nick feigned falling and was able to swipe his sword at Evan's right side, but then quickly swung his body on the rope to Evan's left. His sword nearly hit Evan's shoulder, but struck what was still considered his chest, so Nick got the twenty points for it, making the score "BIO BOTS IN THE LEAD! STILL WITH FIFTY-FIVE TO ZERO!"

Evan was furious. The crowd below was laughing, bellowing, jeering, and cheering. Nick wished he could see Madison and his friends, but he was concentrating. He tried to fake out Evan again, but Evan wasn't fooled. He jabbed Nick in the chest.

"FIFTY-FIVE TO TWENTY, BIO BOTS!"

Nick was unfocused, he had let Evan get him, and now he had to truly redeem himself. He still felt where Evan's sword had pierced him straight in his chest, leaving him in pain where the sword hit. He wished he had made a chest plate. In the corner of his mind, it seemed that something deep inside his sweatshirt, inside himself, like a distant flame, knew he was hurt. Nick jabbed his sword again at Evan, who was protected by his team's Defender.

"FIFTY-FIVE TO THIRTY-FIVE! BIO BOTS!"

"Come on, Nick," he growled. Nick swung backward, creating force, and then propelled himself forward, a little bit left, letting Evan parry his blade. He swung backward again as Evan lunged and Isabella held up her shield.

"SEVENTY TO THIRTY-FIVE!"

He raised his sword with both hands, planning on striking Evan's chest, but Evan nailed him in the chest instead. More pain emanated from the area. His iron sword glowed slightly more. And so, it went on like that, until they were tied with one hundred-twenty points each. They were both swinging about, trying to cut the other's harness, the crowd growing louder with cheers and screams. Nick's chest was searing with pain and he was trying his hardest. He couldn't lose. He couldn't let his team down. Trying so hard, dodging with all of his might, he finally took a risk, abandoning blocking his own rope from the other boy and charging Evan's. Evan's Defender beat his blade and Nick was thrown off guard as Evan was blocked by Isabella. Since the score was still tied at one hundred thirty-five, Nick decided to take another risk. He had to succeed. If he didn't, it was over.

Just then, Evan took his chance and swung his sword at Nick's rope. However, at that exact moment and before Nick could get into position to block Evan, he felt a force within him that he could not explain. All he knew was that he could not just hang there and let his team lose. As Evan's blade swooshed through the air and began to rip his harness, Nick's sweatshirt started to glow powerfully with a bubble of fire. Nick knew bad things were coming.

A forcefield of flames burst from his sweatshirt, knocking Evan's steaming sword out of his hands and sending him flying. With his harness singed, he tumbled away from the platform and into the lake. Nick's forcefield dissolved, sphere of fire and all, with his own harness burnt, and he dropped into the lake after Evan.

10

The Secret Facility

"Arrrrggghhhhh!" Nick hurtled toward the lake, his bubble of fire dissipating around him. His harness, burnt to a crisp from the flames of the forcefield, hung uselessly above him. With a great splash, he hit the water. Every inch of him was drenched in water so cold that he was overcome with a prickling pain. Evan Mester was already swimming back to shore, looking mutinous. The campers on dry land sounded furious, but also appeared scared and confused. They didn't understand what they had seen, yet they didn't like it. Angry voices filled the air as Nick struggled to swim to the shore. The counselors looked dumbfounded, but Coach Razan looked let down.

Nick pulled himself onto the sandy shore, a reddish tinge all over his skin. His friends had rushed in to help and they dragged him fully out of the lake.

"Nick, what was that?" someone asked.

"I-I don't know," Nick stammered. He was in a state of shock, confusion, and disappointment. He had ruined the match. His dumb, unexplainable powers ruined it. But did they?

"D-did it count?" he asked shakily. "D-did we get the w-win? Technically, I-I cut h-his rope before he c-cut mine. . ."

"I don't know, Nick. I don't know what they're going to do."

Nick felt weak, but he couldn't pass out now. He had to fix this. He kept pushing aside the wet hair that drooped over his eyes. Slowly, he got up and walked with the others toward the crowd. Counselor Philip stood there. He shook with what was either anger or fear – Nick couldn't tell which – but the next moment, the counselor said in a low, controlled voice, "Silver, come with me. Medical Cabin." He grabbed Nick's arm gently and led him away from the ogling crowd of campers.

Nick was grateful for this because his legs felt too weak to walk on his own. The creation of the forcefield had really drained him. "Take off that sweatshirt, Silver. We'll throw it in the wash." Nick pulled it off silently, feeling a little less damp and heavy.

Once they reached the Medical Cabin, Counselor Philip lowered Nick onto a bed and passed him a towel. He picked up Nick's sweatshirt as he left the room, saying, "I'll go tell Fletcher what happened to you. Don't move." Nick felt sick. He was too weak and fatigued to respond. He just rested there, dreading what his punishment would be and what would happen to the Bio Bots.

An hour or more later, he woke up. He still felt weak, but not as much, and a little bit drier. He heard Nurse Fletcher say, "You can go now, Mester. That was a pretty bad fall. But you're fine now. Ah, Silver, you're awake."

"Uurrggh. Hello," Nick groaned, sitting up and still wrapped in the towel.

"Well, Silver, here is your sweatshirt." He noticed it was dry as she placed the garment on his bed. "And now you can return to your cabin. I won't hesitate to say your cabinmates have a lot of questions. I also would ask you to change into different clothes when you reach your cabin."

Nick pulled himself out of bed. "What happened after I left?"

"Well, Silver," she began, "you created a pretty big scene. Everybody's talking about it. Looked like you exploded a balloon or something. Or a solar flare, perhaps. Anyway, the rest of the match has been postponed for now. Now please, go back to your cabin."

Nick walked through the door of Cabin B, still holding his sweat-shirt. As he entered, shock exploded throughout the room as scared and confused campers yelled. There were angry voices, too, but he strode past them all to where his friends waited. His sister sat on his bed.

"So," he started off. "Did we win?" They all looked at one another. Finally, Madison said in a quiet voice, "Well, when…uh…everybody, the counselors and all, saw you explode something, they had no idea what had happened and blamed it on a freak accident resulting from rough construction of the arena. So, they didn't blame you," she added, seeing the look on Nick's face. "So anyway, the counselors, um, couldn't help noticing how you knocked that Evan kid's sword out of his hands. They thought that…well, you were cheating. Because you're not really allowed, to…um…knock swords out of your opponent's hand. They said what you did was cheating when you caused his sword to fly out of his hand, so they, well…er…took off the points for it."

"Don't tell me," said Nick grimly. "Don't say we lost!" The look on her face said it all. "We, um, didn't win. One hundred thirty-five to one hundred twenty-five. They won."

"It wasn't my fault!" protested Nick furiously. "I didn't mean to do that. I just . . . lost control!"

"We know," interrupted John. "It's just…the other counselors and kids, well…they don't. Three hundred-forty to two hundred-thirty, Nick. Don't worry. When the match continues, we'll still be in the lead."

"I guess," said Nick grimly. "Well, that was better than I thought! It was so much fun, except for the forcefield, you know . . . it was so satisfying and, well, crazy."

"I knew you'd like it after you got so excited – like the time you sliced my pillow in half with that toy sword!" Madison reminded him.

"Whoops!" said Nick, snorting with laughter that was joined by Dylan and John.

"Oh, wait. Tomorrow's the trip to the Klark Cave, so the cheapskate – er, counselor in change – can make a quick buck and use it for the reconstruction!" exclaimed John.

"True," Dylan instantly agreed.

Madison checked the time. "It'll be dinner soon. Let's just have fun outside." Nick grinned and nodded as the group headed out, determined to enjoy the evening.

But Monday morning dragged by slowly for Nick. First, it was passing the whispers of other campers, then trying hard to ignore them while eating breakfast, then staying calm as Evan Mester came up and yelled at him for "trying to kill me." After that, Nick and Evan were basically enemies. Evan taunted Nick whenever he could. In turn, Nick annoyed Evan, showing him his sweatshirt, which usually flashed brightly whenever Evan sneered at him.

At half past ten, three buses finally arrived, one for each cabin, and drove the campers to the mountains where a long, hollow, rocky cave stood. Each of the campers was given a nylon sack before entering. The cave was like a maze. Nick got lost twice but managed to find his way back. Unfortunately, the third time he got lost, he fell through a wide hole and landed right smack onto Evan Mester's leg, just as Evan found a piece of iron ore. Evan fell backward as Nick crumpled on his back in front of him and noticed the iron. While Evan struggled to get back to his feet, grumbling, Nick grabbed the iron and happily climbed back through the hole as Evan yelled after him. Stuffing the iron into his sack, he walked back to where he and his friends and sister had separated.

The Klark Cave managed to be wet, cold, and rocky, with sharp edges and everything else that a group of eleven to fifteen-year-olds would hate about a cave. At half-past twelve, Counselor Philip finally decided to call them all back. It took twenty minutes for everyone to escape the menacing cave before they drove back to Camp CrystalFlake for lunch.

Of course, the construction had started up again since it was only stopped on Sunday for the first match of Swaying Swords. They all had to eat in the cafeteria and, surprisingly, it had been cleaned. The walls were less grimy, the food wasn't sickening, the benches were comfortable, and the floors were only regular floors. Nick didn't hear as much whispering about him, but he did overhear Evan Mester whispering something to his friends, who all glowered at Nick. When lunch was over, Counselor Philip announced that all of the minerals sold had paid off most of the construction and handed out prizes – to a fifth year and two third-years who had collected the most minerals. Just baskets of candy; nothing too special. Nick and the others got up and were the first out the door as Evan Mester and his friends started strolling slowly over to them.

Nick's group decided to visit the holes. They were even bigger, with slime oozing all over the grass and the wood planks that separated them. They looked rockier and rougher, too. Then they walked to the lake, where the Swaying Swords arena still sat. The construction workers were now chatting with the counselors in the Counselor Cabin, so more kids were outside. The four were discussing what they thought would be built first when Evan and his friends approached and yelled something Nick didn't hear.

"What's it to you, Mester?" replied Dylan angrily, taking a step towards Evan.

"Well, I'm spreading the word about you. Telling them what really happened between us. What sorcery do you have now, huh?"

Nick joined Dylan. "Get lost, Mester."

"Oh, but me and my friends here don't want to end the fun early, do we?" His gang guffawed.

"How about you go, or…" Nick began, but Evan interrupted, "Yeah, sure. That was a freak accident, and you know it. I'm not deaf, you know."

"Yeah, you dopey little kids. Now you three get lost, we're talking to Silver here," said a new, cold voice. Nick suddenly remembered who it was. "Name's Luke. Luke Oralles. Now, you three, GO."

Nick's group didn't move.

"Fine, we'll just have to make you, then," Luke growled.

Dylan snickered, "Make us. Oh yeah. Indeed. Oh no. I'm terrified. How are you gonna…" In the next second, Luke charged at Nick, who was unprepared and got knocked over, thrown to the edge of the lake. POW! Nick leaned up as he heard the sound, watching Luke stagger after being punched down by Dylan, who was seething.

"You maniac! How could you be friends with that…that…" bellowed Evan at Dylan as he rushed to Luke, who was on his feet again.

Luke Oralles charged Nick again, but Madison had jumped in the way and stretched her arms out, pushing Luke to the side. Evan howled in fury and jumped at John, who dodged out of the way quickly, causing Evan to crash on the grass, where he groaned.

"Relax!" John yelled. It looked as if the crowd from Cabin A would retreat, but they didn't. Avery, the Captain of the Airforce Rangers, let out a roar and lunged at Dylan, who was thrown to the hard ground by the force of his charge. Evan let out a sudden crow-like laugh and then jumped at John, who had no chance to dodge this time.

"No!" Nick yelled. He willed a forcefield to appear where John stood as he rushed forward, but nothing happened. John fell backward into the lake with a splash as Evan steadied himself at the edge and walked away laughing with his friends, back to their cabin.

"Jerks! And they know the counselors here won't do a thing about it. . ." Dylan murmured, then proceeded to call their adversaries very specific words, repeating them louder as Nick pulled John out of the lake.

"Eh, it's fine. It wasn't really a hard hit," muttered John as he got to his feet.

"C'mon!" exclaimed Madison. "Let's go before people come and ask questions."

John changed into dry clothes before they quickly ate dinner with the rest of the camp, and then the four spent the next few hours drawing in the Arts & Crafts Tent, where they doubted they'd be found. It was mainly silent until Nick, who had been thinking about something all day, decided to say it out loud. "Hey, guys?"

"Yeah?"

"Do you think...do you think I should read more of that Zorblin book?"

"Why?"

"Well, I've been thinking. I want to know the truth: why my sweatshirt has powers, why I faced death that night, why I summoned a forcefield yesterday – basically making me an outcast here."

"What's your point?" The sun was setting as they started to leave the tent, still conversing.

"I want to raid the Secret Facility." Nick didn't mean to say it so bluntly. He wanted to slowly build up to it, since it sounded so immensely dangerous, but he accidentally dropped it all at once.

"You what?"

"You can't!"

"Yeah, and kill yourself? Don't bother."

"I knew you'd take it like this," Nick muttered, staring at the wall.

"Nick, this is insane. We don't even know where the Facility is!"

"Oh yes, we do," Nick said quietly. "The Quarren Forest. I already told you my theory. Give me a chance." It became darker out, as stars appeared.

"You see, Nick," said Madison in a careful voice. "The Secret Facility is, well, called the Secret Facility for a reason."

"I'll find it!" Nick assured her confidently.

"Just stick to the facts, Nick. That's a suicide mission!" interrupted John.

"Sounds fun and all, but that's not possible," said Dylan in a mono-tone.

"Yeah, I know – but still, after all of this, don't you think I deserve to know the truth? Don't you think I should know how and why I'm, well, different?" sighed Nick.

"Nick, I know – but just listen…"

"Guys, look, I know it sounds stupid, but I think I'm going to go for it! I want to know. Just in and out, that's all. I won't stick around." Night fell upon the camp.

"Well, how are you planning to pull this off, anyway? We only have a shred of proof about this Facility thing. Your sweatshirt, though – I don't know, I can't explain that…"

SLUSH. "What was…?"

SLOP. "What's that…?"

SLORP. SLOSH. "Where's that coming from?"

"That doesn't matter," said Nick impatiently. "I'm going to get my sword and I'm going to find that Facility. Whether Quarzolon is smart enough to hide it well or not…" A terrible pain ran down his spine, but he was getting numb to Quarzolon's curse.

SLOG. "I don't know whether you guys are coming or not, but I've made up my mind, I'm taking risks. I'm going!"

"We're coming," said John.

"Really?" asked Nick, surprised.

"You bet," said Madison.

"We'll follow you to the end, bud," said Dylan.

SLUSH. SLAG. SLORG.

"Okay, seriously…what is that?"

"Uh oh…"

"I'll get my sword," said Nick firmly. The sound stopped. He bolted back into the Arts & Crafts Tent and seized his iron sword from his bucket. He ran from the tent, the moon rising steadily and clouds moving in, but then froze on the spot. Paralyzed with fear, he felt a familiar cold, numbing sensation from his sweatshirt. It grew uncomfortable and the color drained from the fabric as his body temperature dropped.

"Master," croaked a young child, hidden in the darkness of night, as a ghost formed in front of him. "It has risen, it has grown fully. The super weapon." The ghost gave the child a crooked grin. "Good. But that is just the distraction . . .ha, ha, ha!!" The boy stepped back as the ghost laughed coldly and pitilessly. Nick took a great big breath and his body temperature was restored.

The boy and the ghost: he had seen them again. The boy said a weapon was ready, the ghost said it was just a distraction, and then that dark, rippling cold laugh. . .

Nick ran back to his friends, clutching his sword, and was about to tell them what he had just witnessed, but then…

SLEEK! SLORK! SLOORRGG. . . SLAG GLORRRGG. . . SLARRRG. . .

The holes suddenly exploded with oozing slime. The muck was everywhere, and the wooden planks burst apart from the explosion. A huge lump of glistening green slime rose from one of the bigger holes. Shaped like an arm with an attached hand, it dropped to the ground. But it wasn't over. Another arm, lumpier than the first, made of the same muck, had risen from another big, rough hole near the first. Suddenly, a long gleaming lump of a leg came out, then another, then a large torso, the slime sleek and dripping, and finally, a head, the lumpiest of them all.

Its face was horrid: A lipless mouth, made up of darker slosh, and eyes of the dirtiest muck, a darker color than any other part. A monster of slime had risen from the holes. Its right arm lying limply next to a different hole, the monster slowly turned as its slime gleamed in the moonlight and used its left arm to grab the other one and attach it to the useless empty stump where its right arm should have been in the first place.

The climax of the holes, growing in muck and size for weeks, had arrived. They had been the birthing place of a twenty-foot-high monster made of grimy, green, oozing slime. The four watched in stunned fascination as it stretched up high and then bent lower. Slowly, it turned to face Nick, Madison, John, and Dylan, and those dark green eyeballs in the middle of its head were filled with a murderous, violent look. Suddenly, it struck. It swung its arm at Dylan, who crouched but was too slow. Dylan was flung backward so powerfully, he slammed into a nearby tree and remained motionless.

"Dylan!" the others screamed.

The slime monster faced them again. His courage building, Nick lunged blindly with his sword, but the monster raised a foot and kicked him, sending him soaring into the air. He landed, crumpled, in the sand dunes. At that point, Madison and John were smart enough to run for their lives. But little did any of them know that Nick's sweatshirt had begun to glow fiercely. It burst into dim red flames and he could feel the warmth healing him. He rose. Sprinting across the field, he seized his sword, which had fallen on the ground midway between the monster and the dunes and lunged again. This time, he got a hit on the slime monster. And now, instead of a flame-like glow, the sword was burning with actual fire. The monster screamed and thrashed and slapped Nick away.

Dylan rose weakly behind the beast. He feebly grabbed a stick and stealthily crept up to the slime monster. Gingerly, he rose his arm and jabbed the sharp stick straight in the beast's leg. "RAAWR!" cried the monster as Dylan laughed triumphantly, backing up. The monster swung its arm again, but Nick willed himself to summon a forcefield and it worked. A fiery sphere, smaller than the one he had made during the match, burst into sight around Dylan, the tight bubble shearing and burning away the part of the monster's arm where it connected with the fire sphere. John gasped in shock at the sight of the forcefield and Madison froze. The monster, however, decided to go for Nick instead of Dylan.

The bubble of fire suddenly dissolved as Nick lost focus. He thought the slime monster would kill him for sure until John plunged Nick's extinguished sword into the monster's foot and the beast howled and stopped chasing Nick. Suddenly, Madison hurtled out of nowhere just as the slime beast regained focus. She threw fistfuls of sand from the dunes at the monster and it staggered, trying to get the sand out of its eyes, but its slime was too sticky and the sand was already stuck. It roared with rage into the moonlight. When John gave Nick his sword, it burst into flames again. Nick took another risk. He climbed up the monster's leg – which was conveniently easy because of how sticky it was – and onto its head. He plunged the iron sword into its face, which started to melt at once.

"RAWWR!" It threw Nick off as John kicked it in the leg with as much force as he could muster. The monster screamed again in rage and toppled over backwards, right into the dirt, as Dylan leapt on its face and stabbed it with his stick. "RAAWWWR!!" The slime monster thrashed its oozing limbs, but its body gradually lost its form and it melted away, its remnants coating the camp's grass.

The four stood over the slime puddle in front of them, panting with exhaustion and sweating profusely. Dylan had received a bruise after getting slammed into a tree.

"What…was…that?" panted John, leaning his hands against his bent knees.

"Daniel should know that this happened. We should tell him," Nick began as the thought occurred to him. "He's been visiting and watching those holes for weeks. He must've figured something like this would happen. And well, he was right."

"It's too late at night," Dylan murmured. "And obviously, everyone's asleep because nobody came bursting out here when we were being attacked."

Nick straightened up. "Well, I guess it's obvious now what we have to do, isn't it?"

"What do you…?"

"The Secret Facility," Nick reminded them. "I'm going now, not only to find the truth, but to stop this madness. Dylan, don't even try to argue. Whatever that creature at the lake was, it was there for a reason and it almost killed you!"

"Well…I mean, you have a point. . ." Dylan mumbled, wincing. "And if we wait any longer, the whole camp will be wiped out. Look what almost happened to us. We're the only ones that know about the danger we're all in and I think it's time to stop it!"

"You're right," breathed Madison, clutching her side, covered in slime. "Even though it's downright life-threatening to go barging in, I think we'll have to. The Facility's obviously real at this point."

"Well, what are you doing then? Let's go and kill ourselves. Only I hope I die all in one shot. I don't want to suffer, but I guess I'm already suffering with you. C'mon, let's get this done." Dylan panted as he put a hand to his neck and felt it, wincing more.

"Then it's decided. Let's go die in the Secret Facility," said John breathlessly.

"Yeah, you don't have to look on the downside so much," said Nick, half doubtful and half hopeful. And scared out of his wits.

"Sooo, where to?" asked Dylan.

"It's obvious. The Quarren Forest, but we'll have to get in without being detected first," responded Nick.

And so, they marched towards the Quarren Forest, which of course was barricaded after the first few pine trees. Madison looked like she was about to climb over the fence when Nick said quickly, "Don't bother." Then he slashed a large, gaping hole in the fence with his iron sword. The moon was clear in the night sky and by now, Counselor Chris would have already checked the cabins. But would he realize four kids from Cabin B were gone?

The Quarren Forest was different from the Forest of Tappers. The Forest of Tappers was more spacious, with less trees, and had some ponds, while the Quarren Forest was filled with thick pine trees, valleys, and canyons. There was even a mud structure that rose high up and curved in an arch, with a pile of mossy stones below and swampy landscapes surrounding it.

They walked around a bit, trying to find the Facility, until they were plainly lost. Eventually, they stumbled across something odd. The Quarren Forest no longer looked as natural as it had before. The land had opened up a lot more and there were trees, but they were made of iron. And there was a massive lake, shimmering with moonlight in the darkness, despite the fact that it was incredibly foggy. But it didn't look too deep, either.

"Iron," Nick murmured. "Quarzolon's favorite metal, the metal he associated his nature to, was iron."

They looked around the odd area. Trees of iron, patches of iron plates on the ground – what did it mean? They looked around, hoping for clues. But they had to accept that, this time, they were doomed. And when things looked as if they couldn't get worse…CLANG! Walls of iron rose up out of the ground, circling them and the strange area where they stood. They were trapped.

11

Down the Tunnel

———————

"Uh oh..." The walls of iron surrounded them in the Quarren Forest. It seemed as if Ruler Quarzolon did like to stay true to his chosen metal: iron. There was no turning back now, but there was one good thing about this: they now were positive the Secret Facility was in this zone. He must have thought nobody would find this area, thought Nick, otherwise he wouldn't have made it so obvious.

"This is it! Let's start searching."

They looked around, seeking a passageway or something that would lead to the Secret Facility, but the book was apparently right: only someone similar to the Ruler would be able to find the entrance. It was a dark, enclosed area and it was now so late into the night they could barely see. Luckily, when Nick was about to say something about the lack of light, his sweatshirt flared and a glow of reddish-orange fire emanated from it, illuminating the area. At least they weren't hungry or thirsty, he thought, because there was no way of getting food now.

"Let…us…out!" Dylan hollered and banged on the iron walls, which only managed to hurt his fists.

"It's no use," John groaned. "These walls are unbreakable."

Nick had already tried. When his sweatshirt finally became activated after several minutes of concentration, and he felt the power surging through him again, he tried to release it toward the walls, but nothing happened. The dim fire simply dissolved as it touched the surface. Quarzolon must have enchanted the walls, too. But how had he done that? There were so many things they didn't know about Lord Quarzolon and the Mestephans, like what powers they actually did have.

But they did realize something. Every few minutes, the lake would shine a different color. They didn't dare try to swim in it, although they persistently checked the outermost rim, hoping to dig up a clue.

"Ughh," moaned Madison after half an hour. "It's over! I'm done! I give up!"

"Let us out!" Dylan bellowed again.

Nick felt disconnected from the rest of the camp. He remembered how he had daydreamed of having fun, sleeping peacefully, and laughing with new friends, but now he found himself exhausted, injured, trapped, and doomed in the confines of Ruler Quarzolon's trap. He was on the verge of giving up when John finally shouted, "I got it!"

"You did? Got what?" Dylan cried, springing off the wall as Nick's face split into a grin.

"Yes. . . I think I got it, but it's just a hunch. It's not hard, really. Well, sort of. . ."

Madison had been resting on the grass, but suddenly looked more awake now that John thought he had figured out the puzzle.

"Okay, how'd you do it? What do we need to know?" asked Nick.

"Well, you see these iron plates? Count them up and you have exactly fourteen plates. Then look at the trees. Fourteen of them. These are two fourteens, and fourteen divided by two is…"

"Cut to the point, John," said Dylan impatiently. "I'm trapped in a magic forest here, in the middle of the summer, and I'm not really in the mood for a math lesson."

John rolled his eyes and plowed on. "Fourteen divided by two is seven. The seventh tree, which is. . . five, six. . . here! This is the tree that should, if I'm right, be the one that opens the Facility!" It was admittedly a crazily creative theory, but they were all hopeful.

"Wow, John, that was really good. . ." said Nick, awestruck and grateful that they may have found the answer.

Madison added, "Yeah, I'm doing more advanced math than you in school and even I couldn't have figured that out!"

John looked at the seventh tree. "Anyone have a pen, marker, anything?" he asked.

"On me at all times," said Madison, pulling a red marker from her sweatpants pocket. She drew a big 7 on the iron tree.

"Do you just carry that around with you all the time?" asked John, raising his eyebrow in surprise.

"Um, yeah…sort of. Art purposes, you know?"

"When you live with my sister, this type of thing is to be expected," Nick mumbled, then gestured at the seventh tree. "Anyway, how do we activate it?"

"Dunno," John admitted.

"We might as well look, then, shall we?" Dylan murmured. And so, they looked. It had the appearance of an ordinary tree – except for the fact that it was made out of iron. They felt all around the whole tree, getting more anxious as they found anything. And then, after fifteen long unsuccessful minutes, Dylan got annoyed. He aimed two great punches at the tree, which shuddered, and a hatch opened up at the very top. "Hey, wait! Look!" he exclaimed.

"Dylan, you did it! You found the next piece of the puzzle!" He had led them straight to the next clue.

"Now," whispered Madison, "we just need to get up there. Nick, give me your sword."

"Wait…why?"

"Just let me see this. . ."

Although doubtful, Nick handed her his sword. Madison aimed it, balancing it on her arm as she eyed the hatch at the top of the tree. "Now!" She chucked the sword. It soared perfectly up to the hatch and hit something metal inside. It rolled over and toppled with a clunk and a thud. A small metal box with a big red button had fallen onto the grass next to an iron plate at their feet. Madison's perfect aim with hurtling things, even a sword, had caused enough force to knock the little box out. It looked like some sort of remote control.

Unfortunately, Nick's sword was now stuck, its tip slicing into the iron. "My sword!" he complained.

"Don't worry, Nick. We can make a new one. Sorry. . .but let's test this out."

"Are you sure about this?" Dylan asked, taken aback.

"We've gotten this far," Nick mumbled. "Press it, now!"

Beep! The effect was immediate as Madison pressed the red button. Thirteen of the trees, all but the seventh, blasted out jets of blue and yellow light at the lake, which shimmered with the colors as it absorbed them. The four ducked under the trees, but they could still feel wind rising in the vicinity from the power of the blasts. As they watched, the water itself – not just the colors of light – seemed to be absorbed from the lake. They closed their eyes as the jets of blue and yellow light grew louder and brighter. There was a rushing noise and then it stopped.

They opened their eyes and stared at the lake. It was empty. The jets of blasting light had somehow absorbed all of its contents. Nick thought that Lord Quarzolon must be a powerful Mestephan to be able to do that and Madison dropped the remote on the grass. They stood up cautiously and approached the lake. It was like a crater now and at the bottom of the dry pit was a great, iron hatch.

"This is it, guys." Nick uttered breathlessly. "The entrance to the Secret Facility."

They slid down the dried walls of the lake. The hatch read:

MADE: 12 YEARS AGO

THE SECRET FACILITY

PROPERTY OF RULER QUARZOLON

It seemed like Ruler Quarzolon had put a bit of magic into the hatch too, so it would reveal exactly how long ago it was made, whenever the text was read.

"Well, what are we waiting for? Oh jeez. . . here goes nothing!" All together, the four kids lifted the hatch. It creaked and a spider dropped from a hanging web. Using all their strength, they opened the hatch completely so they wouldn't need to prop it open. It was foreboding to leave it open that way, but they knew they had to in case they needed a quick escape.

"Just in and out," Nick breathed, holding the others at bay. "Then we'll escape. Just get the information…maybe kill the Zorblin? After that, we leave – got it?" Once they all agreed on the plan, they plunged into the Secret Facility at last, climbing down a small, stone ladder.

It was just like Nick's visions. The space split off into two hallways, one going right, the other heading left, and there were two rooms in each of the hallways. The ceiling and floor were made of a darker, thinner iron than the surrounding walls. It was dim, but there were still some lights on the Facility ceiling. "Wait," Nick commented suddenly. "If this place was made twelve years ago, then that book…"

"Shh!" interrupted Madison, who was heading carefully to the left hallway. There was a room close to them and they traveled silently, each of their hearts beating faster than usual, toward the tall doorway. They stepped over the threshold slowly and found a room full of books and scrolls and ripped papers: a library. They looked through the materials, but everything was in a different language. They continued to the other room in the left hallway. It was a small, narrow, and cramped room, with rusted buckets and a pile of old sticks that looked like staffs. They quietly decided it must be the storage room and moved on, back to the right hallway.

The first room in the right hallway was cramped like the storage room and seemed like a backup storage space. Further down the hallway, the next room was bigger, like the first one they had entered like looked like a library. Through the high doorway, they discovered that this one was an armory filled with deadly weapons and what they assumed to be powerful, cursed, and enchanted armor. Although they didn't want to stick around long, they each selected a weapon. John took a black staff with two glowing yellow lines down it that stood next to a sign that read "Personal Recreations." Dylan chose a long, thin, rocket launcher, along with a small sack full of ammunition, and Madison took a wide, sharp, purple sword. Nick didn't take anything; he didn't need to because his sweatshirt was already a weapon. They decided the armor may be too cursed, dangerous, and broken to try, so they held their breath and turned the corner with the weapons they carried.

They saw two high, arched doors on the left side, far from each other, and on the right, two same-looking doors, except closer to each other. They crept to the nearest door of the underground facility, to the right of the long hallway. It seemed like a brewing room. There was a line of both full and empty glass tubes, and at the edge of a long table pressed against the wall were five wide tubes filled with a brown liquid. Next to them were about a dozen small, short plastic bottles, with labels that read: CAMP CRYSTALFLAKE APPLE JUICE.

"Hey guys, look." Nick looked horrified as they examined the bottles and the brown liquid in the tubes. "The apple juice…the poison, I mean…was made down here. I knew it!"

"But then how did they get to Philip?" Madison wondered aloud. "He obviously didn't realize there was poison in that stuff. He started panicking and getting all stressed after you passed out."

John took another guess. "So there is a traitor. If you guys remember what I said, the cooks have the best chance of making the poison. Counselor Philip isn't…well, he'd be cheap enough to get them to make it."

"John has got a point, now that I stop and think about it. . ." admitted Dylan, who was admiring his thin rocket launcher.

"Point made," said John, satisfied. "Let's go, then. See what else there is before we leave. And remember, we need to find proof that this place is real. I don't know about you, but I wouldn't want to come back."

They walked slowly to the next room. It was filled with scrap metal and there was a large desk with a lantern propped up. In the corner was a massive robot suit, with a great chest, long, thin legs, and long, stretched-out arms. The top of the torso was much larger than the lower part, expanded out to about twice the size of the bottom half, which was much narrower and had less room. Hammers, screwdrivers, saws, and wrenches hung on the wall, and on the floor was a pile of wires.

They moved on to the next room, as there was not much else to see. They would get the proof later, they agreed, because they didn't want anything weighing them down if they had to run should something, or someone, attack. The next room looked like a hospital room. There were about eight or nine beds lined up against the wall, with empty cabinets. After that, was a fourth room, full of maps and lists. Because of Nick, they spent extra time there. He read a map of Mestephan cities and old Mestephan locations on Earth. There were also battle strategies written down on some papers and two old, worn-out blueprints of the Mezoar Prison, which the Ruler had created and where he had been imprisoned. Nick also found a letter to Ruler Quarzolon that read:

To the Dark Ruler,

I would like to congratulate you on conquering King Cracious. I never liked that king. His choices and decisions were ill-advised. I hope you are a more gracious and worthy ruler. I would also like to say how impressed I was when I saw you fight King Cracious in the Battle of the Lords. I must admit that your battle plans were simply genius.

Again, congratulations on becoming the new king, beating King Cracious at last, and your grand performance during the Battle of the Lords.

Sincerely,

Cornius the Dark

Nick placed the letter back where he found it, thinking that whatever King Cracious had done, Ruler Quarzolon was easily worse.

The others had already moved on to the strange last room of that hallway. There were piles of what looked like dry skin and a large book titled The Simple Monster-Making Guide. This room was darker than the others and a little bit more spacious. There was a symbol on the ground in the corner, made of red lines in a circular symbol. Candles, blown out a long time before, were placed around the lines, making it look like a place where demons were summoned. The room also held moldy buckets of eyes and tongues of different creatures, along with a large jar of teeth and talons. They rummaged through the room before they left. Nick even snuck The Simple Monster-Making Guide in the pocket of his sweatshirt. He was getting anxious because he hadn't learned anything about himself or his sweatshirt.

They journeyed to the next and longest hallway, with three doors on one side and three on the other. Breathlessly, they stepped down the dimly lit hall of the Facility. As they entered the next room, they heard a small, high, cracking sound. They all spun around on the spot, but no one was there. "Just the floors. . ." Nick murmured quietly. This room was large and wide, with iron gates from the floor to the ceiling, blocking the four from getting past. It was dark and misty beyond the gates, and they noticed an empty keyhole on the right side of the wall, with a golden ring around it. A small slit at the bottom of the gates was just large enough for food to be slipped through. Nick rubbed his hands together. If this was really what he thought it was. . .

He was delighted to feel his hands warm up rapidly as they burst into flames, although he was not burned. He waved his hand at the gates while the others held their breath. The fire jetted out toward the iron gates but merely glanced off, just like it did to the walls surrounding the entrance to the Facility. Nothing happened, although they heard a low, rumbling growl destroy the silence even as the space beyond the gates remained misty and dark.

With an uneasy feeling in his stomach, Nick led the others to the next room, which was directly across from where they stood. Sweat was streaming down their white faces. The next room was quiet, and they noticed a veil-like blur in the air. It was similar to a mist, like seeing through a cloudy glass. Dylan said, "I got this, guys" and charged halfway through it before a strong force blasted him backward and he crashed onto the dirty iron floors. "Ouch!" he yelped, clutching the side of his head as it began to throb. Madison ran toward it next, with immense speed, but also got thrown backward, a little farther than Dylan, and crashed to the ground.

"I'll try my powers again," Nick said quickly, before John had a chance to be thrown backward next. He shut his eyes and concentrated on his powers more than ever before. His sweatshirt began to glow and lit up the entire hall. A rumbling noise filled the hallway as the floor quaked slightly. Nick felt a tightening pain in his stomach. . . he had to release the force before it killed him. . .but it was too strong, he couldn't let go. . .

His sweatshirt was blinding all of them and with one terrible yell, Nick released his powers. The hall exploded with fire. The others backed away, yelling and screaming. Nick couldn't see…it was too bright, and there was a sizzling sound and a large bang like a gong. After mere moments, the fire stopped. His friends and sister were crumpled on the ground, their hair and clothes singed. "Sorry guys," mumbled Nick. As they were about to respond, there came another sound.

CA-CAW! RAWWR! TWEET! TWEET! SCREEE! Nick spun around on the spot. "Wha-?" His power had broken the veil and the sounds it had been muffling flooded out the door. This room held cages of all sizes, teeming with animals such as phoenixes, bear-like dogs, fanged cats with two tails with stingers on the ends, small, molten blobs with faces, birds with multiple red eyes blasting beams of energy, and tentacled beasts with horns and small, muscular arms. There was also a large paper on the wall, illustrating another battle strategy that involved

Lord Quarzolon himself, raising and breeding all of these creatures and setting them upon Earth.

Bang! A serpent on the floor shook its tail and with another bang, red energy shot from its tail, bounced off the wall, and hit Nick squarely in the chest. He fell backward, wheezing. The serpent slithered out the door and hissed, spraying some sort of acid on the floor. Bang! More red light flashed at Nick, but he was ready. He quickly dodged to the right, letting the jet of red miss. BANG! A yellow light exploded from the tip of John's staff and engulfed the snake, which was immediately flung aside, writhing in midair, then hit the wall and fell to the floor. Dylan grabbed an empty cage and flung himself forward, landing the cage on the serpent. It hissed.

"How'd you…how'd you do that?" Nick panted.

John shrugged. "I just figured out that if you use your thumb or something to swipe this yellow line on the staff, then it'll work. It just needs a lot of force behind it, though." They made a mental note to never return to that room as they ran to the next. It was small and empty other than a small chamber pot, but that was all. They assumed it was a jail cell or interrogation room and moved on. The next room was also small, but with computers lined up against the back wall. It looked like a security system, with features that controlled doors and rooms, and massive buttons that would allow a user to shut down and reboot the system. But none of it had anything to do with what they were looking for. Judging by the display on the computer monitors, the system looked broken, so that was why the doors were all open.

The next room of that hall was where they struck gold, literally. It was a large, high vault that held stacks of gold and miniature blue shiny pyramids, plus crates of purple and darker gold powder. Madison guessed it was the Mestephans' money. They didn't understand exactly what the collection was meant for, so they moved on, but not until Nick and Dylan had secretly filled their pockets with gold.

Next came a room that was like a long corridor, with only a wall at the end of it. "Hey," said Nick when he reached the end of the corridor. "There's nothing down here!" Dylan called back from the other side. They all took turns feeling around. The iron floor was the same, but there were gray brick walls in the corridor and they found nothing. Very reluctantly, they continued to the last room of the hall, Nick's anxiety now peaking.

"So, Nick…I, uh, I'm not sure if this Facility actually…" one of the others whispered uncertainly.

"No," Nick whispered back. "It has to. It's got to." Although he only said that to attempt to convince himself, he couldn't help but feel that the others were starting to think this mission would fail. In the last room, they came to a big sign that read: THE CASTLE OF RULER QUARZOLON. The room was full of bricks and cement, and notes by Ruler Quarzolon were strewed around. Nick read them, without much conscious thought.

The castle is in further progress. Before I left, I ordered the Querzelan to expand upon the nation of the Querzelan, which I named after the very title I fashioned for myself! I still can't believe the fool who thought his brains were equal to my own. I, who had the Quarelenza disease and emerged stronger? That man never was as brilliant as me. After all, who would be?

And then, another.

The humans tried to fight! I grew careless yesterday and they saw me during construction. Ha! They teamed up on me and they were so unorganized, I killed them. Didn't they know that the only way to succeed is to go it alone? Am I not living proof of that? Haven't they learned yet that having a group to help you brings you down? That is how I designed the entrance to the Facility. The ones dumb enough to work in groups will never have heard of my Facility. And the ones who work alone and do know, will not possess all of the needed traits. They may only have brains, but no one person can have both brains and brawn. . .

"Oh, man," whispered Nick. "He really is a murderer. . ."

Madison nudged him. "Come on, let's go see the next hall."

The next hall was as long as the second one had been. The four of them were really cold by now since the Facility didn't seem to have heat. "Quarzolon must have been a cheapskate, too," Dylan commented, receiving a terrible blast of pain as he did. The next room they entered was strange. The threshold was the same as the floors in the hall, but past that was dirt. A large wooden structure was built above a wide, deep hole. It was a mineshaft. There was even a stack of rails piled in a minecart and pushed into a corner. They couldn't do much with that room, so they stumbled on and entered another one that was tight and cramped. It had a large shelf in the back, stockpiled with ingredients for potions and poisons and maybe even. . . food?

The third room in that hallway was simply weird. It seemed to stretch out and pillars rose up out of the ground, which Nick realized was a solid, brown sand. The pillars were made of a weird substance. It looked like frozen liquid, the color of dark blue. This room gave them chills and made them feel empty and hungry, and even colder than before. They were sinking into the coldness. . . the blinding darkness. . . down. . .down…

FLARE! Nick had risen from the cursed quicksand. His sweatshirt was glowing, and he blasted upward from his own pit as the others sank into their own. His sweatshirt's flames protected him from the room's chills and he pulled John out, who snapped into action. Breathing heavily, John ran to pull Dylan out while Nick pulled Madison out. "Argghh!" John was sinking again. Nick flung a fireball at him, completely by accident, as he raised his hand. The fireball latched onto John's arm and he stopped sinking. Then, instinctively, Nick did the same to Madison as she began slipping downward again. Once they were firmly on the ground and had escaped that room, John gasped, "What…was…that?"

"I d-don't know," panted Dylan, who was shivering. "I felt c-cold, like ghosts w-were flying through m-me, and I felt sick."

John was puzzled. "Nick, what did you do to me that stopped me from sinking?"

"I don't know. My sweatshirt was glowing, I rose, and it protected me."

Madison took a huge breath and added quickly, "Let's never go in there again. But it looked like there is one last room. Should we check it now?"

"No," Nick said firmly. "Let's rest for a bit."

Dylan sat down, but reminded him, "Nick, I thought we came to find out about your sweatshirt. We haven't really learned anything yet."

"It's got to be in the last room. It just has to be! I need it to be." Nick slumped to the floor as the color of his sweatshirt diminished. "Because who's ever heard of a magic sweatshirt before?"

John slid down to the floor and rolled his eyes. "Us, apparently."

"Come on," said Madison, getting back to her feet and pointing to the forgotten weapons on the ground. "Let's see the last room, bring the weapons with us, and show everybody that this place is real. Let them deal with the Zorblin. We can come back with the counselors."

"Nope," moaned Nick. "We're trapped, remember?"

Nevertheless, they all trudged on, stumbling to the final room of the Secret Facility. It was down a short staircase and made out of dark metal, with walls up to the ceiling that formed a giant maze.

"I think we should split up to cover more ground. . ." John began.

"No." Knowing what he did about Ruler Quarzolon, Nick understood why John's plan wouldn't work. "That's what he'd want us to do. He'd think only one person at a time would come and he'd put one trap in the maze that a single person alone couldn't beat. Remember, creating deadly plans is a hobby for him."

John commented, "You really understand him."

"Bits of him. . . after reading what I did." Just thinking of the book filled him with guilt for not reading it all, now that he was actually in the Secret Facility. But together, the group plunged into the dark maze, deep underground. They went straight, turned right, went left down a fork, then turned right again. They reached a dead end. Backtracking, they went in reverse and turned left.

CHARCH! An overgrown worm with horns all over its body whipped around the corner and let out a retching screech. John raised his staff, swiped his thumb, and...BANG! Dylan rag-dolled and was thrown into a wall.

"Oops! Sorry..."

BANG! Chaarrch! The creature was thrown back that time and stayed still for a moment. Suddenly, it pounced on Madison, tossing Nick aside with its horns. Yellow light flashed and the large worm screeched. There was another loud bang as Nick and the worm were both hit by the beam and blasted back. "Run!" shouted John, abandoning the attempt to injure the worm. They tore down the straight path, ran left, right, straight, right, then left, and sprinted faster down another straight path.

"Okay, let's go this way now!" They raced down a diagonal path and turned left. Suddenly, a shrunken horse-like creature with red eyes and covered in spikes galloped at them. Nick concentrated and a dim fiery wall burst into sight. The horse jumped at it, singeing its spikes and letting off steam, barely fazing it. It tried three times before Nick's wall of fire dissipated. BANG! Yellow light filled the cramped hall. This time, the horse's limbs writhed, and it was flung into the wall. It began to get up again and John jumped at it, thumb swiping the line of his staff. The horse hurtled backward and then galloped forward. With another series of bangs, John kept at it furiously, but the small horse was galloping too fast, left and right, dodging the blasts of yellow. There was another bang and a screech, and the animal was launched, but got up after two seconds and stampeded John. His staff went flying and hit the ground, shooting a blast of yellow light at Nick and Madison and hurling them back, Madison's sword still clutched in her hand.

Dylan suddenly flung himself at the horse, his hands working speedily, and...BOOM! He was blasted backward as a burning bullet exploded from the tip of his thin rocket launcher. The noise of the explosion filled their ears as light filled the maze. It hit the horse and it finally burst into tiny bits of stone and a cloud of dust. "Whoa. . ." said Dylan in awe. "That was awesome!"

"We should probably go back," Madison grunted in pain.

"Go back where? No, we have to stay. We're so close. We can't give up now! Something's in this maze and I know it. Maybe something to release us from the area with the gates!" Nick remained hopeful. "We've got each other. The Ruler didn't design this maze for multiple people. He wouldn't have thought people like us would find his secrets. He's actually pretty dumb." A sharp, rattling pain shot down his spine, but he was slightly numb to it.

Madison got up and examined her sword. "Yeah, you're right, Nick. We have to get out of here, but we've gone this far and can't give up now. The fate of, well, a lot of people rests on our dirty, unwashed hands." She smirked a bit as she looked at the dusty mess they had become.

And so they continued – left, straight, right, forward, straight again. The darkness was growing as they tried to go back, right, left, that way, dead end, right, straight, left, down the fork, right, another dead end, left again. The cold was enveloping them mercilessly. Suddenly, a many-tentacled monster with an overgrown snake's head attacked from out of nowhere.

Nick leapt back and yellow light exploded from John's staff. BANG! A jet of yellow light blinded the octopus-snake, but it was so big, it only fell backward. Another bang, but it only toppled over as a long, slimy purple tentacle stretched out. John was swiping the yellow line again. "The monster is too strong!" He tried once more, but the monstered merely rolled over and stretched out more of its tentacles, hissing madly.

"Here!" shouted Madison. She jumped around Dylan and lunged. Her sword slammed into the octopus's tentacles with a powerful slice. A tentacle fell apart as Madison reeled her sword back in and sliced again. It screeched as she tried again, but a purple tentacle grabbed her and yanked her up by the waist.

"No!" shouted Nick, plunging between John and Dylan, who had just been whacked by a large tentacle and thrown to the cold floor. His sweatshirt burst into flames as he felt a rush of foreboding, and a handle burst from somewhere around his chest. Nick seized it and out slid a glowing, iron blade. He extended his arm with his iron sword and charged, managing to plunge it into the snake's head. He felt the monster's tentacle wrap itself around his ankle and he too was hoisted high up into the air.

"Nick, look out!" This time, John had swiped his staff with considerable force and immense focus. A burst of yellow hit the monster and it was hurtled backward. It released Nick and Madison, their swords clattering onto the hard floor. The monster exploded on impact when it hit the wall with a crash. Sparks flew out of the staff and around the beast's remains.

"Wow," said John heavily. "You've just got to really mean it. To focus. To summon all of your willpower into it. . ."

Nick and Madison got up and picked up their swords. Nick admired his, realizing that the iron sword had appeared and been given to him at times when he needed it most.

"Nick, how did you get your sword back?" asked John.

Nick thought for a moment. "Well, I think that even if I don't have the sword with me, if I really need it and I focus enough, it will somehow come to me through my sweatshirt!" He could not think of another way to explain it. As they walked on, he wondered, "Is this worth it? Is this even a good idea?" He knew, even now, that the other three were thinking the exact same thing. Was he leading them to their deaths? Were they ever going to be able to escape the maze and find its treasures? He didn't know, but he tried not to think about what would happen if this really was a trap and they couldn't get out.

An uneasy feeling came over him as they turned left yet again. How long had they been gone? How late into the night or how early in the morning was it already? Would the campers and counselors know they were gone yet? Their weary silence continued until they turned right, then right again, into a small room. It held an ink-black chest, a silver goblet on a small table, and in the corner was a thick, metal, black door. "This is it, guys," whispered Nick. "Something's in that chest. All together now." They all put their hands on the jewel-encrusted lid. A high-pitched snarl came from the chest as, together and with a cloud of dust, they lifted the top of the chest open.

12

The Zorblin's Nest

The chest lid leaned against the cool wall of the small room. The chest itself was large, but all that was in it was a small, golden key. Nick picked it up and observed it. Suddenly, the golden key burned white-hot in his hand. As if a loose wire had touched his palm, he yelped with pain.

The golden key fell to the ground soundlessly and Madison stretched out her sword, sliding the tip through the small hole at the edge of the now-cold key. "Good idea," muttered John. "Now we don't have to carry it." But as it made contact, the purple tip of the sword began steaming, emitting puffs of steam and a whistling sound. Just then, Nick acknowledged the thick black door in the corner.

"Let's just hope this is the way back," he mumbled, not in the mood to take any unnecessary risks. Before Madison could stop him, he reached out to the golden doorknob and pushed the door open. There was the entrance to the maze. The staircase led up, beyond their point of view. "Convenient," whispered Dylan, taking a step forward.

As they all stepped through the thick doorway, they were suddenly back at the staircase, right in front of the maze. Another door, a clone of the last one, appeared in front of the maze and looking back through it, they saw the tiny room they had just exited. They took a step away and, without their touch, it slammed closed and disappeared without a sound. "Really convenient," said Dylan again. The golden key still hung from

the tip of Madison's raised sword. They climbed the staircase and reentered the Facility's halls. Compared to the maze, the halls were lighter.
Nick was glad for this, but they still had barely found anything that was
useful to them. "Okay. The key. Let's go to the gate room. I think it goes
there," John guessed.

They progressed slowly toward the room in the longest hallway, to
the high-arched iron door. The room hadn't changed at all and was still
wide and misty. Balancing the key carefully, Madison tried to get it into
the gold and iron keyhole on the right side of the wall, but it wouldn't
work. When John noticed, he had an idea. "I think I know what to do,
Nick. Maybe try to pull your hand back into your sleeve to grab the key
and put it in the keyhole. Your sweatshirt might protect your hand from
the burns, so grab it through the sleeve!" Nick nodded and pushed his
sleeve further down his arm, pulling his hand inside it before removing
the key from Madison's blade. It worked. No burns.

"Good thinking, John!"

"Yep! Now put the key in and let's see what this does!"

"I hope it's more rocket launchers. That would be fun. Maybe we
could even kill the Zorblin with one!" exclaimed Dylan hopefully.

"Doubt it, but you never know. I don't judge," Madison shrugged.

Feeling a sense of foreboding, Nick shoved the golden key into the
keyhole. It fit perfectly. He twisted the key and there was another snarling noise. Nervously, he removed the key and heard a clicking noise. The
large iron gates swung open magically. The dark mist spread into the wide
room where the four campers stood. They slowly walked forward, sweat
trickling down the backs of their necks, faces pale and cold with fear.
There was torchlight up ahead. And there it was.

Gazing across the larger, spacious room, they saw a pile of singed,
torn, and dirty hay, with more iron bars surrounding an observation deck

that could be accessed by walking up small ramps on the left and right. A huge, snarling, skeletal, and pale beast – long and wide-but-not-too-wide, with a long, pointed, bony tail. It was the Zorblin that lay asleep on the hay.

John's jaw dropped, Dylan jumped, Madison shoved a fist into her mouth to stop herself from screaming, and Nick stared, eyes bloodshot, paralyzed, at the monster he had seen and fended off that one same night. He wished Flame were with him now. He wished his X-Ball Zero, which he had forgotten about during all of the chaos, had told him what would happen if he went to this very place. He knew it would have warned him and he was filled with regret. Just staring at the Zorblin, who looked even taller in sleep, drained any hope he had left. He knew his sweatshirt's power was weakening, too. He looked at his friends, who had given him such happiness and support. He glanced over at Madison, his loyal sister, who had always been with him, and then he looked at the Zorblin, a monster controlled by a monster. Suddenly, his skull seemed to burst open and his skin turned to ice.

"You said it was safe, son!" shouted a cloaked figure at the small child in a wooden room. "I-I checked! I d-didn't know!" the child stammered. Nick saw a ghost who screamed at them in fury as the pair dropped to their knees.

"HOW COULD THEY HAVE GOTTEN TO IT? THEY MUST HAVE HAD OUTSIDE HELP FROM SOMEONE WHO ALREADY KNOWS!"

The cloaked figure, now cowering, whispered, "Dark Ruler, great Ruler, my son…you…you can't be referring to him!"

"I never specifically said I blamed your son, did I? No. I trust the boy. I have seen his work. Seen his powers," sneered the ghost harshly.

"Well…well, then…thank…thank you, great Ruler, but…but that still doesn't explain how they got past!"

"QUIET!" shrieked the ghost, his silvery colors flashing. "Now… you, boy. What do you think of this matter?" The child trembled as the figure and the ghost looked at him. Finally, he murmured, "M-maybe they used a certain force…or…or they had someone from our side give them the answers?"

"Nonsense," said the ghost. "Do you think I would put my faith in a large group of people? No. Like I have said, I work alone. But this… this is just outrageous."

"Do you think…uh, it, my great Ruler, is ready?" asked the cloaked one, kneeling on the hearth rug beside a fire.

"No, your little brain fails you as we speak. No. It will wake in due time. And then, when it wakes on its own, we will unleash it. It can only be woken now by another," answered the ghost harshly.

"But…b-but great Ruler, what if it is woken by them? What if they unleash it themselves?"

"It will not be," answered the ghost calmly. "It is impossible they could have entered the lair itself. They have only found the location. They simply could not have opened the entrance."

"G-good," whispered the figure, staring at the hearth as they knelt. "But should we not go and stop them? I'm sure m-my son would be h-honored to get his f-first task!" They both looked at the boy commandingly and the child slowly nodded, his face growing pale.

"Yes, yes," agreed the ghost softly as he raised a silver hand. "You, boy. Go and stop them." In a flash, the boy disappeared. "Good," hissed the ghost.

"M-my great Ruler. M-may I ask how l-long it will be before our target s-sees this?"

The ghost's face hardened. "With luck, never. But the connection could not have broken, so I would estimate an hour or so after this point in time."

"Very w-well, my great R-Ruler. Shall I...?"

"No," hissed the ghost. "Stay with me. I need to discuss these plans..."

The grip on Nick's skull relaxed as the pain exploded and then stopped. His body slowly returned to its regular temperature as he lay on the hard ground, completely limp. John, Dylan, and Madison were speechless, obviously having noticed his sudden retreat from his own mind. His sweatshirt was as cold as the metal beneath him; actually, it was worse. He pulled it off and felt some warmth spread through him. Madison reached out a hand. He grabbed it as he rose and rocked on his feet, his legs still weak. He stared back at the sleeping Zorblin and he remembered.

"Nick, what happened?" whispered Dylan. Nick explained everything he had seen and heard, chills running down his back, as quietly and calmly as he could. He also explained the vision he'd had with the same boy and ghost that night before the slime monster formed. When he had finished, Dylan said quietly, "Nick, before, when you looked at the Zorblin, your sweatshirt turned gray, your eyes snapped shut, and you collapsed. Your face looked dead – a cold dead. It was a faint blue."

The Zorblin let out a low groan. Its tail curled slightly and its left foot rustled. "Get ready to fight. . ." whispered Nick, but it slept on. Looking around, the four noticed lots of questionable treasures in the Zorblin's pile of hay: a shard of glass, a bone that Nick hoped was not human, a few feathers, a ripped paper, and a worn-out hook. A huff of smoke and a spout of purple fire puffed out of the sleeping Zorblin's middle mouth now, all six of its beady eyes still shut. Its hot smelly breath filled the room. Then, its two other heads breathed deeply and the room smelled of something burnt, with an intoxicating, acidic odor.

The Zorblin was, although the most important, not the only thing in the room. The four kids slowly walked up the ramp on the left side of the misty room. An outside observer, who knew nothing of their journey and what they had learned, would assume they were four kids breaking into a military facility and raiding it for supplies. In reality, Nick Silver, Madison Silver, John Jackson, and Dylan Sheimer were going to do what they came to do, and quickly.

Near the top of the ramp were a large table and weapon rack. A blue and white gun hung from it, but that was all. Nick read the note on the table:

Day 12: The Zorblins are growing restless. We haven't conducted a massacre in a while, and they are getting tired of the usual meat. They want flesh. I plan that tomorrow; I will bring them hunting. I find it will be significantly easier now that I have this place. The Secret Facility has been in my use for twelve days thus far and I do not plan to end it.

The air grew colder. Nick stared over at the Zorblin, feeling hopelessness and despair. "We've been in every room. We never even found the reason we came here," he muttered, pulling the sweatshirt back on. He felt his sweatshirt's power diminish even more. The others were at a loss for words as the Zorblin let out a paralyzing snore as cold as death itself. Nick seemed lost just looking at the monster. His powers weakening. . . his mind swirling numbly. . .

Just as his knees began to buckle, he felt a hand on his shoulder that brought him back to reality. "Right," he said suddenly, straightening up. "We've got to kill the Zorblin. Now."

Dylan stared at him, eyes unfocused. "Not possible. Quarzolon would've done something. I doubt a 'non-Mestephan' or whatever he said would be able to kill it."

"It's the only way," John interjected grimly.

"We have to try!" Nick stated, feeling encouraged. He raised his faint-yellow glowing iron blade. The moment, he knew, had arrived. "Now. . .in three. . .two. . ."

Madison swung her double-edged purple sword before he was ready. With a clash, the blade ricocheted off the Zorblin's hard, stone-like skin. There wasn't even a mere scratch at the spot where her blade had slashed. "I thought…I didn't know…I didn't expect that!" she panted, but Dylan groaned, "I knew it."

Nick slashed his own sword in frustration, swinging it at the Zorblin's pale skin. A clang and a flash of sparks, a rumbling snore from the beast he had just tried to attack – and the sword was reflected off. "What the…?" he said, confused and wondering how in the world Quarzolon's relatives were able to kill any of these things.

"Stand aside," said Dylan dryly, stepping in. He took something from his small sack, stuffed it into his thin rocket launcher, and pointed it directly at the Zorblin. "Alright, guys – stand back." BOOM! The explosion lit up the whole cage. The Zorblin rumbled again and its tail swayed, hitting John and flinging him into the wall with an almighty shove. There was only a very small, faint scar in the Zorblin's back, but everybody else's skin was singed.

"Well," gasped Dylan weakly. "I guess exploding it is out of the picture." He sank to his knees.

"That almost woke the Zorblin," breathed Madison hoarsely. "We can't do that again. Too dangerous. Any other ideas?"

They all quietly thought about it. They decided the staff wouldn't be able to kill the Zorblin, let alone fling it. They also decided swords were too weak and rocket launchers, although able to slightly injure a Zorblin after a few blasts, were way too dangerous and risky. They were only at an advantage over the beast while it was still sleeping, but the problem remained: how to kill it?

And then the answer hit him; it was so obvious, so easy – this had to be the reason it was here. "The gun!" cried Nick. "The power gun!" Before the others could open their mouths, he sprang to his feet, bolted up the ramp, and saw it right in front of him: the blue and white-streaked gun, hanging from the wall. He seized it and raced back down the ramp.

"Nick, what are you…?"

"This is it! Quarzolon left it here to control his Zorblins! It has to be!" Nick stammered. He showed the trio the small device. It had a small dial with three colors. The first was yellow and marked "Stun." The second one was blue and said "Freeze for Time-Span." The last red one spelled out "Kill." He set the dial to red and took aim. "This is it…time to end this madness!" He pulled the trigger as the other three gasped.

GLZZRT! There was an ear-splitting explosion as a blast of ice exploded from the gun but broke apart in midair before hitting its target. Sparkling ice shards flew in all directions and the gun exploded in Nick's hands. Their last hope. Gone.

"What happened?" he seethed as he dropped the remaining fragments.

"The stupid thing exploded!" yelled Dylan angrily.

"How are we supposed to kill it now?" moaned Madison.

None of them noticed the Zorblin twitch slightly, although it remained asleep. Slowly, Nick headed back up the ramp and read from a small dark plate that he didn't notice before, that must have fallen off the wall years earlier.

NOTE TO SELF:

Fix the "kill" setting on Freeze Gun. (Explodes when used.)

Nick read it with displeasure and reluctantly explained the situation to the others, who, like him, were not in good spirits at all. "Wow. How convenient. Yeah, honestly, I didn't really expect anything else, now that I think about it," Madison commented grimly. The mood and atmosphere were darkening when…crack!

"Hey…" Nick remembered that sound. He had heard it earlier in the halls and in his vision just a few minutes before. There was a ripple of dark mist and another sound, softer than the crack, and the air stilled. "What was…?" Suddenly, there was a flash of bright red light and a loud bang from the entrance of the cage where the metal bars were. The light hit Madison and she soundlessly crumpled to the floor, her knees buckling and all of her limbs limp and still. "Madison!" gasped Nick, staring wildly from his sister to the bars.

"Someone's here," breathed Nick. "A kid…a young kid. He came here on someone's orders. I just feel it. He must have been spying on us!" Another ripple of misty darkness shot across the room, along with a whistle of wind. Wind?

"Guys, we need to leave. Someone's here to kill us!" realized John.

"Okay. Come on, guys, help me get Madison up," Nick urged as he bent to lift his sister.

"What about the proof?"

"No time for that," Nick said firmly. "We have to get out, now."

Dylan motioned to the others. "Alright, let's boost her up now. Three, two, one…" They all heaved and slowly lifted Madison just as another swish of red light hit John. He fell unconscious, his arms and legs limp, and crumpled to the ground. Dylan and Nick lost their grip on Madison, letting her fall. "Not you, too, John," groaned Dylan.

"How fitting," said Nick numbly. "It always seems to come down to us, doesn't it? Us getting attacked by that monster, us being the only ones left in the Secret Facility. We're always in mortal danger."

Dylan scratched his head. "Yeah, good point. But wait! Remember back on the first day of camp? When that one counselor came running out of the Quarren Forest, injured?"

Nick nodded. "And I remember when I was in the Forest of Tappers, I heard a voice tell me I would die soon after nearly getting struck by lightning." Dylan gasped. They were struck for the first time by how much they had been through. "But that's it, then!" cried Dylan as the Zorblin twitched again. They glanced at it nervously before he continued, "The monster that grabbed us: it was a slime monster! There must have been more since we saw that one's birth!"

"Yeah!" agreed Nick, just as the Zorblin's third neck twisted slightly, letting out a cloud of acidic breath.

"Come on, Nick. Let's get this done. Get your sister. I'll get John. Leave the weapons behind."

And so, the two struggled to lift up the bodies. But they didn't need to. "Ugghh, what happened?" asked Madison, still sprawled on the floor. Nick let go in shock. Her eyes were still spinning but coming into focus and her pale limbs were beginning to move again.

"You got hit by a red light and were knocked out," explained Nick. "And so did John." Madison stood up, shaking slightly. "What now?" she asked. "We wait," answered Nick and Dylan together. It didn't take long at all. Within a minute, John had awakened, his eyes unclear but his arms and legs moving again.

"Okay. We're leaving. We didn't get what we wanted, but at least we have proof now," said Nick grimly. But something caught his eye as Madison led the others out from where they had come in. "Wait," he called through the mist. He bent down to his knees and searched for it. He had seen something under the Zorblin's fleshy leg. Slowly and carefully, he pulled the white cheese-colored object out of the Zorblin's grasp. It gave a rumbling snore and its leg shifted, allowing the object to be snatched. Nick hoisted the heavy object and held it out. All their jaws dropped. It was an egg.

"This Zorblin…" stammered John. "It isn't, how would you… Not male. It's a female. It's…it's been laying an egg and trying to breed." The dirty, rough egg resembled a doomsday weapon as Nick held it out carefully.

"What do we do?" asked Dylan uncertainly.

"I don't…" Madison began, but stopped immediately. They had heard someone else draw their breath. Someone behind them, back at the entrance to the Zorblin's nest.

"Give me that egg," said a new, sinister, but somehow light voice.

"Who are you?" asked Nick loudly, squinting through the mist only to see a small figure outlined in the darkness.

"That doesn't matter. Now, give me that egg, Nicholas Silver!"

13

The One Behind It All

The small boy emerged from the dark mist so his face was distinguishable. Madison gasped, Dylan yelled, John jumped, and Nick's eyes widened as he nearly dropped the Zorblin's egg. Standing in front of them, grasping a black staff with a glowing red line down the middle and wearing a cloak with his hood pulled down, was Daniel Garring.

"D-Daniel?" gasped Nick, his voice weak with fatigue. "It's been you this whole time?" Daniel stood there silently, his face hardened like stone, and nodded. "Give me that egg, Silver," he commanded.

Nick made up his mind in a split second. "No."

Daniel glared. "Oh, I should have made my point clearer. Give me that egg, Silver, or your friends die." Nick's eyes went blank and Daniel continued, "I know your weakness, Silver. The weakness that prevented you from realizing the true culprit, the weakness that led you here, the weakness that will be, and is, your downfall. You trust people too easily. You believe in them, that they aren't bad."

"No," Nick repeated again. "It can't be you. It just can't."

Daniel's hardened expression curved into an almost uncertain smile. "Like I just said, you have too much trust in groups. That is the weakness the Dark Ruler avoids. He knows that one, acting alone, is stronger than any other."

"No way," Nick retorted, his face going white and his sweatshirt growing dark. "You can't serve him. You can't serve Ruler Quarzolon, Daniel."

"And yet, I do," he smiled threateningly. He raised his staff, which looked like a replica of John's except with a red line instead of a yellow line. "Now, give me that egg, Nicholas, or I will fire."

Deep within Nick's numb disbelief and anger, he found courage. "I'm not dumb, Daniel. That staff can't kill. Only knock out."

Daniel's smile grew even wider, his eyes not moving from Nick and the egg. "This staff can kill in ways other than a direct shot," he said calmly.

"Sure. Yeah, right, Dan," said Nick, his anger pouring out of him before he could stop himself.

"I'll just have to prove it, then," leered Daniel, his eyes widening excitedly. He raised the staff directly at Nick's face. BANG! Nick was too taken aback to attempt to use his powers or to even move. But he didn't need to. At the last second, Daniel raised his staff so the shot missed Nick's head and hit the wall instead.

"I knew it," breathed Nick. "I knew you wouldn't kill us."

Daniel lowered his staff, still smiling. "Not directly." Before Nick could ask what that meant, a familiar sloshing noise echoed through the halls of the Facility. In a few moments, two large slime monsters blocked the iron gates. In front of them, right behind Daniel, were two smaller beasts. Daniel had not fired the jet of light to kill them; he had done it to signal the monsters to come to him. They were going to kill Nick and the others.

"You can't do this, Daniel," said John quietly.

"But I already have!"

"We'll fight, then! We'll fight your goons, Dan!"

Daniel gave a terrible, high-pitched laugh. "I wouldn't do that if I were you. And besides, my father is already on his way."

"What do you mean?" asked Madison, puzzled, but Nick remembered one of his dreams. "Your father is one of Quarzolon's soldiers? Are the other soldiers coming, too?"

Daniel laughed again. "The Dark Ruler, sending his whole army just to kill three eleven-year-olds and one thirteen-year-old?"

Nick thought quickly. "Wait…how would he be able to command them? I thought he was locked up in his prison, the Mezoar Prison!" Daniel didn't laugh this time, but his expression froze, and his smile vanished.

"You wouldn't know," he murmured. "You wouldn't…couldn't…" He stopped abruptly, raised his staff, and snarled, "I'm asking the questions here, not you!" Nick backed up as the slime monsters behind Daniel gave them all murderous looks. "You do realize that it would only take me one lazy flick of this staff to wake up that Zorblin, right? So if I were you, I'd watch my mouth!" Nick's grip on the egg loosened as he listened to Daniel, who noticed and yelled, "And watch it with that egg! Give it to me or die!"

Nick sneered back, taunting him with sarcasm. "No, Dan. You want this egg? Traitors don't get to have omelets at, what, midnight?" Daniel's face was demented with anger. "Not now," Madison warned Nick, whispering in his ear.

"You don't give him advice! Your brother sent you all to a death trap! I don't know how you got in here, but…NO!" Nick had dived at Daniel, but with a bang and a flash of yellow light, Nick was thrown sideways into the wall, straight at an iron bar. John's arm was outstretched, his staff raised. "Nick, I had to. He would've killed you right there and then."

Nick didn't respond. John had a point, but he was too angry at Daniel to care.

"Careful with that egg, Silver!" Daniel warned darkly. Nick was lying on the floor, the egg clutched tightly in his left hand as his right hand picked up a faintly glowing blade that was near him. "I suppose you want answers?" asked Daniel softly. "Well, then. I could tell you that the reason I was watching those holes was to check on that great beast's progress. But, it's gone now."

"Yeah, it is, you liar!" Nick interjected, seething. BANG! Nick went limp, sinking onto the cold floor, but the curse wasn't strong enough to knock him out because Daniel didn't want the egg broken. As it was slipping from Nick's grasp and rolling on the floor, Daniel dived at it, but Dylan got there first. He shoved Daniel aside and seized the egg, kicking the traitor back toward his slime army. Daniel waved his staff in a small circle and Nick was able to move again.

"Why, you...!" Just then, a high-pitched crack split the scene before him as Nick stood up, stepped back quickly, and went silent. A tall, cloaked man appeared next to Daniel. "Father, you're...you're here," he gasped, quickly lowering his staff.

"Yes, I am, son. Now, have you gotten the egg yet?" The scene, which had been dangerous and dramatic, now became almost awkward, and very tense. "N-no," mumbled Daniel.

"Hmm," his father mused. "Well, then. Take the egg and kill them. Actually, let me do it. I have an idea." Daniel stepped back, not looking evil or smug anymore, but now slightly worried and pale. "Well, Nicholas Silver. I see you, your loyal sister, and your friends have managed to get this far. No matter. Your death approaches!" The cloaked man gave a familiar, booming laugh in deep voice. Before Nick could remember who it belonged to, the man pulled his hood down.

"No!"

Camp Director Philip sneered at them through the misty darkness. "The Dark Ruler was right, Silver. You really do trust people easily." Nick felt stupid as the realization sunk in. "Philip, the Camp Director," Nick growled. Counselor Philip gave his low laugh again as Daniel backed away more.

"So, you're Daniel's dad?" asked John quietly.

"Yes," whispered Philip. "But I am also one of the highest ranked soldiers in the Dark Ruler's army. And I see you would like an explanation. Where to begin. . . where to begin. . .? Ah, yes. When I first learned Nicholas Silver was coming to Camp CrystalFlake, I contacted my master immediately. The prophecy of the X-Ball Prototype was finally coming into play. Once I knew this, I told my son, Daniel, that he was going to Camp CrystalFlake, as well. Luckily, he was eleven, also, so he could be with the first years and spy on Silver."

"But...I thought Ruler Quarzolon was thousands of years ago!" interrupted Nick.

"Not thousands. But yes, Silver, hundreds..." Nick's confusion grew as the counselor went on. "Mestephans have extraordinarily long lives. He really peaked in power nearly twelve years prior to today. I, regretfully, was one of his last soldiers to join." Counselor Philip paused as the Zorblin snored again. "Now, back to two weeks ago. You arrived at camp, just as I knew you would. It's now late Monday night and you've already traveled into the out-of-bounds forest and broken into the Dark Ruler's Secret Facility!"

"Not so much of a secret now, is it?" said Nick darkly.

"It will be again, after we kill you," stated Philip calmly, then pointed to Dylan, who was attempting to charge again. "Daniel, blast the violent one." A jet of red light burst from Daniel's staff. It would have hit Dylan if a feeble jet of yellow light hadn't connected with the red streak first. The two exploded outward and away. John lowered his staff, his expression strained.

"Fine, then," Counselor Philip sighed. "Allow me to continue. Around that time, the Zorblin was nearing the end of its sleeping. But it wasn't ready yet and we couldn't take the risk of not having it when Nicholas Silver was here. So Daniel and I dug holes. Before camp started, we went into the Secret Facility on the Dark Ruler's orders and called upon the slime monsters in the Summoning Room. They lived in those holes for weeks, biding their time, growing. As they grew, the holes grew. One of them even grew so much, it escaped. It swam into a large lake and attacked two certain campers..." his eyes lingered on Dylan and Nick.

"But something peculiar happened. When it attacked the second camper, it dragged him deep underwater but was nearly blown apart by a blast of fire. It would have killed the monster if the fire had been stronger and not underwater. It was that sweatshirt. I knew it at once. I've seen how it glows, how it works. Master knows, too." He glared steadily at Nick before continuing.

"Another one of the slime monsters dug a hole into the Quarren Forest and attacked a counselor. And then, on the third day of camp, four pesky kids tried to explore the library to gain knowledge of the camp's beast. Luckily, my son told me everything that morning. You might say I controlled the librarian's mind and made her stop you, preventing you from getting the book that might have ruined everything. That was, in fact, the same reason the counselor was attacked." Counselor Philip stopped, glanced around briefly at them all, then added wryly, "Ironically, I wouldn't know the details that are revealed in the book; I have never read it.

"And then there was the tournament. The night before, I was back in the Secret Facility, working on a poison that I thought would kill the boy and temporarily paralyze his sweatshirt's powers. That tournament was rigged so Silver would progress to that specific challenge. Of course, I also had to rig it so my son would be with him and know which drink to poison. But there were so many ways it could have gone wrong, but was saved by luck. Like how I did not put thirty-five pennies in the sand dunes, but thirty-four, and when I saw Nicholas about to lose, I used a bit of Mestephan magic to place the final penny where he dug. Alas…" he paused and shook his head. "My son almost ruined everything by thinking it would be a good idea to use his powers to crack the beam and make Silver fall and get injured. But if I hadn't held the beam together, he probably would have lost the tournament, disrupting the grand plan. I needn't have bothered, as it turned out. Silver was fine after that – thanks, no doubt, to his sweatshirt's healing powers."

There was silence as they all listened intently, letting Counselor Philip ramble on to reveal all that had transpired. Daniel remained looking even more uncomfortable. "Something terrible happened next, which I only realized earlier today. Silver had gotten an X-Ball Zero, the sequel to the X-Ball Prototype. Luckily, he didn't trust it enough, although I noticed how he could communicate with that extraordinary dog. How that animal got its powers, I admittedly do not know. But on the night Silver returned to his cabin, I accidentally left the hatch open, rushing when I last left. Due to my careless mistake, the Zorblin broke out. It smashed the iron gates in pure fury and escaped through the open hatch. It silently crept into the campgrounds, sniffing out its mortal enemy it was trained against, and finding Nicholas Silver, sensing the boy's energy within him that even he has no idea of. When the Zorblin smashed the window and Silver saw it, its deathly power entranced him."

Counselor Philip looked momentarily triumphant before his face fell in disappointment. "But then, that dog saved him. It protected Silver from the Zorblin, driving it back, and after the two of them collapsed, I came and brought the beast back into its cage, returned it to a frozen sleep, and replaced the iron gates with more powerful ones. The Zorblin was furious, hungry, wanting to kill, but it was too soon. It eventually thawed out but remained sleeping, and I breathed again."

Nick shifted as he listened, remembering that fateful night, and the counselor turned to coldly gaze as him, then glanced around again to be sure the others were still paying attention. "By then, Silver was learning about his powers. I saw what he did to that boy during the match – but of course, that was something he never meant to do. That forcefield was something I hoped he wouldn't learn about that soon. But how he got the sword was puzzling. I kept it from my master, just as I kept the Zorblin's escape and the poison's failure from my master. It must be the sweatshirt, I thought."

He addressed Nick directly now. "But then, earlier today, I realized your powers were becoming easier for you to control. I had a meeting with the Dark Ruler and brought my son with me. Then my son came and watched you from afar, invisible, as you survived in the Secret Facility. Your powers are stronger, and more complex, than we thought. I was quite horrified when my son returned to tell me your powers had broken my master's veil, which had obviously grown feeble from age. But Master could not have been beaten by you, even though I observed the four of you battle the strongest of our slime beasts. I saw you struggle with your powers at first and then use them with ease to beat the monster.

"You asked about my master's whereabouts, Silver. Don't feel so cocky and safe about him being imprisoned. Even though he is locked within the chambers of the Mezoar Prison, the Ruler can become a traveling spirit at will. One of the powers Master created himself, with his special disease, is the ability to divide his soul from his body and wander the universe as he pleases."

"So Quarzolon was the ghost Daniel was afraid of," Nick whispered to himself.

"When Daniel was gone for longer than Master and I expected, I left and teleported right here, in this cage. Don't you understand yet? The Zorblin's Awakening is today."

And Nick suddenly understood it all. He understood everything that had happened since the first day of camp: all of the visions, the dreams, and who the man, ghost, and boy were. His powers. All of it. Almost.

"Shall I mention my initial intentions for taking your sweatshirt with me after you fell into the lake?" asked Counselor Philip curtly, without waiting for a reply. "To examine it. But I couldn't. Some strange magic stopped me. I hid it from Master again."

"For a high-tier soldier of the Quarzolon," Nick commented recklessly, "you really hide a lot of things from him, don't you?"

Counselor Philip took a step toward him. "The Dark Ruler was right. I can see how it would be you. That sweatshirt. . . that gift. . . he wants it very much."

"Why?" asked Nick, knowing already that this would be the one detail the man would refuse to reveal.

"And you think I'll tell you? No, I will not."

Nick wasn't sure what to do next. They were trapped, but they now had what they originally wanted: the truth and answers. Thinking fast, he began, "But why is it me? Why am I the one with the powers...the X-Ball Zero...any of this? Why is it me who needs to be killed?"

"I daresay that you will know that answer in the future. . . if you live long enough," answered Philip icily. "Shall we kill them now, Master?"

To Nick's horror, a ghostly voice echoed and rippled through the chamber. *"Kill the others. Capture the Gifted One. Take him with us."*

Counselor Philip kneeled immediately on the ground and murmured, "Yes, Master." Daniel backed up so much, he jostled against a slime beast as tall as him. "Well, you heard the Dark Ruler!" he shouted to his son and the monsters. "Kill them! Leave Silver to me." He flung himself forward toward Nick. John quickly raised his staff, but Dylan beat him to it. Black smoke and screams cut the air as Dylan pulled the trigger of his rocket launcher. The smoke cleared enough for Philip to see him and bellow, "Kill the one with the rocket launcher, the violent one, first!" There were two more loud bangs as John and Daniel's staffs burst with colors at the same time. The cursed bolts met each other in midair. John's yellow light shrank and dissolved, while Daniel's red light was flung behind him and into a slime monster, who fell over.

"SEIZE THEM, YOU USELESS LUMPS!" shrieked Philip as his shirt caught on fire from another blast of Dylan's rocket launcher. Nick raised his sword and charged as the slime beasts came in. "Nooo!" he shouted, plunging his sword into the chest of one who was charging at him. It melted with a roar.

"Kill them! Kill them!" Philip was pushed aside as the full team of slime monsters roared past him to follow his orders.

"Madison, look out!" A new jet of bursting orange light exploded from the tip of the counselor's long, black, orange-striped staff. Nick charged out of nowhere and pushed a slime monster in front of Madison. The light hit it and it toppled over, dead.

"No!" screamed Philip. "Daniel, get them!" His son ran ahead but another yellow light threw him back to the iron gates.

Nick felt slimy hands grabbing his arms and pulling him away from his friends, but Madison raced forward, raising her sword, and sliced two slime monsters in half. One of them was dead instantly, but the other moaned and stubbornly grabbed her around the throat before falling over, lifeless. "Stop!" bellowed Philip. "Stop!"

The fighting stopped and the remaining monsters stepped back. Daniel got to his feet as Philip stood, also, his orange-tipped staff pointed at Nick's heart and looking warily over at the still-sleeping beast. "If you continue this fight now, the Zorblin will stir before the Awakening and kill us all!" He spoke hatefully, but then his expression went blank and he looked almost frightened. "Where-where is the egg?" he demanded.

Slowly, John pulled the rough, ugly egg from an opening in the pile of hay on which the Zorblin slept. Philip sighed, relieved, until John seized the egg, raised it up high, and loosened his grip, allowing it to dangle.

"You...boy, put down that egg, now! GIVE IT TO ME!"

John didn't move. The Zorblin's egg still dangled from his grasp. "I said to give me that egg, you stupid boy!" John continued to do nothing. Nick realized this was a smart move because Philip wouldn't attack John if it risked breaking the egg.

"It was me," said Counselor Philip quietly. "Me and my son, Daniel Garring, the whole time. After I kill you all – except for Silver, who will be captured – Daniel and I will leave this camp and use Silver's power to free the Dark Ruler at last!" His face was contorted. "Give me the egg," he repeated, "or else you will be killed slowly, personally, by me. Give me that egg or else."

John remained still where he stood, but his arm inched up a bit higher. Finally, he answered quietly, "We aren't afraid of you." He dropped the egg. Philip roared and dived for it before being thrown back as another enormous bang erupted. The egg was about to hit the ground when Nick sidestepped and quickly caught it. Breathing heavily, he faced everyone. They were shocked and he was almost as shocked as they were. Almost.

"Let them go," Nick gasped, "or I'll destroy this. Let us all go, or I will make sure this egg never reaches your hands."

Philip's face twisted in despair. "Very well, then," he muttered, gasping wildly. "Give me the egg and you…you and your friends can go."

Nick edged closer to him, slowly moving between Madison and John. "Don't be lying…" he warned.

"No! If that egg cracks…you don't understand. Give me the egg or you all will die."

"I hold you to your oath. Swear on your loyalty to your master," Nick spoke calmly.

"I swear. . ." Philip hissed.

Carefully, Nick dropped the Zorblin's egg into the counselor's open hand. There was one shivering second of silence when Nick actually thought it was safe to leave, but then Daniel slammed the iron gates closed. Philip looked up, and then whispered to his son, "Get them." Before Nick could react, Daniel raised his staff and swiped it multiple times. BANG! BANG! BANG! BANG!

In that instant, it was their lies that charged Nick up. The situation that put light in his sweatshirt. The betrayal that fueled him. The weakness Philip had told him about and used against him. He shouted fiercely and as his sweatshirt glowed with flames, two long spires of fire exploded from it, slicing straight into the man and the biggest slime beast.

Counselor Philip screamed in agony and fell backward, his cloak burned and a gaping hole where it had been hit. The second spire stabbed at the beast's head, which slipped off of its slimy body, killing it. Nick's sword disappeared off the ground and a dark, silvery-lined handle emerged from the sweatshirt, exploding into Nick's right hand. Without any thought, he pointed the sharp iron blade at Philip, who laughed.

"Oh, Silver. It doesn't work like that, does it?" he crowed as he stuffed the Zorblin's egg into Daniel's open hand. "Forsaken. . . trapped in the Dark Ruler's study, the Secret Facility, as death approaches the impulsive boy who unwittingly survived due to an undeserved gift. . ."

SLASH! Nick had lunged forward and, with experience gained from Swaying Swords, swerved his iron blade around another guardian beast and sliced the hood from Philip's cloak.

"Back off, child. Even your X-Ball says so. Shall we take a look?" Nick was speechless at what happened next. The counselor waved his hand and, with a misty black puff of smoke, the X-Ball Zero was conjured into his fist. He handed the black ball to Nick. "Well, ask it."

"What…what is that?" stammered John, as the others stared blankly and Nick stood still. Nick gazed at the X-Ball and murmured, "Um, does Philip Garring have the power to…kill me?" He shook the tiny black ball and waited. The screen turned green and he read to himself: No, he does not. You alone have the power. You are safe from him in specifics.

Head spinning, Nick noticed Philip's piercing look and the question in his eyes. "Well?"

Nick nervously told him, "It says: Yes, he can kill you. He…um… has the full power." He wasn't sure why he lied, but it felt safe to him. While Philip was contemplating this, Nick slunk to the back of the room and whispered under his breath, "Do I actually have the power to survive Philip Garring?" He shook the ball again and read the words: Answer not found, Nicholas. Why wasn't it working anymore?

"Ha ha! Of course, the answer was expected!" laughed Philip. He flicked his hand and the conjured X-Ball disappeared from Nick's hands in a puff of blackness.

"So what if I actually can survive Philip?" Nick pondered, deep in thought. There's still Daniel, the slime monsters, and the Zorblin, and its Awakening is tonight! If only Flame were here. He could hold the Zorblin. If Flame were here, I'd feel safe. Philip said Flame had powers. If he could use them and save us, we could escape! And if we escaped, that would be great, because right now, the fate of the entire world rests upon our hands.

Philip was distracted as he began giving Daniel and the slime army instructions. Nick pulled the other three to the back of the cage and whispered his plan. "Guys, I know it's insane, but it's our only hope. I'm going to try to summon Flame to us." They all looked dumbstruck.

"But how, Nick?" Madison whispered back.

"Philip said he has powers. That dog has made a connection with me. We even have similar powers."

"Well, it's worth a try. Anything that can get us out..." whispered Dylan.

"Don't worry, guys. I got you all into this mess and I'll get you out of it. Just trust me."

"Saving all of your last words now? Ha! I wouldn't blame you. It's time the Wonder Group gets separated," Philip sneered.

"I guess we're all going to die now," moaned Nick.

"Not you, Silver. You're getting captured and transported straight to the Dark Ruler on Planet Mezort. But your friends are as good as dead!"

Nick told the others under his breath, "Okay, guys. Keep him distracted. This will take all of my willpower." He focused until his sweatshirt gradually began to glow. He heard a faint humming as a terrible tugging feeling pulled at his guts.

Philip, who hadn't heard their conversation, roared as Dylan staged an attack to divert his attention. "What do you think you're doing? Forget this! Daniel, take him." There was a bang. "Well done. Now drag him over to the Sacrifices Room – the one with the dark sand and liquid pillars. Go!"

Nick was distracted by the sound of a terrible struggle. The slime monsters were strangling Madison and John, while Daniel dragged an unconscious Dylan away. "No!" yelled Nick, breaking his concentration. He raised his glowing iron blade as he charged the slime monsters. He vaporized the first and then, feeling a punch, swung his sword frantically at the second, who fell dead. With John and Madison freed, they nodded together and took action.

"CHARGE!" roared John as Madison swung her sword at another slime beast, who wailed in pain. Nick sprinted at Daniel, who had the limp Dylan slung over his shoulder. As Nick leaped on his adversary, Dylan fell to the floor, unmoving.

"Bravo," rang a dark voice. Philip had surveyed the revolt. Nick kicked Daniel aside, desperately grabbed Dylan by his ankle, and pulled him back down the chamber. "You kids are good fighters, really. Just not good enough." The counselor raised his hands and a wave of darkness propelled Nick, Madison, John, and Dylan's limp body across the chamber. "I warned you," he said dangerously. "The Awakening is approaching soon. The Zorblins shall rise again, and you will perish. I would take Silver now, myself, but frankly, I'm not sure if I can trust my son anymore."

Daniel stared at the ground and Philip scowled. Meanwhile, Nick, his weakness evaporating, was lying on the floor, trying to regain his focus. A faint hum rang in his ears as his sweatshirt glowed once more. His head was throbbing, but he couldn't stop now. His stomach was twisting and turning as if there were a whirlpool forming inside of it. The great tug of power projecting from his sweatshirt was hurting him terribly and increasing in force.

"You kids can't escape us. The Zorblin will awake soon, and until it does…" More monsters entered through the gates and guarded the only exit.

"We're doomed," gasped Madison. Dylan's arms began to move, and his legs stiffened as his eyes opened. Lying on his side, he saw a thin rocket launcher and a bag of ammunition, which had been magically refilled, not far away. Although it may be dangerous, Dylan knew he had to take the risk.

John slashed his staff wildly, sending flashes of yellow light that repelled bursts of orange light back at the slime guardians, who fell with every hit. Madison was beside him, swinging her sword at the beasts that were trying to stop John. Nick lay on the floor and the whirlpool in his stomach was mirrored by a whirlpool of fiery light on his sweatshirt that spun around constantly in a circle. He was sweating profusely now and almost…

Philip bellowed, "Enough of this! Silver, come with me!" He yanked Nick off of the floor, shook him madly, and pulled him toward the door just as…

With a loud flourish, Flame, the dog, burst from the whirlpool in Nick's sweatshirt with such force, he cried out in pain. The dog jumped in Philip's face, scratching and biting it. Blinded by fur, Philip let go of Nick and Flame jumped off. Surprisingly strong, Flame clenched Nick's hood with his teeth and pulled him away from further danger. Through the pain, Nick couldn't help feeling proud of himself for successfully summoning Flame.

"HOW?" shouted Philip as he slapped a hand to his eye, staring in disbelief at the fluffy light-brown dog that was now springing up and down and coming to Madison and John's aid.

BOOOOOOOOOMM! All madness broke loose. Dylan had jam-packed the rocket launcher with three bullets and launched them at the slime monsters and Philip. Nick collapsed, unable to move, weaker than ever. "Good. . .doggy. . ." he croaked.

"Stop! Stop!" Philip's voice was hoarse as Daniel took cover behind the slime guardians. None of them stopped…until they heard a terrible roar. A groan. The Zorblin's head twisted, a dribble of acid oozed from its left mouth, and its head fell again. The Awakening was approaching at any moment.

The acid was creating streams in the floor, filling them with puddles of even more acid. Dylan was fighting again, wrestling the smallest slime beasts into the acid. But John had been pushed onto the acid, too, and Flame began healing his injury. Nick was still lying on the floor, weakened nearly to the point of death. Teleporting Flame had been too much for him. Nick and Dylan's stolen gold, that they had taken in their journey through the Secret Facility, had fallen into a stream of acid and incinerated. The book of summoning Nick had found was lost somewhere. More acid was spreading through the cage.

Suddenly, Flame began leaping and yapping as John got up, patted him on the head, and returned to the battle, swiping his staff powerfully. Daniel and Philip were shouting as their minions were battling.

"Guys!" gasped Nick as he saw Madison get pushed in a large puddle of acid and Dylan being punched in the jaw by a slime monster. Two more slime monsters kicked John to the ground, knocking the staff from of his hand. Flame began to bark loudly. He ran around, licking the injured and biting and scratching the enemies. Unfortunately, he was better at healing than fighting.

"Flame, no!" The dog was kicked feet away as a clumpy foot slammed into him. "Nick, I got this!" he managed to convey. But Flame was surrounded. Nick rolled over to his side as a humungous, glistening green foot swung at the dog, a thin wall of fire erupting between them. The foot shattered on impact and was incinerated. Nick was still weak and the closed iron gates remained a problem. They could escape if the doors were opened, but Philip and Daniel were standing guard there. What to do. . .?

"Bucket!" Nick got on his feet as the idea rushed to his head. He wobbled slightly, blood and sweat pouring down his neck. He seized the bucket and swung it in a puddle of acid. He heard it beginning to incinerate and knew he had to act fast. He jogged gingerly toward the gates and flung the acid from the bucket. The splashed iron began to mercifully melt before he stumbled a few inches backward, then collapsed again.

Another roar shook the room. The Zorblin's middle head reared to its right, then left. It rumbled and its tail shook violently. The battle stopped. Everybody turned to look, even the slime monsters, looking confused. The tail swung again. As one more terrible roar was let loose, Philip quickly conjured up a pocket watch. It was old-fashioned but did the job in telling him what he needed to know. It was exactly midnight, now Tuesday. The Zorblin's heads writhed, and it rose to its feet, lifting up its terrible, pale, veined, body.

The Zorblin's Awakening had begun.

14

The Last Zorblin

The Zorblin rose from its nest. It was on its feet now, its tail swinging, and Nick forced himself to his feet again, screaming as his friends and sister did the same. They grasped their weapons and bolted for the melted iron gates. "Run, Daniel!" shouted Philip through the chaos and roars. The awakened Zorblin crashed through the chamber, destroying everything in its path.

It stumbled around, stuck at first. Crushing and stampeding the remaining slime beasts, its first and third heads spat out waves of green acid. The acid melted through the walls and the Zorblin came crashing out into the hall. Once Philip and Daniel felt safely out of the way, Philip laughed in his booming voice, "Slime monsters! Zorblin! You know your orders! Kill the girl, the redhead, and the black-haired one. Capture the boy with the orange sweatshirt and kill the dog!"

A full-blown battle broke out. The four campers and Flame sprinted down the halls as the slime monsters, Zorblin, and the cloaked father and his son chased after them. The Zorblin roared again and its second head let out a burst of purple flames. It stomped down the hall, breathing deeply, followed by armies of living slime. Nick was weak, terribly weak, but he forced his legs to carry his weight. John and Dylan fired their weapons, taking out three or four slime monsters behind them. A burst of orange light shot from the end of the iron hall, instantly slaying another beast. "Keep running!" Nick yelled.

More jets of light. Red, yellow, orange, and spraying green acid and purple flames. Flame was extremely fast, even for a dog. Yells and screams and roars bombarded their ears. The chaos was so wild that Nick was awestruck at how none of the other campers or counselors, although extremely far away, couldn't hear the battle, or else they surely would have come running to see what the commotion was. Nick, Flame, and John dove into the vault as Dylan and Madison hurried swiftly down the hall.

"What do we do?" John gasped, clutching his side. "I don't know," stammered Nick.

"Maybe try to group up and fight back!" whimpered Flame, licking Nick's weakest leg and somehow allowing a nice feeling of warmth to seep through it.

"Flame's right, we need to group up and fight together," Nick told John, who looked vaguely confused for a second until he remembered that Nick could talk with Flame. "Come on!" The three bolted out of the vault and ran down the hall as another loud bang went off. Nick shot a ring of embers out of his palm at three medium-sized slime beasts. They sliced through them and melted them completely. "Cool," he muttered as John swiped his thumb on his staff, blasting away two more slime monsters.

"This is bad," Nick panted as he ran. "You think?" said John sarcastically as another bang went off and a jet of red light missed his head by inches. A bursting orange light shot forward, but Nick shoved John away and ducked. The iron blade fell from his grip. Although Nick's legs felt like jelly and his head was spinning, he kept running anyway as a cold sensation began to spread through his sweatshirt. "Look out!" John bellowed. An oozing fist swung over his head as he took John's advice and ducked aside. He quickly straightened up and continued sprinting. His head whirling with pain, every nerve of his body screaming for freedom, he heard another ear-splitting roar. A burst of purple flames appeared down the hall where they were about to turn. There was a rumbling scream and a blast of acid. Dylan was laughing, the sound of his sizzling rocket launcher cutting the air. "No!" screamed Philip, soaring through the air on a breeze of toxic black smoke, a mist surrounding him.

Nick's bones were in pain. He dropped to the floor as a burst of orange swept past him and missed John by inches. "Nick, get up. Come on!" As Nick lifted himself off the floor, he felt his heart pumping and heard the blood rushing in his ears. His veins bulging, Philip flew toward them, grabbed Nick, and slammed him back down to the floor. Just as suddenly, in a fluid moment and a burst of weak flames, a sword was drawn from Nick's sweatshirt. He slashed the sword at Philip, who stepped back. There was another enormous roar as a long, scaly tail swung from around the corner and swept Philip off his feet, flinging him into a room behind him. Nick ran for it, calling, "Hey, Dylan!"

Dylan, who was halfway down the hall with Madison, whipped around. A dripping green slime beast charged at him, but Madison swiped her purple double-edged sword and sliced it in half. Nick, John, and Flame tore down the hall as the spewing acid began to sizzle. "What do we do?" gasped Dylan, blasting his rocket launcher at three more large monsters.

"Just get to the exit!" cried Nick, stopping to whip his sword at the nearby slime monster as the Zorblin blundered down the hall, its three heads twisting and writhing, its six eyes full of terrible fury. And suddenly, Philip was flying at him again and, with his hand outstretched, pinned him to the wall. "Run!" he croaked at his four watching allies. They didn't.

"You think you can play the hero, Silver?" sneered Philip, his cloak whipping behind him. Nick's breath rasped as the hand remained tight around his throat. "Wait!" groaned Nick. "Before you capture me, just answer this…"

"And what might that be, Silver?" demanded Philip.

"H-how…how did I see the Zorblin's eyes multiple times, in lakes and stuff?" That question actually had been on his mind, but he was mainly asking it to stall.

"That…ah, of course," hissed Philip. "As you may already know, you and the Dark Ruler share a very unusual connection. That is because of his weapon and your gift. You have a distant connection – very faint, yet effective. You were imagining what you saw, Silver. It was actually on his mind then."

Nick had a plan, but this answer threw him off. "We have. . . a connection?"

"Yes, indeed."

"Well…" Nick remembered his plan and used it. With a flare, his sweatshirt shot out small embers and many sparks at Philip's face, causing him to leap back. In that moment of vulnerability, John hurtled over to them and swiped his staff, the flash of yellow removing the orange-tipped staff from the counselor's hand.

"Kill the one with the staff!" yelped Philip, sprawled on the floor. The Zorblin appeared at the end of the hallway and they bolted. BANG! The flash of yellow flung Daniel back, knocking his red-tipped staff into a slime monster's head, where it slowly began to descend into the ooze.

"My staff!" exclaimed Daniel, running at the struggling slimy beast, who was trying to seize the staff in his head. Dylan had also charged down the hall, punching a slime monster, whose shoulder absorbed the attack easily. The slime beast grabbed him and threw him across the room.

"Stop that!" A wisp of weak blue fire swished from Nick's raised arm. He felt incredibly weak now and had almost slipped to the ground when

Dylan pulled him up again. They changed from a quick jog to another full-blown sprint as a spurt of acid splashed the wall.

"Go! Go! Go!" commanded Daniel as he led an army of slime monsters down the hall, his cloak ripped, with staff back in hand. Nick tried to run faster but a booming red light hit the side of his leg, and the curse, weaker than intended, made him fall. Dylan seized his hand and dragged him down the hall quickly. Sweating, he felt his pants tear slightly, but other than that, he was relieved to not have to use his leg for the moment. But soon he was up again, rushing into the robot room with Dylan.

Purple flames flashed through the doorway as Dylan and Nick hid behind the wall while more of the slime army rushed past. Dylan had been clutching his weapon tightly all of this time, Nick realized, as he saw Dylan pull it into his sight and then, to Nick's shock, load it with dozen four bullets. "Let's go," whispered Dylan, preparing the launcher.

When more yells and screams hit the air, Dylan and Nick zoomed out of the room. Dylan shot all of the ammo at the now gigantic army of slimes with one ear-splitting explosion. Nick felt weightless for a second. Then, surrounded by the purple fire that flashed around the hall, the screams and roars of the now dead and dying monsters, and the bellowing Daniel, he felt slightly stronger.

"KILL THAT ONE!" screeched Daniel, pointing straight at Dylan. Nick willed a thin wall of fire to rise, shielding them completely from the other side of the hall.

"Yeah, Nick! Great!" celebrated Dylan, but too soon. The Zorblin had hurtled down the hall behind them. They were cornered behind Nick's wall. "Drop it!" Dylan urged. "I don't know how!" cried Nick frantically. He tried to touch the wall, but it gave him a second-degree burn and he recoiled his smoking hand. He quickly realized if he hadn't been wearing the sweatshirt, he would have gotten a lot worse than a second-degree burn. A jet of purple flames exploded from the Zorblin's second mouth and as the two ducked automatically, it struck and broke the wall. Seizing the opportunity to escape, they tore down the hall. Nick's lungs were searing as another bang went off. They turned the corner and saw Madison and John in the middle of a mob of monsters, battling.

Nick drew his sword and slashed. A quarter of the mob vaporized. Another bang, and half of the remaining monsters were blasted apart, chunks of slime shooting in different directions in a flash of yellow. "ARRGHH!" A slime monster had wrapped its long arms around John, who was sending bolts of light out of his staff wildly, unable to finish the beast. Madison swiped her sword and a gash formed in the monster's side. This one was strong, but it took only two more slashes before the monster was cut in half.

Flame burst into the mob to heal Madison and John, who were both injured, enough to allow them to stand. "Are you ready, Nick?" growled Flame softly. Nick nodded. "Charge!" They all ran toward the approaching monsters and sliced, zapped, slashed, and vaporized them. Just when they thought they were relatively safe, a bolt of red light flashed past Madison's ear. "What the…?" Daniel emerged from the end of the hall. His cloak was wet with slime, torn and dirty. His face was grimy, he was bleeding, and there was a gash along his left eye. His staff was raised, and his face was twisted with rage. Nick took a step forward.

"Daniel. You don't have to do this. You can do whatever you want to do. You can choose."

Daniel let out a yell. "That's what you think about everyone, Silver! You keep giving them too many chances. Now look at you!"

"That means nothing right now, Dan," said Nick honestly. "And you know it."

"You know nothing!"

"I do. I know more things than you think I know. So, if working for Quarzolon is really paradise for you, then why were you so terrified of him during your meetings?"

Daniel didn't respond. Nick had stumped him. John raised his staff. "Not yet," Nick whispered in his ear. He turned back to Daniel. "I see. So, you are only doing this because of…?"

"Quiet, Nich - Silver! Dad, they're over here!" Philip hurtled around the corner as the Zorblin roared again out of sight, and the five took off once more. Weapons went off at rapid-fire. Nick was leading, then Madison, then Dylan and John, weapons raised. Flame was running behind them all, trying not to go too fast, but when a flash of light almost hit him, he sped up considerably. They then ran straight into the Zorblin, who roared, bent down lower, and shot out gallons of acid, which hit the incoming slime monsters, incinerating them all.

Daniel was chasing Nick, who suddenly got a good idea. He abruptly stopped moving and Daniel came crashing straight into him. He swung his sword at Daniel, ripping his cloak in half. Daniel kicked away the shredded remnants and raised his staff to swipe it at Nick, who ducked and leapt forward, pushing him over. The staff flew from Daniel's grip again and Nick seized it, pointing it straight at Daniel. "Do it now," a voice in his head thought. Nick threw the staff instead. It landed far down the hall, where the Zorblin stampeded over it. Daniel's furious shout was drowned out by the Zorblin's sudden roar, as it lifted one of its feet to reveal two snapped sticks, red sparks shooting from them, stuck in its skin.

It roared again and whacked the wall with its tail, then came rushing down the hall at the two fighters, who ran again. Nick's sword was gone, but he knew it would just take a little bit more power to have it reappear.

He pulled a handle that poked out of his sweatshirt, revealing his iron blade. Pulling it out this time was more difficult and painful, but still possible. Daniel, running next to him as the Zorblin chased them, tried to lean to the side and snatch it out of his hands, but Nick was too quick. He slashed the sword at the air and Daniel pressed himself to the side of the hall.

The Zorblin had chased the two into a corner at the end of the long hall. They seemed doomed. As the Zorblin took one step, the broken staff in its foot exploded with a powerful burst of red. It was knocked over and the two enemies ran down the next hallway. The Zorblin's three heads screeched and it momentarily stopped chasing them. Its foot was scorched and marked, but it still moved fine otherwise. BANG! BOOM! Nick and Daniel were saved as John and Dylan fired. The strong yellow light smacked the Zorblin's face and forced it backward. Exhausted, John stumbled, too. Dylan's rocket launcher then shot a half dozen burning bullets, two of them exploding in each mouth of the Zorblin. The force of the explosions blasted Dylan into a slime monster, which tore at his neck.

"Let's go!" yelled Dylan.

"Don't let them escape!" ordered Philip from somewhere down the hall.

"Get to the hatch!" screamed Madison. They ran down the hall, passing various rooms as they went. Nick got an idea and nodded at the others, dodging, ducking, and sprinting until he reached the Potions Room. He rapidly searched around, abandoning his sword on the floor, and grabbed two purple bottles and one bright pink one. He charged out the door and easily found his friends. A crowd of slime monsters had them cornered onto the wall exactly opposite the exit. Nick let out a battle cry and chucked the two glimmering purple bottles at the monsters, hoping it would work. The two bottles smashed onto the hideous crowd and suddenly, they became paralyzed. Once they did, Madison and Dylan went to work on getting rid of them before they were able to move again.

After they had cleared the room, Dylan replenished his ammunition by snapping his fingers. "Convenient," he murmured weakly, unsure but grateful. It sounded as if more slime beasts were there somewhere. But how? And Madison was badly injured. Her leg was bloody and cut open.

Nick still had the pink potion. Was there a chance that it could thoroughly heal Madison? Suddenly, as he thought this, a faint glow emanated from the potion. He carefully pulled the cork out of the glass bottle and tipped it to let the thick pink goop stream into Madison's mouth. The air brightened slightly as a scorching hot feeling enveloped his sister. In a few seconds, she was healed. "Nick…what was…?"

"Healing potion," answered Nick firmly.

CRASH! "Uh oh."

ROOAAR! The Zorblin's roar echoed through the air. What little hope they had left seemed to be draining.

"KILL THEM ALREADY!"

They had no way out now.

"FIND THEM!"

"It's over, isn't it?" Nick thought hopelessly.

John thought otherwise. "Now! Run!" They all shot out of the room, rushing to the ladder, which led to a hatch miraculously left open. But a hand dragged Nick back down. Daniel stood behind him, with his hand clutching Nick's sweatshirt.

"Give it to me!" bellowed Daniel, yearning to own Nick's mysterious power.

Rapid, broken flashes of piercing red shattered the misty air. There were more yells and when the red cleared, no one was knocked out except the watching slime monsters. Daniel was breathing heavily, his eyes changing from confusion to anger. It seemed as if he were contemplating what he had done, still trying to comprehend Nick's apparent gift: the only reason he was still alive, but the reason he would die. The Zorblin's appearance destroyed the silent moment. Daniel swung around and Nick grabbed his allies and ran. The beast's large tail swung widely and more purple flames cut the atmosphere. And in a ripple of darkness and with a high-pitched crack, Daniel was gone.

"Keep going, Nick!" reminded Flame with a yap. But when they turned the corner of the hall, heading reluctantly away from the only exit, they stumbled into about a dozen more monsters. How was this possible? And then it clicked. At the same time, John and Nick understood. They exchanged looks and led the others to the room they now desperately wanted to find.

"Where are we?" stammered Dylan.

"The monster-making room," replied Nick and John simultaneously. "That's how those slime freaks are multiplying."

Still relentless, Philip glided over to them through the air, his cloak ripped, and hood torn off, with his pocket bulging slightly because of the egg.

"Separate!" said Nick. "Flame, stay with me and Madison. You two, stop the spawners!" Dylan and John agreed and ran off. Madison and Nick stood their ground with Flame.

"Philip!" shouted Nick, and the chaos ceased. The multiplying beasts froze as Madison and even Philip stopped. "What, Silver?" he barked, landing softly on the ground. Daniel appeared at his father's side. "What's happening?" he asked.

"I want that egg," said Nick plainly. "Or we'll use force."

"Oh, no! Two kids and a tiny dog! I'm terrified!" sneered Philip.

"Get lost," snarled Daniel, yet shaking as the Zorblin came right behind him.

"Give us that egg, or…or…" stuttered Nick.

"Or what? Or nothing! You don't know. You have no plan! Now, get out of the way, Silver, so I can blast the girl to smithereens!" Philip raised his deadly staff.

"Just give us the egg. We'll make a deal!" Nick offered quickly.

"Alright. Fine. This'll be fun. Duel with Daniel, then. Swords. You win – you get the egg and escape. You lose – no egg, you are captured quietly, and your friends, sister, and dog die."

Nick and Daniel stood, staring straight at each other on separate sides of the single long hall. In a burst of flames, the handle of Nick's sword reappeared. He seized it and pulled the full iron sword out, glowing a faint yellowish-orange color. Daniel waved his hand and with a cloud of dark mist, a long, jet-black spear appeared in his hand, circled with red electricity, its point deadly sharp. The edges of the spear were slightly curved with a sharp rim. The two bent lower, extending their weapons further out.

"Alright!" called Philip, holding out the egg. The Zorblin had backed up, so Nick had room. "The duel will begin with the challengers each at their own side of the hall, which will be their safe zone. When the duel starts, the two will come forth, into the middle, where they will fight. First one down to the floor, or completely disarmed, loses." Nick listened carefully as he and Daniel glared intensely at one another. Philip cackled with laughter. "The duel starts in three. . . two. . . one! Fight!"

Just as Dylan and John burst from around Daniel's corner, the two duelers approached each other. Nick swung his iron blade at Daniel's raised spear, which pierced Nick's chest and blocked his sword. Nick quickly backed up and then leapt forward, lunging his sword at Daniel.

It hit his shoulder and slid off, but the gash wasn't deep enough to affect him. Daniel slashed his spear, which hit Nick's leg sideways. He gasped, retreated, ran back, and swung his sword again at the spear. It ricocheted off and he swung at the spear once more, shoving it aside and nailing Daniel in the stomach. Daniel stumbled away, then teleported right in front of him and dug his spear into Nick's chin, releasing a spurt of blood that quickly cleared up as Nick retreated to his safe zone in a spark of fire.

"Cheater!" yelled Daniel. Philip watched intently as the cut on Nick's chin began to heal. "I'll allow it," said Philip coldly. Nick bolted out of the safe zone as Daniel was distracted, slashing his sword. Daniel, swinging his whole body, parried his blade to the side and leapt at Nick. His spear would have hit him directly in the heart if Nick hadn't curved his sword in that split second when his spear deflected off of Nick's wider weapon. Nick's allies looked on, terrified yet intrigued. Daniel swung his weapon at Nick and cut his shoulder. Nick gasped in pain, doubled over, as the spear pierced his forehead. He sprung away, rubbed his forehead hastily, and charged again, slashing his sword at Daniel's spear and knocking both weapons aside. The iron blade lunged at Daniel, piercing his neck. He stumbled and waved his spear out of frustration at Nick's head. "Traitor!" Daniel brandished his spear again, cutting Nick's cheek. Nick curved his sword next to Daniel's spear and, with knowledge gained from Swaying Swords, sliced it at Daniel's nose, which now bore a vague cut.

"FINISH HIM, DANIEL!" bellowed Philip.

"Get him, Nick!" retorted the others. "C'mon, Nick! You've got this!"

The duel continued. Nick felt a burst of adrenaline and eventually backed Daniel into his safe zone, only to have Daniel spring at him and knock him over sideways. Just before Nick hit the ground, he aimed his iron blade to stop the fall and lifted himself up, leaning forward.

"You've always been soft…too trustworthy," Daniel taunted. SLASH! Nick slit a large gaping hole in Daniel's shirt. Daniel roared in pain and swung his spear at Nick, smacking his right arm with so much pressure that Nick yelped. Daniel smiled and lunged as Nick dodged and circled around him, swinging his sword at random. Daniel, unable to finish Nick as he weaved in and out, grew in fury.

"Do it already, Daniel!" bellowed Philip angrily.

"Looks like a great father and son relationship you have there!" yelled Nick sarcastically, throwing Daniel off-guard. As he paused, Nick lunged but Daniel lazily blocked it. Nick spun in a full circle and extended his sword arm, which hit Daniel's spear arm, knocking the jet-black weapon out of his hands. Nick stood, relieved and shocked, as he watched the black spear flip in midair and fall back down into Daniel's grasp, who looked furious.

Nick looked at Philip, expecting his face to be angry, but in fact, his expression was calm. He looked at Daniel, who was clutching the spear again, and said quietly, "Since the spear didn't hit the ground and reached its owner's grip again, the duel is still ongoing."

"Seriously?" yelled Madison.

"SILENCE HER!" screamed Philip, but the slime monsters were nowhere to be seen. He looked at Madison's slimy sword and Flame's untidy fur, which had slime on it also, and became enraged as he understood. Madison and Flame had finished off the slime monsters around them while Philip was distracted with the duel. But John wasn't there, either. Neither was Dylan. Nick, a smirk flitting across his face, realized why more slime beasts weren't coming back: the two had broken the monster spawner.

Philip growled, "Finish him, Daniel!" Daniel teleported again, but Nick was ready for it this time. He instantly backed up and lunged his sword at the misty figure in front of him. He heard a wail of pain, and as Daniel and his spear materialized and came into view, he stabbed Nick in the chest, paralyzing him. Daniel smacked the flat of his spear hard into Nick's chest, making him kneel on the ground in pain, then touched the sharp edge of his spear directly above Nick's heart.

"Now, my son. . ."

Daniel didn't move. He wore the same blank expression as before, as though contemplating his decision. As he began to slide his spear upward, Nick curved his sword at Daniel and lunged. Daniel stumbled and almost hit the floor, but as he fell back, he teleported with a quick crack behind Nick and lunged his spear into his back. Nick spun around and waved his sword at the spear, hoping to somehow knock it out of his hand. Nothing. Because Daniel was back in his own safe zone – and then he wasn't. Nick backed up quickly as Daniel appeared before him, his spear surrounded by red electricity and lengthened to twice its size. Daniel extended his spear to Nick's head, which seemed to explode with pain, then backed up a bit, his spear raised high above their heads, and it shrank to its normal size again.

Nick was frozen, paralyzed by pain and the realization of how much chaos and danger he had stumbled into. Before Daniel could disarm or knock him over, the Zorblin returned to the hall, behind Nick, and spat out two jets of poisonous acid. Nick ran for it, passing Daniel, completely forgetting about the duel. "NO!" boomed Philip, running at the Zorblin, trying to restrain it. The Zorblin kicked and thrashed, its heads squirming and writhing, acid spewing out and covering the dueling hall.

The counselor waved his arms at the mutinous monster, trying to stop it from moving anymore. It roared again and a burst of purple flames exploded through the air. "Arrgh!" struggled Philip, his son darting to his aid. There were crashes and bangs and calls for help as the Zorblin's struggling kicked Philip away. When Daniel rushed towards it, its large, skeletal tail swung and swatted him away like his father.

It wanted meat, Nick thought, as it had been restrained from proper food for years. It wanted flesh, blood, and bone. The last Zorblin was fighting her way past her commanders. But it didn't seem to want only meat. Something was odd about the Zorblin's red, deathly eyes. They were wider, their glow was stronger – even stronger than the glow in the eyes Nick had seen days before. There was a blinding fury, controlled by something, in her eyes. And then Nick saw it. The last Zorblin's six beady eyes were all focusing on Philip Garring and the egg. The egg she had laid, the one stolen from her nest. She roared and thrashed, spitting out flames and acid towards the counselor.

"Help!"

"Dad!"

"ROAAR!"

"Son…!"

The Zorblin disobeyed Philip. It attempted to kill him to get her egg back. "She wants her egg!" cried Nick at the stubborn man, who still refused to surrender the lumpy egg.

"No! The egg must hatch! Not to be blubbered over by that beast!"

The Zorblin attacked. Philip, screaming and yelling, struggled to dodge the spouts of acid and roars of purple flames while forced against the wall as the Zorblin blocked all other ways of escaping. "Get BACK!" he screamed, struggling as the Zorblin kicked its stumpy but strong right foot flat on his face, smashing him back into the wall that he tried to teleport away from. "Get off me, you…"

But the last Zorblin would not leave him alone. It wouldn't stop until it had its egg, and it seemed like Philip knew this, too. He raised the egg and chucked it at Nick. The Zorblin stopped attacking him and its three heads twisted. Without thinking, Nick caught the egg with both hands. Then, Philip sneered and the others watched in terror as the Zorblin began to chase Nick down the hall. Nick sprinted away with all of his might, for his very life. When Nick reached the end of the hall and turned on his heel to race back in the other direction, the beast spun around and blasted out gallons and gallons of acid. The green spray washed over Nick. He screamed in agony, his vison blurry, then his eyes forced shut, as the acid burned all over him. The last thing he saw was Philip screaming as he pointed his murderous staff at the others, preventing them from helping Nick. Flame barked as Madison screamed and Dylan and John shouted. But Nick was coming to a halt, still clutching the egg, hoping to destroy it when he had the chance, and knew he was dying.

As more acid sprayed over him, he screamed, skin burning, eyes shut, legs failing him – yet he felt a strong surge of power. The last thing he remembered was the incredible glow of an orange blast of flames that was coming from him, not just the sweatshirt. And there was an explosion of black, the sound of crunching, the flash of more green liquid, the loud sizzle of dark smoke, and the faint picture in his mind of an unrecognizable woman, handing him something very small. But what?

15

The Robot Suit

Nick was sprawled on something hard, but yet soft. His body ached as he had been dropped into a vat of stones, then microwaved and sprayed with a coating of pure ice. But still, he finally noticed, he was alive. He was lying face down on something both ticklish and rocky, and his face felt muddy. Who was it he had seen? Where was Daniel? What happened to the Zorblin? Where was the egg?

He felt chilly now, as a steady breeze swept over him. He was weak and hungry, but had enough strength left to roll over. What he saw were thick trees covered in dark green leaves, and patches of the dark, starry sky above. He was hot and cold at the same time, head aching. A torturous numbness was attacking his every nerve. Finally, he traced the feeling of cold, raw torture to his dim sweatshirt. He managed to yank it off, lying flat on the grass in the Quarren Forest, and he felt normal. His headache subsided, his swirling numbness dissolved, and even his sweating stopped. He understood now that his sweatshirt was not completely dependable. It had brought him headaches, pain, and visons, along with powers to protect and attack.

As for the woman he had seen, he didn't know who it could be. As he lay there, he considered his mother – but no. It seemed like something or someone beyond his own family. And what had the mysterious woman given him? The sweatshirt? The X-Ball Zero? Maybe even

Flame? He didn't know, but he had a slight feeling it was none of those. And then he remembered everything else: the fight, the Zorblin's Awakening, the duel, the egg, the acid, the pain. . . his friends. They were all still trapped down there! Madison, Dylan, John, and Flame. Or were they? He had obviously been moved out of the iron hall, out of the whole Secret Facility entirely.

His sweatshirt had saved him and yet it nearly killed him. He had to stop relying on it too much. But his sword…where was it? It must still be down there, too. Or, like it had earlier, it disappeared. He wasn't sure, but he began to worry. He had to save the others. He had brought them to mortal danger. But was he really in the Quarren Forest? He could have been transported, straight to the Mezoar Prison, like Philip had said.

Philip! Camp Director Philip was Daniel Garring's father. The two had betrayed them all. That's why Daniel always watched the holes.

He felt dead, yet dimly, he knew he was alive, still on his own planet. But what to do now? He knew he had to save the others. But how to do it? He didn't even know where he was, for starters. He may be in the Quarren Forest, but where in the forest? Were they already dead? Nick had no idea. He wanted the X-Ball Zero more than ever, to ask it questions – things he wanted to know after entering and somehow escaping the Facility. He trusted it now. And he had learned why the Zorblin's Awakening had taken place that night, because of the egg. It would lay the egg at midnight and when it awoke, its senses triggered, it would be stronger than ever because of the egg being stolen. The Zorblin's anger would have multiplied its power by tenfold. So, then, the Zorblin's Awakening had to have been something else prophesied, wasn't it? The silvery moon hung over the stars, illuminating the dark night, as he tried to think straight.

"Help," moaned Nick. "Help me." He tried to get up but fell back again. No use. He was completely weakened by the acid, but lucky to be alive. He needed to save them, and now. The realization fueled him. He seized the crumpled sweatshirt, pulled it on over his head, and although he felt a swirling numbness and pounding headache return, he felt slightly stronger and more protected. He got to his knee and finally lifted himself up onto his feet. He wobbled for a second and then stood still, sweating again. He walked slowly through the night as the moon shone through the shady trees.

Nicholas Silver traveled through the Quarren Forest at a steady pace, stepping around the trees and through the leaves. In the silence, he heard the sound of crickets chirping and owls hooting their dull, soft hoot, hoot. The soft crunching of leaves echoed through the forest as Nick walked over them carefully. He had to find it; he knew it was here somewhere. . .

And finally, he found the entrance. There were patches of iron plates and a large, empty, dried crater in the ground, with an open hatch leading into a tunnel. He could hear muffled screams and shouts. The iron trees still glowed, and the wind still blew lightly. Nick slowly approached the odd location, noticing the iron walls had fallen. Could the others have broken the security on the computer in that one room? No. Couldn't have. Perhaps they were just temporary, then.

He descended into the crater, slid down carefully, and crouched low at the bottom. The dust swished around him as he stopped. He thought about how Camp CrystalFlake, so close, was so calm. He wiped his forehead and climbed down the ladder into the tunnel. His feet hit iron yet again, and more screams and bellows hit his ears, knocking him off balance. He shook his head and headed back into the Secret Facility.

"GET BACK HERE!"

"Guys, run!"

"ROOAAR!!"

"Oh no!"

"RUN AWAY!"

BANG! "John!"

"Sorry…"

And then they all stopped moving and talking. Philip looked dumbstruck and Daniel looked like he was staring at a ghost.

"NICK!" His sister and friends ran forward, not noticing their frozen enemies for that moment. "How…?"

"How are you still alive?" snarled Philip, shocked.

"I-I don't know," mumbled Nick. "My sweatshirt, I guess."

"That sweatshirt can't save you from that! Nothing can survive a Zorblin's acid!" Philip challenged him, looking angrier and confused than ever. "Daniel, get him!" As his two enemies ran at them, Nick whipped his arm out and half of a wall of fire burst into sight and burned their faces, knocking them over. "HOW DID YOU LIVE?" exploded Philip before grabbing Daniel and lifting them both up again and commanding, "Forget the others. Capture Silver, get his sister and friends, and we will bring him to the Dark Ruler!"

"Wait! Where's the egg?" cried Nick. "You smashed it when you fell," murmured Madison, pulling him down the hallway. Philip was flying again, soaring straight at Nick. But the Zorblin beat him to it. The three-headed beast thundered down the hall, roaring. All six of those beady, pitiless red eyes were staring straight at Nick and he knew it was because the Zorblin saw him smash the egg when he fell over. The Zorblin rammed Philip out of the air as the cloaked man flew. There was a boom, but Dylan's rocket launcher was incredibly weak now compared to the fully awake Zorblin, who was determinedly chasing the person who had accidentally smashed her egg.

"ROAAR!" Out of desperation, Nick spun around and concentrated, willing a small beam of fire at its necks. It stopped and writhed, smoke sizzling in the air, giving him time to run some more. "Nick," panted John, trying to keep up with him. "When you got splashed with the acid, we thought you were dead. The Zorblin went rogue. Daniel tied us up and Philip brought the Zorblin to its cage. After Daniel left us, Madison slipped out of the ropes and retrieved your body. She brought it somewhere in the Quarren Forest and when she came back to get us, we heard a roar and the Zorblin came running down the hall with Philip and Daniel chasing it. They saw Madison untying the ropes, we all broke out, and a chase started. Ten minutes later, you're back."

"That would explain a few things," Nick gasped. "Thanks, J-" He was interrupted by a long, skinny bolt of red light that hit John in the back and took him down. "JOHN!"

"Get back here, Silver!"

But Nick was sprinting like never before. Daniel was behind him, chasing him with a new staff, and suddenly he stopped and turned around. Nick didn't bother looking back, but continued to run, eventually bursting into the robot room. There was a button on the wall that Nick hadn't noticed before. He pressed it and a white door slammed the room shut, making things dimmer. "Phew," he sighed, leaning against the wall. "How am I supposed to get past the Zorblin now? It hates me more than ever. I need something, like a power-up. Like…" Looking to his left, he found what he was looking for. Grinning slightly, he walked over to it, climbed up the side, and hopped into the mechanical suit labeled Iron Titan.

The suit lit up blue. He squeezed his arms through the arm holes, and what should have been heavy magically felt lighter. Light enough to raise without breaking a sweat. His body fit decently in the suit and when he squeezed his legs through their holes, they magically felt lighter, as well. There was one trigger in each hand. He pulled the first trigger, on the left. Ropes with large hooks at the ends shot out and hit the wall. By retracting the trigger, the ropes sank back into the Iron Titan's knuckles. He pulled the trigger of the right hand and a jet of liquid-like ice shot out of the palm. "Sweet," whispered Nick. He noticed a small label next to the frost trigger, saying it was unstable, which he disregarded. Trying his best to straighten up, he began to march around the room. It was fairly easy walking in this; a little weird, a little hard, but not that bad. He punched the button for the door with his left robotic hand and the door sprang open.

Crashing through the doorway, past the threshold, he broke into a run down the hall with a clink, clunk, clink, clunk, clink. The Zorblin roared again and Nick heard flames shooting and spreading, and more screams. In the robot suit, he now stood double his normal height and he peered around the corner. The Zorblin had trapped the others into a corner of the Facility. He craned his neck to see Philip and Daniel watching at the other side of the hall, waiting for the Zorblin's final move, killing them. The Zorblin's heads seemed to lengthen and its tail shook as it opened its mouths, baring teeth. Philip laughed his low, booming laugh.

The Zorblin's heads drew breath and as the terrible combination of fire and acid blasted from its mouths, Nick charged it in the robot suit and extended his now mighty arms, strangling the creature. "ARRRGGGHH!!" The Zorblin struggled against the suit's grip, the fire and acid spitting uselessly onto the floor.

"WHAT? NO!" shouted Philip from far away. Nick kept the metal fists clenched on the Zorblin's sides as it roared, heads thrashing, fire burning the floor but not harming or even hitting Nick's suit at all. But then its tail swung into the side of Nick's suit and made him dizzy, and the beast slipped out of his and the Iron Titan's grasp.

"Nick! What…"

"How are you doing that?" asked Dylan, awestruck.

"Get them!" cried Nick, trying to contain the Zorblin in a headlock with the suit's arms around its squirming necks. As the allies whipped around, they saw the dark figures tearing across the hall. There was a terrible struggle as Flame bit, Madison slashed, Dylan shot, and a now-conscious John blasted the demonic father and son. And beside it all, a ten-foot-tall robot battled a large, skeletal, three-headed, bony-tailed monster spitting out flames and acid.

"THIS IS INSANE!" bellowed Dylan as he blasted his rocket launcher again into Daniel's face, who released a muffled yell. The flash of yellow forced Philip to the floor, not powerful enough to fling him. "YEAH, VERY!" John shouted back as he directed another flash at Philip, who had pulled out his orange-tipped staff.

Nick kept his robotic arms wrapped tightly around the wailing Zorblin, trying to throw it to the floor. The Zorblin whipped and pushed, tossing Nick to the floor instead. The two tall fighters lost balance and rolled over before Nick was boosted to his feet by the writhing Zorblin. He straightened up and swung his fist multiple times, trying to release the Zorblin from his long, metal arm. The Zorblin slipped off, got up, slashed its tail, and charged. It rammed Nick back and then she jumped onto him, crushing the suit slightly to the floor, where it fixed its eyes on Nick's. Slowly, those beady red eyes met Nick's brown ones. Hope was swirling down a pit. It had awakened...there was no hope. . . they were dead, surely. . . Ruler Quarzolon would return again. . .

"No! Get away or else!" Flame growled at the creature. He had retreated from the struggle to help Nick battle the Zorblin, but not physically. Flame glowed at the suit's feet and Nick suddenly felt a glow inside, as well. He was rising again. He was stronger. He had hope. "TAKE THIS, UGLY!" he shouted, balling up his left fist and pulling the trigger. Winding ropes hooked themselves onto the Zorblin. Cutting into its skin, they pulled the Zorblin back as it tried to escape and held it at bay. And when an orange burst of light missed Flame by about an inch, Nick's reacted. He let go of the trigger, the hooks and ropes shooting back up the Iron Titan's knuckles, and leapt at Philip, who brandished the staff again. Nick hit him and he crumpled. The Zorblin began to race down the hall and Nick swung the robot's foot at the cloaked man, who screamed and was launched. Maybe, Nick thought as Daniel pulled out his red tipped staff to stun, we can go to that one weapon room and get the same staffs for ourselves. . .

But he had bigger problems now. The Zorblin was escaping, and although the threat of Philip was neutralized, the Zorblin's threat rose dramatically. The creature fully recognized Nick now as the one who had shattered its egg because when Nick fell from the acid that should have killed him, the egg fell with him. The Zorblin turned back wildly, heading right for him.

"GUYS, RUN!" bellowed Nick, as he attempted to kick at the Zorblin's raised leg.

"No! We won't leave you!" Yellow light whizzed out of John's staff and hit the Zorblin, moving it back by mere inches and making its heads twist toward John. Nick gasped and bolted forward, strangling the Zorblin from behind. It roared in his grasp, tail thrashing madly, stumpy feet kicking. Nick was thrown backward as one foot and a skeletal tail kicked and swung at the Iron Titan, knocking him down. As the last Zorblin advanced on the fallen robot suit, blasts of burning bullets shot at its first and second heads, making it wail and back up. Madison charged with her sword, but the Zorblin's middle head spat the cursed fire at it and destroyed the weapon, just missing Madison herself as she jumped backwards.

Nick was up again. He let out a battle cry and kicked the Zorblin, making it bend lower and spew out acid. Nick dodged, punched, avoided more sprays, lunged, and missed. Madison disappeared, but Nick had no time to register this. Philip and Daniel began to fight again and the three of them battled together. Flame jumped at Daniel, who made him temporarily freeze, while Dylan and John kept Philip at bay and Nick defended against the Zorblin from within the protection of the iron suit. Philip had a smoky aura three times his size around him, mimicking his movements and knocking down John and Dylan. Suddenly there was a yell as a shining purple battle-axe slashed through the air and Philip stepped back in alarm. Madison was holding the battle-axe now, swinging it wildly.

"FOR THE DARK RULER!" Philip proclaimed loudly, sending a shockwave of black electricity through the air and throwing back his foes. The fight momentarily froze. Philip's hands were held high, bolts of black lashing out of his fists. "Final Zorblin, kill all the campers!" He directed a bolt at the Zorblin, who squealed and ran toward the tunnel. It smashed through the iron ceiling, through and up the small tunnel, breaking the hatch right off of its hinges, and climbing out above the Facility into the crater. The final Zorblin was escaping and now going to kill its prey.

Philip cried out, his smoky aura dissipating completely, and then both Garrings disappeared, teleporting to the top of the tunnel and clinging onto the ladder. "We have to stop them, don't we?" moaned Dylan.

"Yep, I guess so," answered John grimly. Nick jumped out of the tunnel with ease; The Titan shot upward through the hole the Zorblin had made, right into the dry crater. John, Dylan, Madison, and Flame followed him.

"But how can we get out of this crater…?"

"I got this," said Nick confidently. He picked up John and Dylan in one hand, Madison and Flame in the other. All four hung onto the robot suit's arms. In a swishing movement, both arms swung forward and the four were rocketed up and out of the crater, landing on the hard grass above. Summoning strength from himself and the suit, Nick jumped high, up and out of the crater. The walls still hadn't risen again. Good.

The group raced through the Quarren Forest, searching together for the three terrible enemies that now ran loose. It wasn't hard because the Zorblin wasn't very stealthy. They all heard a crackle of liquid, a seething noise, and the thuds of a half dozen trees falling over. They sprinted through the thick and wild trees, around poisonous bushes, past the fallen trees and a puddle of acid, and finally, to the edge of the forest, where the Zorblin lurked, and the man and his son stared across the camp.

"Daniel, how do you think we should invade the camp?" they heard Philip ask. "Let the beast run wild? Silently sneak through the camp and kill them ourselves? Release all of our power at once?"

"Uhh…er…the f-first one?"

"Good idea, son. Relax, then, and let the last of its kind run amuck!"

"NO!" Nick threw himself forward, kicking Philip over, shoving Daniel to the mud, and tackling the Zorblin, which put up a fight. They rolled over, back and forth, left and right, until they tumbled straight out of the forest, knocking over the fence and heading into Camp CrystalFlake. How the noise didn't wake anyone up right away, Nick had no idea, but as the two continued to struggle, he noticed Philip conjuring a blurry mist that was encircling the three camper cabins and the Counselor Cabin.

The Zorblin lurched to its side and its stumpy foot kicked Nick's suit with such force, he was flung backward. BANG! The Zorblin rolled over. There were more bangs and flashes of light and the Zorblin barely moved. All it did was roar and spit out waves of acid at John as he drew nearer. John dodged as Madison struck with her axe, swinging at the Zorblin. She slashed a gash in its foot and was kicked away. Nick raised himself in the robot suit and jumped at the Zorblin, pushing it over but getting whacked aside by two squirming heads. The Zorblin was clearly stronger than them. "EAT FROST, UGLY!" screamed Nick. He pulled the trigger on his right hand, shooting a blast of ice. It would have hit the Zorblin's third head if it hadn't squirmed away at the last second and let the frost hit Cabin C instead. The wooden roof was covered in ice, with icicles dangling all around. The bubble of mist still encircled the cabin. "Maybe I won't use that trigger, then," he muttered to himself.

The Zorblin bent lower and reared at the Iron Titan. Nick surged forward, but the Zorblin grasped the suit with its tentacle-like necks and tossed it to the side. The Zorblin wailed as it was hit with another blast, spun around, lost balance, and toppled over. But it was back on its feet again even faster than it had been knocked off, even though it was clearly in pain.

"RUN!" bellowed John. They sprinted across the fields, up the small hill beside the lake, past the holes, and through the dunes as the Zorblin thundered onward, close behind. When Nick saw it lunge for Flame, he punched the beast in the side of its second head and it turned on him again. Counselor Philip and Daniel reentered the fight just then. Dylan's rocket launcher fired at Philip, who dodged it, and the burning bullet soared past him into a far back pine tree, which exploded at once.

"HOOK, LINE, AND DIE!" Nick cried as several hooked ropes propelled out of the suit and wrapped around the now wailing Zorblin. More hooks latched onto the beast's necks. Seeing this, Philip took out his anger out on Madison, who barely dodged his wave of black energy and ran out of its reach. Daniel waved his sleeved hand, washing a wave of force and red electricity upon Dylan that made him double over in pain. The rocket launcher fired again at Daniel, hitting the edge of his shirt. The last Zorblin jumped for Dylan, and although most of the hooks had separated from its skin, some still held it at bay, preventing it from moving farther. Nick struggled to hold the Zorblin still as the suit's left arm began to stretch and splinter.

"No…stop…go away. Go back to sleep…back to sleep. Come on, please. . ." whispered Nick as he began to slowly slide forward toward the restrained beast. There was another bang behind him.

"Ouch! Nick, help!" cried Flame. Nick's senses tingled in his sweatshirt and it glowed softly as he understood the dog's pleas. He saw Daniel's attacks on the dog, but he couldn't get to them.

"Madison, Flame!" Nick shouted to his sister, who was closest to Daniel and Flame. She began to run, extending her battle-axe. Daniel yelled and fired a feeble ray of red smoke, then ran toward his father.

Crack! The bionic arm splintered more. The Zorblin was furious and the remaining ropes were beginning to snap. Nick could not hold the Zorblin for much longer. He somehow noticed the silvery moon as it hung over the shining stars and felt a warmth in his heart and sweatshirt. He was weak and as this sudden feeling spread, the ropes binding the Zorblin finally snapped and it thundered across the campgrounds.

"Nooooo!" Madison was almost stampeded by the monster, her axe swinging, but the Zorblin didn't notice. It continued to run, wailing. Nick watched as it ran around blindly in large circles, a large deep gash in its foot. The colorful bursts, loud explosions, and flash of weapons continued.

"Help! Anyone, help!" Nick called out, but nobody came to help. The blurry mist Philip had cast around the cabins blocked any sound from entering. Nick wished there were someone…anyone…who had power to match that of their enemies. Someone older and wiser who had experience with something like this. He thought wryly that the X-Ball had been right again when he first arrived at camp. This was, indeed, the most special summer yet, but not in ways he had expected. Camp CrystalFlake was doomed.

A column of the cursed purple fire, meant for his head, missed and hit the blurry mist around the Counselor Cabin instead. A weird jagged-edged shape formed in the mist, shattered right in front of the cabin's door. The booming sound shook the wooden cabin and suddenly, there was a yell from within. The door creaked open. Counselor Robert, the same counselor who had been attacked in the Quarren Forest on the first day of camp, stepped out, looking terrified and slightly angered. He gasped, looking up at the Zorblin, and began to scream aloud.

"MONSTER! MONSTER! THE LEGEND IS REAL! Counselors, wake up! Help!" He ran wildly toward Counselor Philip as he looked around, not comprehending, and implored, "Help! What's going on, Camp Director?"

Philip appeared just as shocked as Counselor Robert. The Zorblin slowly walked over as the frightened, clueless counselor turned around and screamed. Acid drooled onto his head and two more jets of acid drenched him completely. When the Zorblin stopped, the acid stilled and the counselor dropped to the ground. It could not have been plainer that Counselor Robert was dead.

16

The Mestephans Flee

Counselor Robert's body remained still on the grass, his body smeared with smoking and sizzling acid. The Zorblin let out a low rumble, then a high-pitched groan, and reached down to eat. Even Philip looked horrified. "Stop! STOP!" ordered Philip. Reluctantly, the hungry Zorblin stopped. The same leg Counselor Robert had injured two weeks prior was already half gone. "Shame," sighed Philip in a low voice. "Probably my favorite counselor." The scene was horrible as the Zorblin hung her heads over the body while Philip stood contemplating. Daniel Garring looked sickened; his eyes bloodshot. "Is h-he-?"

"He's dead," Philip told his son dryly as he raised a hand and the crack in the misty blur around the large cabin resealed. The night was darker than ever. Nobody knew what to do or what to say.

The Zorblin stared hungrily, its feet shuffling, heads twisting. Nick finally went to make the first move. "ATTACK!" he cried, springing at the beast. "Stop!" screeched Philip, and in a swirl of black energy, Nick was blinded and still for a few seconds.

"What?" asked Daniel. "Why did you stop the fight?"

"Because I think these campers have gone further than most mortals. I want to reward them," Philip Garring said slowly.

"You want to what?" asked Madison, confused.

"You four, and the dog, I suppose, have fought valiantly. Unlike most humans, you have managed to survive for longer than ten minutes."

Why does he keep calling us "humans" like he isn't human? Nick wondered.

"Your power is great – great for the Querzelan. Yes, it would be, indeed. How unfortunate it is that you are humans, however." There was that word again.

"You keep calling us humans, as if you're not," Nick pointed out.

"Oh. . . how right you are, Nicholas Silver. . ."

"Grruuhhh," groaned the Zorblin, still staring at the body. Philip glanced at it almost pitifully and then continued.

"But we, Daniel and I, are not mere mortals. We are two of the most recently born Mestephans."

Nick and the others gasped. "But, how…well, that's how you flew!" That explains all of their powers, Nick thought to himself silently. They aren't human – but wait! I still don't even know what a Mestephan is.

"But…what exactly is a Mestephan?" John asked before Nick could open his mouth again.

"What is a Mestephan?" Philip laughed loudly. "Yes, I know about the book you found. What it didn't tell you…well, look!" With a snap of his fingers, a moldy, leathery book shot out through a small hole in the roof of Cabin B, straight into his hand. "This book would have told you if you kept reading it. But now it's too late." With that, he threw the wide book at the Zorblin, whose third mouth swallowed it whole. Acid dripped from its large, vertical mouth, and the monster rumbled again, satisfied.

"Hey, you promised us a reward!" barked Dylan. "So tell us about you Mestephan people!"

"Well, then. Alright. A deal's a deal, I suppose. Mestephans are like humans, except they have no flesh, no bones. Their blood is dark, nearly black, like a tarry liquid. Their sweat is similar. A Mestephan is made up of cold and hot, pitch-black, very thick glittery smoke. The thick, smoky insides keep us standing and give us our powers. Our brains are the same as mortals, but Mestephans have three lives. Master is on his second, I believe. When a Mestephan dies of age, they are reborn again, back to the youngest age. When they die on the third life, they are gone, dead completely. I believe murder also applies to this. Or maybe murder keeps them at their same age. I don't believe so, however. The smoke inside of a Mestephan is so thick with multiple layers that, with practice, they can unleash powers. Sometimes, not usually but not extremely rare, the powers released from a Mestephan can vary, depending on their soul. The strongest of Mestephans have the ability to create their own powers."

Of course. Just our luck that Mestephans live longer lives than normal people, Nick thought angrily as Philip droned on. "I am not sure of this, but some Mestephans might be born with the extremely rare chance of immortality. But to my knowledge, there are ancient legends of only one very old, immortal Mestephan. They are only born from Planet Mezort, a planet with a curse, where birthing works similarly to this disgusting planet. It is a planet cursed to be its own, with people cursed to be what they are: Mestephans, darkened in spirit, soul, and mind." He paused, with a look both somber and arrogant. "And that, Silver, is what a Mestephan is," finished Philip in one hiss.

Nick thought to himself wearily, debating silently at some length, "Mestephans. We know what they are now, but does that even help us at all with killing the Zorblin and stopping them, too? Alright, think! How did Ruler Quarzolon's relatives kill it in the book? I don't think it included how…or I can't remember. How did he tame them, at least?"

He pondered deeply, tossing ideas around in his head. "There was that freeze ray thingy, but it's destroyed now. Think…think. Wait! The X-Ball Zero! That could tell me what to do. Well, maybe not, but it's worth a try! No, that wouldn't work. How would I even get the X-Ball without being noticed? Well, that pushes that idea out of the picture for now, anyway."

Then he remembered something, still talking to himself. "Wait… there is one way I could do it, but it's risky." He recalled when he had tried the right trigger of the suit earlier and the label he had noticed but disregarded at the time. He focused, trying to remember the words that were written, until it finally came to him. "That's it! The frost launcher is unstable and can backfire on the whole suit itself. But what other choice do I have. . .?" he muttered under his breath. Instantly, he jumped out at the Zorblin, startling everyone, and pulled the trigger – or tried to, at least. It was jammed.

"Noooo!" he cried. As the Zorblin charged, yellow flashes soared past Nick's suit and collided with the monster, who stumbled slightly and began to run again.

"I've just got to get it working again…" murmured Nick, racing from the charging beast. BOOM! The Zorblin stumbled again, its left foot bent, then jumped up, roaring and spitting wildly. There was another bang and Nick quickly froze to look for a streak of yellow, seeing if it would hit the Zorblin, but instead it was a burst of orange directed at a distracted Dylan's head. Nick ran forward and stupidly tried to kick the orange lightning out of the way. A terrible crunching, searing sound split their ears as the orange bolt hit the large metal boot. The suit's left foot crunched with a few searing sparks and a small explosion as the lower calf and foot broke away completely from the Iron Titan.

Nick clunked backward in the suit, balancing mainly on the right foot with his left foot hanging limply, aching with pain. He was in view of the Zorblin, face-to-face just a short distance apart. Nick swung the right metallic arm out and pulled the trigger. It was still jammed, moving only slightly. He ran again, avoiding a splash of that poisonous green acid.

"That's it! Acid!"

As stupidly and insanely risky and reckless as it was, it was the only option. If Nick could get just a little bit of acid on the trigger, it would dissolve whatever was jamming it and, with a bit of luck, allow him to pull the trigger and kill the last Zorblin.

Meanwhile, Philip watched at the edge of the camp below, observing as his son battled the other four at once. Daniel blocked the purple axe, sidestepped a jet of light, ducked as a rocket launcher fired, and flung the small dog out of the way. He fought with his spear again, red electricity swirling around him. It was the same spear that he had used during his and Nick's duel.

Purple flames spread silently as acid bubbled on the grass. Nick jumped around the Zorblin, taunting it for some acid, as the creature roared and kicked, unable to finish the boy in the tall robot suit. "Hey, Three-Head!" jeered Nick, jumping up and down. The Zorblin's heads whipped around toward him. "Over here, boney! C'mon, try to spray me. You've got no aim!" Suddenly, as he tried to escape another blast of fire, his working foot slipped. The suit lost balance on its one leg and toppled over. SSSSSSSSPLASSHH! The robot suit was burning, dissolving, and breaking apart as the acid bugged its system while the Zorblin blasted its cursed fire at the twisting Titan.

Determined to still take Nick alive as a prisoner, Philip attempted to stop the Zorblin from killing him by launching a misty wave, filled with spikey black dots, at the beast. It missed and hit the acid-wet robot suit instead. "Ouch!" yelped Nick as larger dots appeared all over the suit as it twisted, turned, and crunched, leaving him unable to move. Philip cursed from below and fired another hex at the leering Zorblin, who bellowed in pain and began to twist and writhe just like the malfunctioning robot suit.

Nick attempted to pull the trigger again. As it was burning, twisting, and melting, he struggled to lift the robot suit up, but the spiked curse made it fall again. The legs were snapping apart and the already weakened left arm shook so violently, it broke off as the chest piece began to crack and split into pieces. With as much effort as he could muster, Nick leaned up and pulled the righthand trigger. An angry burst of frost backfired on the robot suit, freezing the acid and the flames and even shattering the curse, while simultaneously shooting at the still twisting, black-dotted Zorblin, which roared and spat out its cursed fire at nothing. The ice hit the creature and, with a sealing crackle, the last Zorblin froze into a shiny sculpture, icicles dangling from its mouths, tail suspended high and arcing over the dunes.

Metal pressed into Nick's chest painfully and his breathing was obstructed. And as the robot suit broke completely apart from the pressure of the icy frost, Nick crawled out, sweatshirt shining brightly, sweat and blood smeared, pants ripped open at the knees. He stood up as the flickering light miraculously healed his wounds. His head was beginning to throb icily as the distant spirit was consumed with rage. There was a burst of flames from his sweatshirt and without hesitation, he gripped a handle from his chest and slashed it through the air. A fiery glow surrounded the blade and Nick jumped forward, slicing the sword through the ice mountain created by the frozen Zorblin. In one clean stroke, the long iron blade first melted and then cut through the frozen, three-headed monstrosity until finally, the fire in the sword went out and the ice mountain was cut in two. The top half, which consisted of the necks and heads of the Zorblin, collapsed, falling to the grass, while the distorted bottom torso remained frozen, standing up in front of the sand dunes. Ruler Quarzolon's final Zorblin was dead at last. Nick stood staring until he began to feel his sword burn.

Philip Garring's scream of pure fury mingled with the yell of a distant spirit: the one who had created and relied upon the creature that was now dead. Nick felt his sweatshirt freeze numbingly around him, but it barely affected him as his faithful friends and sister ran towards him to celebrate. Their joy was cut short. Stepping from behind the destroyed and crumpled Iron Titan suit were the cloaked Mestephans, Philip and Daniel, who both looked demented.

"It's not over, Silver! We have you now! Prepare to watch your friends die and then you will kneel at the foot of the Dark Ruler!"

The threats were silenced as sirens wailed and red and blue lights flashed. Police cars rushed into Camp CrystalFlake. The sun slowly rose, and the moon set as Philip stared blankly, his anger and excitement vanishing. Then, in a puff of dark smoke, he disappeared. Daniel clumsily twisted on the spot before, with few feeble sparks of red energy, a smaller puff of smoke, and a soft crack, he was gone, too. And as the police stepped out of their cars, Nick's grip slackened, and his sword fell from his fist. He felt a rush of pain, but the sun was beginning to shine. He felt stronger than he had in a long, long time. His powers were shining freely, his sweatshirt flaring with golden power. It was over.

17

The Last Day of Camp

Even only hours later, these moments seemed to be a blur as Nick looked back on them. The police asked hundreds of questions before they left and then the campers celebrated and laughed until their parents were summoned to pick them up. Camp was fun again, even if only for a little while. The real counselors were in control of the camp now and the Mestephan camp director was gone. And through all of the chaos and excitement, only a few people realized that Philip and Daniel Garring had vanished.

It started off with the cops finding Counselor Robert's body, the ice sculpture sliced in half, and the hexed pile of machinery, remnants of the Iron Titan robot suit. The officers conversed with each other for a while and then began to interrogate Nick, Madison, John, and Dylan. They were understandably very suspicious of how the group had "found" their weapons – an iron sword, purple axe, thin rocket launcher, and long, yellow-striped staff – but the four decided to tell them exactly what happened.

They explained the Camp CrystalFlake legend of the Zorblin, how they had found the book, how Nick had been poisoned, and what had happened during the lake trip. They described finding the mysterious book, how they saw the holes growing every day, how Nick could talk to Flame, and how he saw the Zorblin up close.

They went on to talk about Nick's visions and the encounter in the Forest of Tappers, how Counselor Robert was attacked in the Quarren Forest two weeks prior, and Nick's forcefield during the first match. They finished by talking about their battles with the slime monsters, their discovery and exploration of the Secret Facility, and how they learned the truth and fought fiercely, right up until Nick killed the last Zorblin.

The police were baffled and speechless. As much as they didn't believe that the legend could actually be true, the evidence was right in front of them: the sliced mountain of ice, the Zorblin's body frozen within, John's magic staff, the destroyed robot suit, the purple flames, acid puddles, and small but noticeable ice mounds. The weirdest thing was that a few of the police officers already knew about the legend of Quarzolon, because strange afflictions had been rupturing through the earth lately. They were finally convinced after the other campers, who were set free from their cabins when Philip disappeared, ran out and explained how they suddenly couldn't hear anything outside, that a leathery book had flown from someone's mattress through a small hole in the wall, and that there actually was a legend about the Zorblin. They described Nick being poisoned and how he had cast a forcefield around himself during the first match of Swaying Swords. When the police had absorbed all their details and finally believed their story, they called for the campers' parents.

In the meantime, firefighters had been summoned to put out the cursed purple flames, which took a very long time. After they left, all of the counselors gathered to discuss what was next for the camp and what to do with Counselor Robert's body. In the end, they decided that Camp CrystalFlake would continue but would be cut short for the rest of the year, with reconstruction being postponed and starting up again in winter. The dead counselor's family were notified and would soon be there.

It took a while for the police to clear everything up before they finally finished loading the two frozen halves of the Zorblin onto a large truck and drove away. Nick, Madison, John, and Dylan headed to their bunks, utterly exhausted, and slept deeply for a few hours. After they awoke, the counselors threw a party for the four saviors of the camp. Since it was the first day of July, everybody was doubly happy. There were balloons, fireworks, and a party full of fun that lasted all day. The activities included a soccer game between the cabins and practice for next summer's Swaying Swords. After a decently lengthy round, Nick narrowly won. Sword fighting during the Battle of the Facility, as the campers had started calling it, definitely helped his sword movements. And Nick was also glad that no spheres of fire burst out of his sweatshirt during practice.

After each cabin's team had their practices, a delicious grand lunch was served. Refreshed at last, the four found Flame running through the dunes, sniffing the sand. The day was sunny, with a slight breeze, and perfect. Nick looked at Flame and scratched his head. "Oh, Flame. I have so many questions for you now." But Nick couldn't talk with Flame the same way anymore. It was weird. It seemed as if, after all that the sweatshirt did, some of its powers couldn't be rekindled so easily. There were just a few moments that warm day, for only a few seconds at a time, that Nick could talk with Flame. Unfortunately, it was always when Nick least expected it, preventing him from asking questions.

At nightfall, everybody went to sleep again, sinking into dreams and resting. But while everybody else was sleeping, Nick sat in bed, thinking about how, just a few days earlier, he had seen the same beast outside the window that he had killed just hours before. He then thought of another question. Where were Philip and Daniel? What happened to them? They were Mestephans, Nick thought, so they could be anywhere by now.

Wednesday morning arrived and the camp was washed over with brilliant heat under a cloudless sky. The counselors decided it would be a good idea if the campers could get some refreshing entertainment. So, after a pancake breakfast, they brought in a large crate filled with rafts, pool noodles, and water guns. The Swaying Swords arena had been moved temporarily into the Forest of Tappers for the rest of the summer so, an hour and a half later, the campers all took a swim in the lake, where they had plenty of room to frolic.

Nick was having a pool noodle fight with Dylan when Evan Mester swam by on a raft he had stolen from someone else, yelling and shouting at campers as he passed. "Dylan, you ready?" asked Nick as he lowered his pool noodle. "You bet," replied Dylan.

The two swam towards Evan's raft as he yelled, "Watch it, freaks!" Evan's gang came over to stop them, but John came out of nowhere and bopped Evan on the head with a pool noodle. "Hey!" bellowed Evan. Evan's gang was much larger than before and some were even older than him, but before they reached Nick and his two friends, Evan's boat suddenly flipped upside down.

"That was very worth it," Madison chuckled as she resurfaced from the spot where Evan's raft had just been.

"YOU…!" Evan sputtered, but the four were already gone, laughing the whole way back to the shore. Madison left to find her friends while Nick, John, and Dylan joked around. "Well, at least we overturned the S.S. Mester, or whatever he called it," Dylan smiled.

Lunch was hot dogs and hamburgers. Although Madison remained with her friends at the other side of the long wooden table outside, Nick and his friends were happy all the same. Flame sat by Nick's feet, waiting eagerly for the small pieces of hot dog that he ripped off and dropped for him. After the barbecue, the four visited the holes again. The slime had been cleaned up, it seemed, and large bags of dirt were piled next to the holes because the counselors wanted to fill them up.

They had also learned that the new Camp Director had been selected. It was a man who looked to be in his fifties or sixties. He had short, grizzled dark hair, a wrinkled face, and blue eyes behind a pair of spectacles. He wore a heavy brown jacket, a red buttoned shirt, and long black pants, with a neat brown hat on his head. And he was nothing like ex-Counselor Philip. He was friendly, made jokes, and laughed a lot. Finally, Nick actually could say aloud that the Camp Director, named Thomas, was great.

Nick, his sister, and two friends were practically famous at Camp CrystalFlake by Thursday. Not many people knew that Flame had been part of the fight, but those who did were shocked to hear how the dog had been summoned. Only a very few people had heard the story from Nick's point of view, however. He didn't like talking about it too much. He still had two painful questions on his mind: One, why and how does he have the sweatshirt and X-Ball? And two, why didn't he die when sprayed with acid? The Battle of the Facility kept his head buzzing.

The new Camp Director, Counselor Thomas, kept glancing at Nick from time to time, during meals and free time. Everybody was eager to see what Counselor Thomas had planned for Friday, which was the Fourth of July, since the counselors kept saying it would be a great time. Those last few days at Camp CrystalFlake were Nick's favorite ones. Evan Mester tried to corner him again with his gang at the Big Tree, but Nick skillfully climbed up the trunk, jumped, and landed right behind the gang, away from the small spot where he would have been surrounded. Evan jeered and yelled at him, but Nick didn't care; he was impervious to those insults by then. Thursday night was relaxation at its best. Cabin B was the perfect temperature and Nick was extremely tired, falling into a restful and dreamless sleep.

On Fourth of July morning, Nick was awakened by a sparkler in his face. "What the…?" he murmured as he stumbled out of bed. John told him, "C'mon, Nick, they're giving out the sparklers now!" Dylan pulled his sparkler away from Nick, urging him on. Nick got dressed at lightning speed and quickly opened the door. Campers were running around with sparklers, some trying to throw theirs through suspended rings while others attempted to juggle theirs. The counselors were passing out the sparklers and hosting competitions. When Nick received his sparkler, he hadn't even done anything with it before it exploded with light, firing sparks everywhere. Every camper's head in the vicinity turned. And Nick wasn't surprised to see his sweatshirt's faint glow already receding.

They had a great breakfast of bacon and eggs and afterward, the counselors let the campers practice lighting a campfire for another event that was planned for later. The four enjoyed roasting their own marshmallows in the meantime and the day continued with confetti and fireworks launching into the air. Every single camper was prepared for a big surprise during dinner. Midway through their pizza and cupcakes, Counselor Thomas walked over to the packed outdoor lunch table, grinning.

"Well, campers, according to your counselors, this has been a very, er, interesting summer," he said. "And you may not know this, but before Counselor Philip became the Camp Director, I was the Camp Director, but I had retired." Nick listened carefully, trying to understand how he now had the position again after retiring from the same job. "And so, we leave here, tomorrow at noon, to depart for the summer. Camp CrystalFlake will be closed until next summer, June fifteenth."

Many moans and groans of complaint echoed across the table. None of the campers, except the four who fought in the Battle of the Facility, had known about this.

"However, I have very good news regarding next summer's time here." The fifth years groaned now, wondering what they would be missing, until Counselor Thomas reassured them. "But don't worry, my fifth years, for this may not be your last year here." Most of the senior campers looked up hopefully. "My fellow colleagues have informed me that the previous

Camp Director had already paid for Camp CrystalFlake to return with a whole new look and a large building right there," he pointed at the holes between the two forests, "plus a few observation towers." A murmur of talk buzzed through the table.

"But that is not all," said Counselor Thomas lightly. "Next year, Camp CrystalFlake will have new and improved group activities. Campers in each group will stick with their own ages" – Nick and Madison exchanged glances at that – "and I believe you will all enjoy them very much." There were more whispers back and forth as he continued, "Every camper will join at least two activities, since, I do admit, I was not impressed when I heard how your previous Camp Director planned very little activities with you all."

A few campers nodded in agreement as they talked with their friends and siblings. "And I see," Counselor Thomas continued, "that our fifth years still wonder what their news is. Very well, then. Camp CrystalFlake is being extended to a sixth year." A happy cry rose from the fifth years at the thought of returning for one final year. "Sixteen-year-olds are now welcome to join us at Camp CrystalFlake for next summer," Counselor Thomas finished. "And that is all of the news I have for you, campers. In twenty minutes, please meet up at the campfire." Counselor Thomas took another split-second glance at Nick, who was sure he had something to say to him.

Ten minutes later, all the campers were back in their cabins, discussing the news. "So, guys. New Camp Director, new activities, new year, new stuff," summarized Nick happily.

"Yeah," said Dylan, lying on his bed. "Should be fun, let's try and do all of them, if we can!"

"Well, I guess you'll have to do it without me, then. You heard what he said about the age groups," Madison reminded them.

"Oh, right. . ." Nick remembered.

"Honestly, though, I'm fine with it. I'll do stuff with my friends. One of them left the camp after the first year and now they're coming back. And besides, I get enough of my little brother at home anyway," she grinned.

"Yeah, Counselor Thomas seems way better than Mr. Mestephan. Hopefully, those new buildings will be something interesting," John commented. "And tomorrow's the last day, so that was our last dinner here for another year."

"Oh, right. The dinner. Oh, how I loved eating here," Nick chimed in sarcastically. "And the camp apple juice was marvelous! I simply loved getting poisoned by the Camp Director!"

"And I loved getting my leg cut up by a slime guy!" added Dylan in the same sarcastic tone.

"Somehow, I think I'll actually miss this place, though," said Nick, staring out the window as the sun slowly set and the stars began to shine. He closed his eyes, and, for an instant, he saw flashes of the recent battle: the Secret Facility, the Zorblin charging, a small Mestephan firing a curse, and a tall Mestephan flying in midair. He opened his eyes and the image went blank.

When Counselor Chris came into their cabin and told them they could come out now, they had barely taken six steps when they saw a flash of red and heard a crack and laughter. Nick froze, his eyes scanning for any traces of Mestephans, but feeling returned to him when he saw that it was only a firework launching and Counselor Thomas laughing together with the other counselors. Nick relaxed his tense muscles and made his way toward the wooden stumps around the fireplace, in the same spot where he had sat for attendance during the first day at camp.

It was plain to see that after his time at the camp, his senses had definitely sharpened.

"Fireworks!" announced Counselor Thomas to the oncoming campers. Fireworks launched into the night sky as the campers excitedly watched. There were colorful bursts of all shapes, sizes, and hues zooming upward, sometimes one at a time and sometimes all at once. They all crackled to life in thrilling explosions of bright red and orange light, not deathly and cold like the lights that shot from the staffs during the battle. And so, it went on. The campfire was lit, the fireworks continued traveling at weird angles, making interesting shapes in the sky, and the Fourth of July passed in one warm summer breeze.

Saturday morning seemed cold and misty after all the fireworks from the night before. Nick woke up, shuffling around, trying to get back to his comfortable position. "Eh, what time is it. . .?" he mumbled.

John, already dressed and leaning against the wall on the side of his bunk, muttered, "I dunno, but I do know breakfast is," his sentence was punctuated by a yawn, "soon."

The last day of camp was slightly breezy again and Nick was a bit chilled as the campers trooped toward the long wooden table beside the glinting lake.

"Tired," muttered Dylan as he slumped in his seat.

"Yeah," agreed Nick, brain swirling, hardly aware of what he was agreeing to as he yawned widely. "At least we have some breakfast food to wake us up. Not too hungry but, meh, I'll have some," he said, sliding a waffle and sausages onto his plate.

As breakfast ended, something did indeed wake Nick up. Counselor Thomas stepped closer to the table from behind the other counselors and asked clearly, "May I have Nicholas Silver, please?" Nick froze and so did the other campers.

"See you," Madison whispered in his ear.

Nick got up and walked toward the new Camp Director. "Good. It's nice to see you, Nicholas. Come with me, please," he said. Silently, the two headed towards the Counselor Cabin and, once inside, Nick saw a front desk with two rooms on each side. One was a large kitchen on the right. The left room had a set of couches and two tables, stacked with papers and pens, sitting on a hearth rug beside a familiar fireplace. Counselor Thomas led Nick up a flight of stairs that was behind the desk and into a large wooden room.

The counselor's office was big, with a wide desk, a door in the back leading to a balcony, a copy machine, two plants, and other things – including a long, green-tipped staff. Nick quickly spun around. Counselor Thomas laughed softly. "Sorry to scare you, Nicholas, but yes, that is one of the Mestephan staffs."

"But…how…you…?" stuttered Nick, about to attempt to summon his sword.

"Don't worry, Nicholas. I am not here to kill you or harm you in any way. You see, I have experienced things similar to what you witnessed on Tuesday."

Nick steadied himself. "Okay. . ."

Counselor Thomas smiled. "Good. Now that we are on the right track, please, Nicholas, take a seat." Nick sat down in a comfortable chair in front of the desk. "I once met an army of Mestephans years back. I tried to fight back, but I was losing. I was being outnumbered when suddenly, in a flash of flames, a small dog appeared at my side. The dog licked my injuries, healing me. The dog fought, distracting them. I was dumbfounded, bewildered. . . and then I realized this dog couldn't be a normal dog. As it distracted the Mestephans, I was able to steal the staff," he gestured lightly to the staff leaning against the wall, "and used it against the Mestephans. The staff definitely caused a distraction, but I did not stay to watch. I fled. The dog disappeared. I took the staff and kept it all of these years, to use it in case the Mestephans that claimed to be part of a cult ever found me again. And after all those years of searching, I finally was able to again see the dog that saved my life years ago."

When Nick spoke, he found that his throat was dry. "Flame?" he asked.

"Yes. I believe you named him Flame? A fitting name."

"But…but do you know anything else about Flame? And my sweatshirt. Do you know about that, too?" asked Nick quickly.

Counselor Thomas chortled. "I know few things, very few. However, I regretfully inform you I cannot foretell now."

"Cannot foretell now." The same words the X-Ball Zero had told him. Wait, Nick thought. "Do you know anything about the X-Ball Zero?" he asked.

"Again, I regretfully – and I know you hate to hear this – must not tell you now. And please, I do not advise you to use it until the time is right. I also would like you to know that phones and such are easily trackable by Mestephans."

"When the time is…?" Nick began.

"Please. Now, the police have informed me of your story. However, I need to know your side of the story."

And so, Nick told him. Even the part about the X-Ball Zero. It took a while, and when he finished the full story, Counselor Thomas nodded, his eyes gleaming.

"How long did it take you to be able to control the sweatshirt's powers as well as you did?"

Nick, taken aback by this question, answered slowly. "I started getting pretty good control of its powers in the Facility," he said honestly.

"Good, good. I thought as much. Its powers will feed off your emotions and brain waves to activate easier when necessary," Thomas sighed.

"Oh, okay," said Nick. "But one last question," he began, heart starting to pump, "why am I the one with the sweatshirt, the one with the X-Ball, the one who had to be brought to Quarzolon?"

"Again, I hate to tell you, but that is another thing you should not know now."

"Really?" replied Nick sadly, too disappointed to stop himself.

"Yes, I am sorry to say, but I think the information you think will help you live may end up killing you. But as you ponder that, know that in due time, you will know. That is all I have to inform you of. You have impressed me deeply, you have shown me courage, and you have led an army like a leader. For that, I give you my everlasting faith. That is all. Goodbye, Nicholas Silver. Good luck."

When Nick returned to Cabin B, he told the others everything the new Camp Director had said as quickly and breathlessly as possible. "W-wow, Nick," said John, awestruck.

"That's great!" said Dylan.

"That's actually really good! Now we know someone at camp who actually understands us and what happened!"

"And will happen," sighed Nick. The others glanced at each other as Nick stared at the floor.

"Well, Nick," began John as they headed outside, "whatever does happen, will happen. And we'll stop it again."

They walked back over towards the dunes, one of Nick's favorite places at Camp CrystalFlake. He was still worried. "But Daniel. He betrayed us and Philip's gone. They're going to tell Quarzolon what happened and he's going to do something about this."

"Nick, you need to understand the world isn't all dark. We have each other. We stand strong and we will fight back! That's how we survived in the Facility. You said it yourself. Quarzolon believes nothing about groups achieving triumph, but look what we did!" said John, his voice lifting.

"You're right," shrugged Nick. "We can get through this. We just have to let time pass. We simply have to stand strong and wait for what's coming next."

"Good," said Dylan happily. "Now that you've stopped thinking we'll all die a painful death" – Nick actually laughed a bit at that – "I think we should get each other's phone numbers so we can talk during the school year!"

"Good idea!" agreed John.

They exchanged phone numbers as the sun beat down their backs in the midst of the sandy dunes, tall green grass rising high up. Nick mentioned how phones are trackable by Mestephans again, and everyone promised they would be careful about it.

"ALL CAMPERS IN CABIN A, PLEASE COME TO THE ENTRANCE TO BE PICKED UP!" announced Counselor Thomas's voice through a megaphone.

"We'll be next, then," muttered Nick, tightly clutching the paper with his friends' phone numbers. He and the others marched to their cabin and started collecting their things, even the weapons from the Facility. Soon, it was their turn.

"ALL CAMPERS IN CABIN B, PLEASE COME TO THE ENTRANCE TO BE PICKED UP!"

The four of them walked together toward the camp entrance, a small brown dog watching devotedly from afar. Nick's sweatshirt glowed as brilliantly as the sun that shined down on them and he took a last look back, meeting the gaze of the Camp Director as he waved his hand up high and smiled.